What others are saying.

"Readers are welcomed with open arms to the fictional town of Ruby in author Cynthia Herron's sweet romance, *His Heart Renewed*. I wish I could enjoy a real visit to the wonderful community Herron's created in her series set in the Ozark mountains. Her characters become friends in a story that reminds you falling in love requires a heartfelt combination of trust, forgiveness, and hope — while choosing to believe the best of others."

Beth K. Vogt, *Christy Award-winning author*

"In *His Heart Renewed*, Cynthia Herron pens another charming tale of two wary hearts and the healing that finally brings them home. I adored revisiting the friendly, small-town setting of Ruby, Missouri, where humor and faith abound and delicious food fills every plate. Erin and Mike's bumpy road to happily-ever-after reminds us that God's grace is for all the days of our life, not just our best. Well done!"

Kerry Johnson, *Publisher's Weekly Best-selling author of Snowstorm Sabotage and Tunnel Creek Ambush*

"As delightful as the cupcakes from Charla Packard's Pennies from Heaven deli/bakery, Cynthia Herron's *His Heart Renewed* is a sweet story that will leave you watering for the next Brewer family romance. Another memorable journey to Ruby provides a respite in a small town readers will love to visit where something as ordinary as a firewood delivery can change two people from frenemies to friends with the potential for a partnership to navigate life's difficult pathways. Highly recommended."

Tanya Agler, *author of Caught by the Cowgirl*

"Three big cheers for Cynthia Herron who returns readers to the glow and glory of small-town romance, life, and healing in her latest Ozarks' based **Welcome to Ruby** tale. This time, in *His Heart Renewed*, Herron takes readers on an extra charming, heart-tugging journey showing how opposites who attract light the best fires when they finally take a chance on love. Such a satisfying, heart-lifting unfolding of renewal and hope. Settle in and enjoy."

Patricia Raybon, *Christy Award-winning author of All That Is Secret and Double the Lies of the Annalee Spain Mystery Series.*

His Heart Renewed

Welcome to Ruby!

Blessings,
Cynthia

The Welcome to Ruby Series

His Heart Renewed

The Welcome to Ruby Series, Book Four

By

Cynthia Herron

His Heart Renewed
Published by Mountain Brook Ink
White Salmon, WA U.S.A.

The website addresses shown in this book are not intended in any way to be or imply an endorsement on the part of Mountain Brook Ink, nor do we vouch for their content.

This story is a work of fiction. All characters and events are the product of the author's imagination. Any resemblance to any person, living or dead, is coincidental.

Scripture quotations are taken from the King James Version of the Bible. Public domain.
ISBN 978-1-953957-36-8

The Team: Miralee Ferrell, Tim Pietz, Kristen Johnson, Cindy Jackson
Cover Design: Indie Cover Design, Lynnette Bonner Designer

The Author is represented by and this book is published in association with the literary agency of WordServe Literary Group., Ltd, www.wordserveliterary.com.

Mountain Brook Ink is an inspirational publisher offering fiction you can believe in.

Dedication

For Jeff, Rachel, and Elizabeth
For Mama and Lisa
For Nikki

For the ones with shattered hearts and mended dreams.
God restores.

In memory of Wendi—my precious sister—
my best friend forever.

In memory of Todd—my beloved cousin—a treasure to all
who knew him.

See you in the morning.

*"Even the youths shall faint and be weary, and the young
men shall utterly fall: but they that wait upon the Lord shall
renew their strength; they shall mount up with wings as
eagles; they shall run, and not be weary; and they shall
walk, and not be faint."*

Isaiah 40:30-31 KJV

Acknowledgments

As authors often say, because it's so true, writing a book—seeing it to fruition—is a team effort. It does, indeed, take a village to write our stories and make them the best they can be. With *His Heart Renewed*, this fourth novel in the Welcome to Ruby series, it's no different.

While I could share about how very difficult it was to ultimately finish this book—the extreme duress as I wrote to deadline—I'll save that for my author note at the end of this story. It's pretty unbelievable how life events unfolded, and how, too, God ultimately crafted this project into something worthy and beautiful.

As always, without special people to cheer me on, this story would still be mere words languishing on a laptop screen. A heartfelt thank you to my husband and children for their continued support and encouragement as I wrote through the deep fog of grief. I love you dearly.

Thank you, precious Mama—who, even in your own sorrow—tethered me to the place that shelters us from countless storms and forever remains our source of strength. The Solid Rock will endure until the end of our earthly days and into eternity.

Thank you, Lisa, my dear cousin, for your uplifting calls, texts, and messages during your own sojourn in the valley. You'll never know how much your thoughts and prayers boosted me on the loneliest of days. I love you.

Deepest appreciation to my editor, Miralee, and the entire Mountain Brook Ink family. Your wisdom, insight, and support bless me. Thank you for helping me expand my talents in ways that add value and appeal.

I'm especially grateful to my agent, Sarah, and the WordServe Literary team as we continue partnering together to take my stories to new heights.

Thank *you*, dear reader, in your faithfulness for giving my words wings as you share my heartfelt, homespun tales with your loved ones and friends. You make our time together between the pages, sweeter.

Most of all, to my Heavenly Father, thank you for setting me on this publishing journey and for allowing me to share the stories of my heart—stories that start first with a kernel of an idea—until they sprout into a full-grown novel, and at last, become a book.

Chapter One

Somewhere along the gold-rimmed skyline, beyond the scarlet treetops, lies a fertile land steeped in heritage and tradition. It's been said that the Ozarks region is the cherry on God's earthly masterpiece—the place where folks can come to meet a friend and make a home in the hills and hollows of heaven on earth.

If she hadn't seen it with her own eyes, Erin wouldn't have believed it. Was that a naked man standing at the edge of her front lawn?

Well...never let it be said that Erin Shaye was a prude. Maybe, though, she was imagining things. She closed her eyes. Waited ten seconds. Opened them. Okay. Not a completely naked man. To his credit, Dander Evans wore...a Speedo? Flesh-colored that blended with his skin tone.

Good gracious. He had guts. She'd grant him that much.

The local barber, a mid-fiftyish gent, appeared to be taking a break...of sorts. Pausing, he checked what Erin guessed to be his Fitbit—perhaps for heart rate and steps logged—reached toward the cloudless, blue sky and stretched, then resumed his morning jog down the sidewalk toward town.

Since Erin arrived in Ruby over a year ago, Dander had lost some excess weight and he appeared to be on a mission to get in shape. Good for him. His daily runs seemed to be working. Still, his choice of running attire baffled her. Usually, the fellow wore sweats or sometimes knee-length, athletic shorts. His choice today bordered on outrageous, and judging by the swaying tree leaves, the October breeze agreed. Even with the bright, warm sunshine on this glorious Saturday morn, it might be fifty degrees. Certainly, too cool for so much bare skin. Then again, Ruby—this charming, small-town gem, tucked deep within the Missouri Ozarks—served up some dandy peculiarities.

Take Mike Brewer, for instance. When Erin initially moved to Ruby, the handsome homebuilder welcomed her with opened arms. Of course, those arms weren't actually extended toward her. At the time, they'd carried a gigantic fruit basket wrapped in red cellophane and a mondo-sized bow. A fruit basket, not solely from him, but from the Chamber of Commerce and local businesses, welcoming her—Erin Shaye, DVM—to their fair community.

Now, Mike barely glanced at her. Despite the fact they attended the same church, shopped at the same market, and ran into each other at the same locales in town. Oh, and not to forget that Erin had purchased Mike's sister's cottage last month when Mel married. One would think that shared bond might draw the guy into conversation, but nope. Oddly enough, the brown-eyed bachelor with dimpled grin spoke nary a word when their paths crossed. Peculiar, indeed.

"I don't know what I've done to offend him," Erin lamented one day to Ida Mae Farrow at the Come and Get It Diner.

"Bless your heart, honey." Ida Mae returned with a

smile. "You haven't done anything to offend that fella. You've simply knocked him for a loop, and he doesn't know what to do about it. That hasn't happened since Sally Sue Messmer took him for a ride twelve years ago and then ditched him." The Come and Get It proprietress rubbed her protruding stomach, ripe with twins, as if recalling details. "Broken hearts can be slow to mend. I should know. Only that's a story for another day. That boy'll come around. You wait and see."

"Oh, no. I didn't mean that I—"

"Have a thing for him?"

"Yes. I don't."

"Uh-huh. Remind me sometime to tell you all the folks around here who said that very thing."

"Why? What happened?"

Ida Mae's blue eyes twinkled. "On the way to the altar or after?"

Erin sipped her coffee, remembering her new friend's words. Could it be? Could Mike Brewer, confirmed bachelor, actually like her? If he did, the guy certainly had a funny way of showing it. Twelve years seemed like a long time to pine after a high school sweetheart. On the other hand, what did she know about love? Veterinary school had left little time for dating, much less anything more. She didn't count the horrid sting of a broken engagement. Been there. Done that. Old news.

Ruminating before the picture window of her cottage, Erin nearly choked on her coffee as the focus of her thoughts hastened down the street in his Chevy Silverado. Mike slowed the vehicle as he approached her place, and proceeded to back into her driveway, next to her SUV. Firewood—maybe a rick —filled his truck bed. He shifted into park and cut the engine. *What on earth?*

He paused for a minute to grab a pair of work gloves from the dash and then hopped down from the cab of his pickup as if sprung from a toy Jack-in-the-box.

Erin moved closer to the window. Did Mike intend to restock last year's wood pile? She hadn't ordered any. She'd barely been in the cottage five weeks, having finally moved from the back room of her veterinary clinic in town, and she hadn't yet come up for air. She'd heard the Brewer family, specifically Mel Brewer's dad and three brothers, enjoyed serving the community in this way. Where they found time, in addition to their day jobs, one could only guess. Still, Mike hadn't mentioned anything about a wood delivery. Having mostly avoided her for the past year, this charitable act puzzled her.

He unlatched his truck bed and went to work. Yep. That's exactly what he intended to do—deliver and stack the wood in the very spot where a few logs from his sister's supply remained.

Thick, brown locks fell across Mike's forehead, accentuating an otherwise well-trimmed haircut. Erin couldn't help but notice the way his blue denim work shirt clung to his muscular, toned frame as he set to work. With spot-on precision, he gathered and stacked the wood like a man on a mission. A mission to get 'er done and get out of there as fast as he could.

If he didn't want to be there, why had he come? Erin tightened her fingers around her coffee mug. She should step outside and say something. At least offer a thank you. Yet, judging from his hurried air and mechanical movements, would Mike even acknowledge her? Everything about the man said *Don't bother me.* Hmm...

Still, a kind deed merited a kind word.

"What do you think, Miranda? Should I risk it?"

Erin's ten-year-old white and gray shorthair blinked and purred contentedly from her perch high atop her cat condo.

"You don't say?"

All right. She'd give it a go. After all, Aunt Bea didn't raise her in a barn. Good manners were worth their weight in gold. Or firewood, in this case.

Erin set down her mug and stepped outdoors. The cool morning air nipped at her nose and raised goosebumps on her arms. Why hadn't she thought to grab a sweater? Oh, no matter. She wouldn't stay long.

If Mike heard her step outside, he didn't let on. In fact, he never even looked up from his task. His gaze remained fixed. His efforts, a blur of motion.

Strolling toward the rising stack of wood, Erin paused in her tracks. Again—as it had during previous encounters—Mike's height and Mack truck physique fascinated her. Noticeably over six feet by a good couple inches, with solid, sturdy limbs concealed by favorable-fitting work clothes, he possessed an understated appeal that might captivate many women. Good thing she wouldn't let herself be sidetracked by such surface attributes. Erin stepped forward again, and this time, cleared her throat.

"A-hem." By then, he obviously knew she stood there, observing. When Mike didn't speak, Erin tried again. "I really appreciate your kindness. I'll pay you."

"Glad to help." He tipped his head, acknowledging he'd heard her, yet still didn't glance her direction. "No payment necessary."

"Bu...but you're doing all this work. Besides, that's

seasoned wood, right? I know it probably costs a pretty penny."

"Not a problem, ma'am." Still, he refused to meet her gaze.

"Well, it's very kind of you. At least come in for a cup of coffee when you're finished. Or maybe you'd prefer something cold?"

"No, thanks."

"It's no troub—"

"No."

What was his problem? Despite the other Brewer siblings' pleasantness, Mike won the oddball award. Where Gabe, Garrett, and Mel were chatty and cordial, their brother nailed the opposite. Adjectives like reserved and aloof jumped to mind.

Ida Mae must have pegged it wrong. *Knocked him for a loop?* A loop, her fanny. The man liked her about as much as a bowl of turnip greens. She got it now.

"Suit yourself." Erin turned back toward the door, muttering under her breath. "How about a thump on the head then? Maybe that would be more your preference."

Mike almost snorted. Yeah. Gabe and Garrett called it. The attractive veternarian with blue-green eyes the color of Jaden Pond, and short, trendy bob—more strawberry than blonde—definitely gave off interesting vibes. A thump on the head, huh? That might prove fun. One never knew. What was she? Maybe five-feet-six-inches tall on Sunday morning in high heels? Made no difference. Erin Shaye might be looking. He wasn't. Landing a wife pinged his radar about as likely as a UFO flyover. Still, he hadn't meant to hurt the gal's feelings. He simply hadn't wanted to encourage her.

Should he apologize? He let it percolate in his mind as he plopped down a final log and secured a waterproof tarp over the firewood to repel moisture.

Come to think of it, a cup of coffee didn't sound half-bad. Though, then they'd have to talk, wouldn't they? He slid off his gloves and slapped them against his jean-clad thigh, thinking. Surely, two thirty-year-olds could pass fifteen minutes. To be fair, he'd heard through his sister Mel that Erin was twenty-nine, a hair shy of the big 3-0. Nevertheless, the point being, polite conversation between two grown adults shouldn't be a problem. Forget the fact they'd started off on the wrong foot this morning.

He could ask how business was down at the clinic, however, he suspected he knew. Right dandy, by word on the street. He could inquire about her family—usually a good ice-breaker and a safe subject. He understood she'd been raised by an aunt. Aunt what-was-her-name? Oh, and the cottage. That'd be a sure bet. She'd probably yammer up a blue streak about his sister's previous home. There was something about Doc Burnside's old cottage—be it its vintage appeal and good bones or its walls laden with history—that charmed folks. Erin had told his sister from the get-go that if she ever thought to sell the place, she'd snatch it up in a hot Ozark minute, and when Mel married five weeks ago, she did.

Fitting the cottage should revert back to Erin then who'd also purchased old Doc's clinic. 'Course, Doc Burnside, God rest his soul, had practiced people doctoring, not veterinary medicene. Still, the beloved physician who'd delivered half of Jewel County would probably be tickled pink to know he and the new owner shared a common thread.

Mike grinned. Yeah, they could chit-chat about all

that. He closed the pickup's tailgate, the sound making a light thud to match the sudden hitch in his pulse. *Buddy, all you have to do is accept that cup of coffee, exchange a neighborly howdy-do, and be on your way. Nothing to it.* Then why did his brothers' teasing jabs taunt him—the ones that inferred the recent Ruby transplant had piqued his interest as much as he, they teased, had piqued hers?

Aw. Phooey. What'd they know? He had Blackie, his cabin, and more business than he could spit at. What more did a man need than his dog, his abode, and his work? Unless one counted emerald eyes to drown in, arms to hold him, and a heart that beat in sync with his?

Mike shook off such thoughts. Craziness, that's what it was. Bachelorhood had suited him well all these years, and he wasn't about to fritter away the good life for a feisty redhead, brilliant and gorgeous though she might be.

Best to get on with this. He had other things to do today. Tromping to Erin's back door, he gave it three sound raps and waited. Maybe she hadn't heard him. He rapped again. Once. Twice. Thr... With the force of a gale wind, the door jerked open and there she stood, her cheeks, cherry tomato red. Her lips, firmly sealed. Her ire, clearly etched in the frown she now wore.

Mike's hand paused in midair.

"I...uh..." She was upset? What had he expected? He'd spurned her thanks and a simple cup of coffee. He'd hurt her feelings and that bothered him. "May I take you up on that cup of coffee?"

The pretty veterinarian's eyes singed him. "Anyone ever tell you that you need an attitude adjustment?"

Mike gulped. For the love of pickles, did she have to be such a stunner? "I was rude. I'm sorry."

"Yes, you were."

All right. She wasn't going to make this easy. He guessed he couldn't blame her. Since the woman had moved here last year, he'd done his best to avoid her. "Am I forgiven?"

Erin cocked her head to one side, as if she had to think about it. He noted the small scar—a little less than half an inch or so, a slight raggedness above her left eyebrow—against otherwise flawless, fair skin. He'd never noticed it before. Possibly because, other than initial introductions a year ago, he'd tried not to focus on the newcomer. The very striking, *very available* newcomer who'd tripped his heart like a thousand-volt cable wire.

"Absolutely." She rolled her shoulders, as if his apology was insignificant.

"Why do I think you don't believe me?"

"Dunno. People say a lot of things to ease their conscience."

But he really meant it. He couldn't be sorrier. He'd known for a while now the woman liked him in more than a friendly way. Not her fault he wasn't interested. No one got under his skin like that. Until...this minute? *Duh. Way to go, dimwit.*

"You're right. Only I *am* sorry. It goes against my grain to be discourteous."

Erin quirked an eyebrow.

"I'm not at my best today."

She raised the other eyebrow.

"I had a rough night." Not a lie. He'd lain awake most of the night trying to think of ways to appease his conscience for acting as he had toward the new vet. He'd hoped maybe a wood delivery would pave the way for a fresh start.

"You've had a rough *year*." Erin snapped. "I'd like to

know what I've done to provoke you."

"Nothing. It isn't you. It's me." He fiddled with his work gloves, recalling various instances when Erin had tried engaging him—at church socials, community events, the market, the diner, and so on. No way could she possibly understand. He didn't understand it himself. The likely explanation had to be Sally Sue Messmer—his former high school flame...and more.

Sally Sue had scalded him and cured him at the same time. When it came to long-term relationships, he'd never make that mistake twice. Didn't matter how appealing he found Erin. It'd never work. Still, it wouldn't twist his drawers to be civil. Hopefully.

Erin expelled a breath and tapped her foot. "Is there something else?"

He should gather what was left of his pride and hobble away. Any self-respecting man would do just that.

Blast it. Mike refused to accept defeat. He didn't want to leave things like this. "Okay. No coffee. Got it. How 'bout a stack of pancakes, a slab of fried bacon, and some ice cold OJ? I'm not picky."

Despite her best efforts to the contrary, a smile tugged at the corners of Erin's lips—rather nice lips, at that.

"Missed opportunities stink, huh? Nevertheless, I'm sure the Come and Get It can accommodate your hankering. In fact, that's probably their morning special. Plus, all I offered was coffee."

"Great. I'd love some. Thanks." Mike quelled the laughter that bubbled up within his chest. He'd outsmarted her. He resisted the urge to fist-pump the air.

Except...Erin flashed him a full-fledged grin and shut the door. *Good job, bud.* So much for his cocky brilliance.

Effectively silenced, Mike turned to go. Lesson learned. Good guys still finished last. Check that. He hadn't been good to Erin Shaye. He'd been a jerk, then tried to counter it with bravado and humor. *Way to go, fella.* He ambled away like a scolded pup, berating himself for his initial crustiness. When the door suddenly whooshed open, he swung back around.

"Here." Erin extended her arm and offered an insulated coffee mug. "You can return the mug later."

A peace offering? He wasn't no fool. Mike quickly retraced his steps and reached for the thermal mug. "Thank you."

"Hope you like pumpkin spice. It's my favorite flavor this time of year, and it's all I had in the house." She didn't invite him inside like earlier, but something bright sparked in her eyes.

"It's perfect. Thanks again." As he took an exaggerated sip through the slitted lid, the fib tasted sour on his tongue, along with the horrid brew. No way was he going to tell her the truth. He loved pumpkin pie. As coffee? He'd rather guzzle a mud puddle. Surely, the good Lord's punishment to keep nasty attitudes at bay.

"Certainly. Thanks for the rick of wood," Erin replied. "Oh, and for the record, I had cinnamon love knots warm from the oven—guaranteed to melt in your mouth. Too bad you missed them." She waggled her fingers and retreated back inside.

The air sizzled. A lightning bolt zipped down Mike's spine and his belly clenched. Same as a year ago—when they'd initially met—only this time, his reaction mirrored a full-blown electrical storm.

Cinnamon love knots? Have mercy. The animal doc threw a mean sucker punch.

Chapter Two

Erin stroked Miranda's soft, furry coat and nuzzled her sweet girl's face with her own. The low rumble of a purr pierced the late morning silence and communicated unadulterated love.

"I love you, too, precious."

It never failed to amaze Erin how her beloved pet possessed the innate ability to center her sometimes frenzied world. Not that this morning ranked up there with the unpredictability of day-to-day events at the clinic. Still, her encounter with Mike Brewer tipped the proverbial apple cart enough to throw off her equilibrium. That the guy was too above having a cup of coffee with her for fear of what Erin might draw from it, grated on her—even two hours later. Who did he think he was—filet mignon on a silver platter? *No way, buster.* More like canned soup with a side of stale crackers.

She hoped he thoroughly enjoyed the brew she sent with him and that he drank down his prior smugness with each sip. *Enough of this.* Erin gave Miranda a final nuzzle, grabbed her jacket and purse, and headed toward the door. Saturday errands wouldn't take care of themselves, and Mister Unattached-and-I-Intend-to-Stay-That-Way could carry on with his Christian duty somewhere else for all she cared.

"Hold down the fort, Miranda. I'll be back soon."

Miranda meowed and curled into a ball, ready for her morning nap. *Ahh, to have the life of a feline princess.* The cute, cuddly furball regarded her with sleepy eyes, and within seconds, began to doze.

Stepping outside, Erin closed the door and crossed the short distance to her Honda CR-V. As she slid into the driver's seat, her eyes landed on the nearby woodpile, skillfully stacked, the top few rows lightly covered with a blue tarp to prevent moisture, but also, to allow the stack to breathe. Having only been in the cottage a few weeks, and considering it was still early fall, Erin hadn't needed to light a fire yet, except now she could hardly wait.

"Besides the amazing picture window in front, the fireplace is one of the home's best features," Mel had mentioned. "It'll keep you warm and toasty during the winter, for sure. Plus, it'll lower your overall heating expenses if you decide to use it on a regular basis."

Mel Brewer—Enders now—had been one of Erin's first friends when she'd moved to Ruby last year. Friendly, helpful, and single at the time, Mel had introduced her to others in the small, close-knit community of Ruby. Immediately, Erin had grown fond of the quirky, loveable locals, including Mel's family with their penchant for fun, food, and gab. The Brewer siblings, especially Gabe and Garrett, exuded warmth and generosity. Mike, the youngest of the unmarried brothers, however, remained distant and detached. Until today. Until Erin had called his hand and doled out some of his own, much-deserved medicine. Then, he'd attempted to backtrack and regroup.

No matter. Just because the guy bore a strong resemblance to Chris Hemsworth and had the physique of a superhero didn't mean he had a winning personality. Nope. He fell short of the mark on that trait. Like way short. Which, Erin found odd because his parents, Jake and Billie Gail, oozed goodwill and kindness. Whether or not that Sally Sue Messmer person played a role in Mike's frosty demeanor, one could only guess. From what Erin had observed in public, he wasn't that way with everyone.

Only her. With everyone else, he seemed relaxed, affable, and even charming. Good thing she'd quelled any attraction she might have initially felt for the man. She'd much rather remain single than hitched to an iceberg.

Erin started her vehicle and eased from the driveway and onto the tree-lined street. Almost eleven-thirty now, her stomach growled and gurgled. It'd only been a few hours since breakfast, though with her morning interruption, she'd barely finished half of her cinnamon love knot, and the remaining pan of goodies she'd covered and set aside for later. Mike's arrival, and subsequent cold shoulder treatment, had killed what was left of her appetite. Now, she regretted that. Why let one sour apple spoil the fruits of her labor?

Erin tootled along the Norman Rockwell-worthy lanes and considered stopping in at the Come and Get It Diner for an early lunch where there were sure to be tantalizing specials-of-the-day. Why not? It would be the perfect time to beat the crowd and grab something delish that she didn't have to prepare. Not that she didn't like to cook. Just that once in a while she enjoyed being lazy and eating others' culinary delights. Especially Ida Mae's and Chuck Farrow's creations. Rumor had it that Chuck's recent cookbook had garnered praise from well-renowned foodies. Imagine—a celebrity in Ruby's very midst. It made Erin smile. This genial town continued to surprise and delight her in extraordinary ways.

Of course, the charm faded when she detoured to the Come and Get It and wandered in only to find Mike Brewer's rump plastered to one of the red bar stools at the luncheonette counter.

For the love of pickles. Erin Shaye could light up a box of wet matches. When the woman flounced in with her energetic vibe and mega-watt smile that could melt ice cold butter, the bite of biscuit lodged in Mike's throat. *Mercy.* He choked and reached for his water glass.

Briefly, Erin's gaze flickered toward him. Then, she spun in the opposite direction and headed for a vacant booth. She slid across the vinyl seat, with her back to him, and waited, presumably, for a menu.

Okay. He fully admitted that he must have been out of his ever-lovin' mind to rebuff her kindness this morning...or for that matter, at other times too. He'd had a few hours to wade through the muck he'd made of Erin's generosity, and his attitude didn't bode well with him. He'd been raised better. Would she even listen if he tried to explain?

Mike set down his glass, the biscuit finally working its way down. Gathering his half-eaten bowl of beef stew, along with his courage, he made his way over to where Erin sat.

"Mind if I join you?"

She glanced up, surprised, her smile vanishing.

He waited as she mulled over the idea.

"I suppose that would be all right. Though...why?"

So, the gal was gonna make him eat crow. Fine. Mike slid onto the seat across from hers, removing his phone from his shirt pocket, and switched it to vibrate. He placed it on the table, screen-side down, eliminating one distraction. "Because I'd like to get something off my chest."

Erin's right eyebrow shot up.

"No, not my phone."

"Well, don't let me interrupt." Ida Mae plunked down a menu and stood back, tucking her hands into the crisp pink apron that barely circled her very pregnant belly.

Framed by faux blonde ringlets, her face bore the glow of many a mother-to-be, and a grin that said she couldn't be happier about this unexpected blessing. Twins, at that. At forty, she and Chuck had finally gotten their happily-ever-after. Good for them.

Mike gave a chuckle. "You're not interrupting, Ida Mae. I imagine, though, Erin would like some time to scan the menu."

Ida Mae nodded. "Why, of course. You take a few minutes to decide, darlin', and I'll be right back. Oh—and special of the day is beef stew and biscuits. Apple pie for dessert. Which, by the looks of it, you'll be ready for soon." She pointedly glanced at Mike before waddling away.

"Is it as delish as it smells?" Erin tipped her head toward his bowl.

"Sure is. The biscuits are especially tasty."

"Guess that's what I'll order then." Erin didn't bother opening the menu. Instead, she relaxed against the booth and pinned him with her gaze. "Finished with firewood deliveries?"

"Yes'm. Thanks for the coffee. Warmed my bones." It had, at that. Though pumpkin spice-flavored brew would never be his drink of choice, he'd finished every last drop and thought of Erin the whole time. To run into her again so soon must be God's idea of a do-over. He hoped he didn't mess it up. "I have your insulated mug out in the truck. I'll wash it and return it to you."

"No hurry. I have others."

"Oh." The conversation—if one could call it that—would never make it past the starting gate if he didn't think of something in a hurry. Clearly, the gal wasn't about to make his efforts easy. Mike fiddled with the spoon in his bowl of stew and tamped down his jitters. "I really appreciated your thoughtfulness. Regarding the coffee, I mean."

Erin's left eyebrow shot up, accentuating the small scar above. "Really? Good to know."

"Nothing like a hot cup of coffee on a chilly morn. I'm sorry I missed the cinnamon love knots."

"Not a problem. All the more for me."

Way to go, bud. She's not having it. Obviously, him coming over here was a bad idea. Mike let his spoon drift back into his bowl of half-eaten stew. "Look, Doc—Erin—I'm sorry for my earlier rudeness. It had nothing to do with you. I wanted to do something nice for you by delivering wood, and then I blew it."

"Yeah, you did. Except you've already apologized, so I'm not sure why you feel the need to revisit this."

"Maybe it's me, but you're giving off some pretty icy vibes."

"Pardon me for being direct. What is it you want?"

She had him there. What did he want? "Well...I...er..."

"Exactly." Erin laughed. "You're absolved. I don't hold any grudges. I got—get—the point."

A slow warmth built in Mike's chest. For the past year, he'd fought his inclinations toward the perky redhead. Stuffed down any romantic inklings he might have for her. Now, like a stray lightning bolt, suddenly, it smacked him dead-center between the eyes. "It" being the reason he'd run the other way like a wayward young'un every time their paths crossed. *Glory be.* The woman had tweaked his heartstrings. Something he'd sworn would never happen again.

Erin placed her order when Ida Mae returned.

"You got it, honey." Ida Mae jotted down Erin's selection, then pointed her gaze at Mike. "Warm up your stew for you?".

"No, thanks. I'm good."

Good? His features flushed like he'd run a marathon, and a thin sheen of perspiration dotted his forehead.

"You sure? I could bring you a fresh bowl. Hot, straight from the kettle."

"I'll finish this first, Ida Mae. Thank you all the same."

"Sure thing."

Ida Mae toddled away and Erin prompted, "Please go ahead and finish your stew. You don't need to wait until mine comes."

Mike placed his palms on the table and leaned forward, his brown eyes, solemn. "I'm a dummy. Have been since you arrived in town. This isn't the place to go into it, but years ago, a bad experience colored my perception of things. Specifically, romantic relationships and the like. It has nothing to do with you. Never did."

Erin's skin prickled. "Romantic relationships? You flatter yourself. We barely know each other."

"*Sheesh.* I said that wrong." He heaved out a sigh and shook his head. "I *mean* I know we've been aware of each other. You know, as men and women are."

"Keep digging. That hole's getting bigger by the minute."

Another flash of color stole up Mike Brewer's neck and spread along his jawline. "Oops."

Despite her annoyance, Erin laughed. Clearly, eloquence wasn't his strong suit. "Assumptions. The word's led to the downfall of many a well-intentioned soul."

"Right. Sorry." Mike picked up his spoon and stirred his stew, which had to be cold by now. "The deal is..." Again, he let the spoon drift back into the half-eaten stew.

"I'll speak from my own perspective. From the get-go, you rattled me. Don't know why. Well, I think I know why, but that's beside the point. I handled those feelings badly and I'm sorry about that."

What was he admitting? Erin reigned in her laughter. Hunger pangs faded as Mike's tone registered. Slight awkwardness mingled with complete, unbridled sincerity, tempering further honesty. Though he didn't appear to regret his words, he shifted in his seat, training his gaze on her.

Like an unexpected hand of cards, Erin's emotions reshuffled, presenting unforeseen options along her periphery of possibilities. Authentic contrition would always win, hands-down. In that instant, she saw the man's heart. Maybe Mike's apologies hadn't been the stuff of romance movies, but he'd spoken with conviction, and that counted for something. A lot, actually.

"Thank you for sharing all that. It gives me some insight into what's been going through your mind."

Mike nodded. "I'm glad. 'Cause I'm feeling mighty embarrassed. For the past year, you must have thought I was a jerk."

"Not exactly. Well, kind of. Your initial welcome to the community, followed by your aloofness, made me wonder why the reversal."

"Yeah," he paused, a slight smile playing at the corners of his mouth. "About that. As Chamber of Commerce President, it's my duty to officially welcome all new businesses to town."

"Your duty?" Erin teased.

"Er...my pleasure. Ruby needed a veterinarian. Lord knows, kids and critters need their doctoring. Nice to know I don't have to run Blackie twenty miles down the road for his check-ups and shots anymore."

"I see."

"That and...besides what I already told you."

Yes. Erin wouldn't make him repeat it. At least she had a better idea of what made the handsome homebuilder tick. Or rather, what—*who*—got under his skin. *Her.*

She'd barely had a chance to digest the fact before Ida Mae delivered a passel of goodies from an oversized serving tray.

"I brought extra because I know Mike's is colder'n a berg now." Ida Mae sidled up as close as her girth allowed and began plunking down glasses of iced tea, dishes of stew, baskets of biscuits, and dessert plates with slabs of apple pie.

"Thank you kindly, Ida Mae." Mike helped steady the tray as she emptied it. "Say, should you still be doing this? Aren't you getting close to your due date?"

"I know I'm plump as a fritter, but nope. I still have eight more weeks to go."

"Chuck's okay with this arrangement? With you being here on your feet all day in your condition?"

"Oh, brother." Ida Mae cast her gaze heavenward, then fixed her eyes on Mike. "For your information, this is the twenty-first century. Pregnant women work all the time. Granted, I'm a tad older than most, but this isn't my first rodeo."

Erin knew the story. As a teenager, Ida Mae had placed her first child for adoption, and in recent years—through somewhat of a miracle—they'd connected. Though the baby wasn't Chuck's, after decades of pining away for one another, he and Ida Mae had finally found their way back to each other, too. A poignant, true-life narrative neither shied away from. The Farrows's fairy-tale had been a long time in the making, and not without its ups and downs. Townsfolk couldn't be happier for the couple when they announced they were having not one, but *two* babies. Sometimes, fact eclipsed fiction, and God transformed and redeemed even the most poignant of circumstances. Something that Erin should remember on nights that seemed way too long and her cottage a bit too lonely.

"Sorry, Ida Mae. Didn't mean to insinuate you weren't up to the task," Mike was saying. "Expressing my concern is all."

"Not to worry. In fact, as of next week, I do intend to scale back my workdays, per my obstetrician's advice. Chuck and our co-manager will handle things here while I kick back a while at home." Ida Mae blew some wayward blonde strands from her face and gave them a wink. "Actually, Hubs is cutting back on his hours, too. Between penning his next cookbook and readying the nursery, he says the home front is calling him. Then when these angels come..." Ida Mae patted her stomach. "I'll reassess. I may come in a day or two during the week. We'll see. Well, let me know if you need anything. Otherwise, I'll be back to check on you two lovebirds. Enjoy."

"Oh, we're not..." Erin tried to correct her assumption, but Ida Mae waddled away before she could finish her sentence.

Chapter Three

From his vantage point, Mike's two-story log cabin gleamed in the late afternoon sunlight. As the steep, pebbled lane wound around the tree-shrouded hillside, leaves and vines gave way to the sun-dappled clearing, revealing the home of his heart—the masterpiece he'd spent the better part of a year building. Two stories— three—if one counted the small, cozy reading loft perched high above the second level, overlooking town below and blending seamlessly into the wooded backdrop of Ruby's hills and hollows.

Why, as a self-confirmed bachelor, he'd designed and built such a mammoth spread remained a mystery to most everyone, including his own family, except secretly, Mike still yearned for things he couldn't yet express. No shame in that, he told himself. No shame a'tall, save for the fact he and Sally Sue were history—had been for well over a decade—yet the past held him in a chokehold and refused to release him.

At least that's how it had been...until Doctor Erin Shaye waltzed into town, turning his right-side-up world upside-down. Now, he could hardly think straight. The woman addled him. Seeing her again this morning set his mind to wondering *what if*. *What if* his past was meant as a learning experience rather than a lasting impression? *What if* an old story was granted a new beginning? And more to the point, *what if* he could rewrite the chapter "Left at the Altar" and retitle it "Right on Time"?

That would be a supernatural wonder. A miracle, for

sure.

Mike drew closer to his abode, conscious of the prime, unsullied timber that sheltered the craggy path—each tree somewhat symmetrically the same, yet each one unique in its story and design. In the distance, a wide-eyed doe paused and sniffed the air. She hightailed it away over some fallen tree limbs and underbrush, leaving only a memory of where she'd been.

While earth, rock, and foliage bore testament to the hillside's distinctive palette, each crack and crevice of this centuries-old mount teemed with hints of mystery and hues of color. Stamped with the Maker's thumbprint, this was the stuff of daydreams, and while some audacious souls might be tempted to sell this land to the highest bidder, Mike vowed he'd never be included in that lot. He valued nature's beauty more than financial gain.

He eased up the incline and into the garage, shutting off the engine. Another day. Another dollar. Another night alone. Just him and Blackie. Not that he didn't love his two-year-old Lab. He did. Loved him mightily, in fact. But sometimes, on days such as this—October gems that promised bright harvest moons and crisp, chilly nights— it'd be nice to cuddle up with someone other than his pooch. 'Course someone like Erin Shaye would fit the bill in fine fashion.

Are you nuts, man? The look on her face at the Come and Get It when Ida Mae intimated their relationship status communicated volumes. Astonishment. Or at the very least, strong surprise, mixed with obvious distaste. Erin had quickly recovered, however, the way her eyes darted from Ida Mae to him, and then back to her meal after Ida Mae hurried away, left no question. He'd blown any chance he might have with Ruby's newest citizen. Erin had barely looked at him as they ate. There'd been only small talk—polite niceties to curb the uncomfortable silence during the awkward transition.

Way to go, idiot. If you'd reigned in your dummy tendencies, you guys might have become friends...or maybe more.

She'd been interested and he'd tossed away potential. He'd kicked opportunity out the door and Erin's feelings with it. *Blast it.* For too long, Mike had married himself to work, preferring it over dating and its entanglements. At least work exhausted one in satisfying ways. Romance muddied up one's mind. Or it had. Could it have been different with Erin? He'd never know.

Mike grabbed a few items from his truck seat and bounded from the cab. Blackie met him with a happy bark at the mudroom entrance, tail wagging to beat the band and tongue going to town as he licked his dog dad's hands.

"Hi ya, boy. What'd you do today besides make good use of your doggie door here and chase after squirrels?" Mike rubbed the scruff of Blackie's neck and tossed his key fob, a folder, and an assortment of mail on the counter beneath the bank of oak cabinets.

Yap. Yap. Yap. The Lab's deep woofs pierced the room's silence as he proceeded to tell Mike all about it.

"You don't say? So...you ate, slept, and made merry while I earned the day's wages? Ahh, you lead a charmed life. Good thing we have a partially fenced area around the cabin, or you might've been tempted to take off into the hills and make a deer friend or two."

A chuckle tickled the back of Mike's throat. *This is what I've been reduced to. Conversing with my dog and expecting him to answer.* Well, no matter. No one here to josh him about it.

Mike tugged off his jacket, hanging it on one of the many wall hooks beside the door, and reached in his shirt pocket for his phone. *Empty.* No wonder there'd been no calls to field since lunch.

From the Come and Get It, he'd checked on a building project north of Ruby, then he'd spent the last few hours visiting Mel and Matt over at their place. He must've left his cell on the table at the diner. Unusual for him, although admittedly, it hadn't been a usual kind of day. 'Course it wasn't that late yet—around four-fifty or so. He could head back to the Come and Get It. Being a Saturday, it'd still be open for another hour.

"You'd probably like supper first, huh, boy?"

Woof!

"Yeah. I thought so. All right, you spoiled goofball. Follow me."

Blackie beat a path into the kitchen, a cavernous, yet comfortable space, which still held scents of early morning coffee and last evening's pot roast. The canine's entire body trembled with excitement as Mike advanced toward the pantry—a huge walk-in affair—lined with endless shelves which boasted pots and pans, boxed items, canned goods, staples, and whatnot.

Woof! Woof!

"Patience, boy. You normally don't eat for another hour. What's the hurry?" At two, Blackie shouldn't be experiencing another growth spurt, nevertheless, maybe he was. Mike made a mental note to discuss that with Erin at his annual checkup in a few weeks. He'd made the appointment some time ago—deciding now that Ruby had a veterinarian in town, it was high time to transfer

Blackie's care. Not only would it benefit small business, it would keep his patronage local. Not to mention shave off the twenty-five minutes it normally took to haul his pet into nearby Sapphire.

Mike dished up the high-end dog food, sliding the stainless-steel bowl back into the fancy feeder, and the critter immediately began chowing down. "Enjoy, big guy."

Blackie paused for a moment to lick Mike's hand, leaving remnants of food plastered between his fingers. *Yuck.* He appreciated his pet's gratitude, but he could do without the slobbery kisses at least until after Blackie finished eating.

He gave the Lab's head a final pat and retraced his steps to the mudroom where he quickly washed up. As he washed, a fleeting image danced across Mike's mind. Erin had a pet. A cat. The feline had watched him this morning from its comfy perch inside. A curious critter, Mike had noted, as the cat affixed his eyes to Mike's every move. He'd meant to ask Erin about her—or him—although there'd been no time for that. He'd squashed any chances of small talk that might have been. Still...he'd like to have asked the cat's name. Did it keep her company at night the way a faithful companion might during those long stretches of loneliness and silence?

Mike shook his head, attempting to clear his wayward thoughts. *Who are you, bud, to draw any conclusions as to the state of Erin's personal life?* Maybe she didn't experience solitude the way he did. Maybe she had a full and active social life which negated the need for periodic introspection. He'd always been an odd duck in that way. Wasn't that why Sally Sue left him standing at the altar alone twelve years ago on what was to be their wedding day? Because she'd suddenly realized that she didn't want to be tied down at such a young age to *"someone who acts so old."*

However, Mike knew the truth. When Sally Sue discovered she was no longer pregnant the week before their wedding, she had no further use for him. *"This couldn't have worked out better really."* They'd met at Cusick Park away from probing eyes and well-tuned ears. His fiancée had turned to him in the dewy glow of a September morn. *"Now, no one will know the truth—about the baby, I mean. We can say we had a parting of the ways and leave it at that. We're both so young. People won't think a thing about it. In a month or two, the good folks of Ruby will have moved on to other topics. A little ol' broken engagement won't hold a candle to the market's rump roast sale or some equally fascinating subject."*

Mike recalled the emotional sucker punch in vivid detail. Instead of relief that day, bile rose in his throat and his gut churned. *"This isn't funny, Sally Sue. Baby or not, we love each other. Have all during high school. I still want to marry you. Make a life together."*

"Are you sure? Really sure?" She'd fidgeted with the engagement ring, still nestled on the third finger of her left hand.

"Of course, I'm sure." Then, Mike had taken her hands in his, giving them a squeeze. *"You're the only one for me, Sally Sue. Always have been, always will be."*

"I feel the same way. I just wanted to give you an out." She'd gazed up at him, fluttering her golden lashes. *"I guess it would be a shame to let a three-thousand-dollar wedding gown go to waste."*

Except one week later, that's exactly what Sally Sue did. Along with the wedding, reception, and honeymoon. *Wasted.* All of it. Expense. Effort. Time. *Love.* She'd stood him up at the altar in their childhood church before the entire town of Ruby, leaving behind a handwritten note on the dressing table in the bridal room.

Mike closed his eyes against the torment of that day. Though he no longer pined for the girl from his past, the memories marked a poignant chapter in his life. The chapter called *The School of Hard Knocks*. Until recently— say, one year ago—when Erin Shaye bebopped into town, he hadn't had cause to revisit it.

Maybe it was time.

Tires crunching on gravel snapped Mike back to the present. *Who in the world?* He didn't receive many callers. His out-of-the-way location deterred visitors and he somewhat liked the fact.

Quickly drying his hands, he turned to peer out the window and his jaw dropped in surprise.

Erin. Why had she come?

Maybe this was a mistake. When Ida Mae caught Erin before she left the diner and asked if she'd mind taking Mike his phone, it seemed like a simple request. Now, Erin wasn't so sure. What if he didn't appreciate the intrustion? Anyone who lived this far off the beaten path—on practically a mountainside, no less—surely didn't want to be bothered.

Still, considering they'd eaten lunch together, as a gesture of goodwill, it seemed only fitting that Erin indulge Ida Mae's request. "Certainly. I can take Mike his phone. Can you give me directions?"

The twinkle in the woman's matchmaking eyes should have given Erin a clue. "You bet, and thanks for doing this. I'm sure that boy'll appreciate it. It isn't like him to forget something so important, but in all fairness,

I found the sucker beneath his dinner napkin. Don't know what lit a fire under Mike's tail to vamoose in such a hurry. Good thing I caught you." Ida Mae rattled off a couple highway names, street signs, and landmarks. "Don't go by your GPS. It's not the best route. Trust me. Oh, and I'd give him a few hours before you head there, or he might not be home yet. Saturdays are errand days."

Yes. Erin could relate to that. With the clinic being closed on the weekends, that was when she usually tried to accomplish other tasks, too.

Now, she cut off her engine and sat spellbound. Ida Mae had directed her to Mike's cabin, no problem. Though, Erin had no idea that by "cabin" what the Come and Get It proprietress really meant was *castle*. A mansion. Technically, a log cabin, but that was semantics. *Oh my.* Erin sucked in her breath at the sheer beauty and vastness of the home.

Despite the dwelling's enormity, an undeniable warmth emanated from the massive log planks that melded beautifully into the forested background. Magnificent covered porches wrapped around the cabin's entire upper and lower stories, affording stellar views from any given point. Abutting the west end of the cabin, so as to possibly catch those glorious Ozarkian sunsets, was a generous deck which boasted a picnic table and benches, a pair of Adirondack chairs, a gas grill, and a wood storage chest. The domicile could easily swallow Erin's entire cottage several times over.

Had Mike built all this? Of course, he had. Every aspect, every detail, smacked of his personality and preferences. She knew enough about the guy that while he might not be a fancy fellow, he took pride in quality and craftmanship. This portion of paradise was purely his brainchild.

Extraordinary. But wasn't this rather extravagant for only one person? Maybe he hosted a lot of family gatherings, or perhaps, liked to entertain. Possibly, she'd misjudged his reasoning for building so far off the beaten path...yet she didn't think so.

Well, she wasn't here to assess his abilities or his penchant for solitude. She'd return his phone and be on her way. Judging by the raised garage doors and a glimpse of his truck, obviously, Mike was home.

Erin grabbed the object of her intent and exited her vehicle. Immediately, the heady scent of earth and woods tickled her nose, drawing her back to another time— simple, carefree days she'd spent as a child adventuring with Mama and Daddy. Hiking, camping, nature jaunts. They'd done it all. Before...the accident. Before...her life changed forever. *Before* she'd gone to live with Aunt Bea in St. Louis.

Erin touched the scar above her left eyebrow—the only reminder of that summer she'd turned twelve. What she wouldn't give to relive that last trip to the lake with her parents. *Oh,* how she longed for a do-over. When the giant buck leaped out of nowhere, naturally, no one expected it. In a flash, it was over. *It* being the wreck that upended Erin's world.

"Well, hi there." Mike strode from the garage and raised his hand in a wave. "Wow. Three times in one day. To what do I owe this pleasure?"

Erin held up his phone. "You left it on the table at lunch."

"Ah. Nice of you to deliver it all this way. Thanks."

"Ida Mae asked me to br—"

Before she could finish her sentence, a black blur

zipped around the fenced side of the cabin and descended upon her.

Woof! Woof! Woof!

"Blackie!" Mike hollered. "Come 'ere, boy." Instantly, the dog stopped in his tracks and returned to Mike's side where he'd opened the gate. His tail continued to wag, and his pink tongue lolled from side to side as he sized up their company. "Way to go, sport. Good boy." Then, redirecting his attention to Erin again, Mike shook his head. "He's harmless and he can't jump this chain link fence, but sorry for the scare. He loves his doggie door. You may have guessed."

What a beautiful Labrador. He'd make five of Miranda.

"So, this is Blackie?" Erin approached slowly, holding out her hand so the dog could take a sniff. "No worries. He simply caught me by surprise." A smile found its way to her lips as the sleek-coated Lab bestowed kisses on her outstretched palm. "I'll be seeing you soon down at the clinic, won't I, fella?"

Woof!

"Yes, ma'am. I scheduled his yearly exam for the end of the month per your receptionist. By the way, he probably smells your cat."

"Why, I bet you do." Erin petted Blackie's head. "Aren't you a handsome one? Look at that shiny coat, bright eyes, and moist nose. And lots of healthy teeth and pink gums, too. You're about what—two?"

"Good call, Doc. I'm impressed."

"And you nailed it, as well. I'm sure Blackie smells Miranda."

"Miranda. Now, that's a nice name. I like it."

"I rescued her from a no-kill shelter when she was a few months old. I considered changing it, but that was her given name, and I thought it was kind of pretty." She handed him his cell phone. "Here."

"Thanks again. I really appreciate you delivering it. I guess my mind was on other things when I left the diner."

"Yeah, you scooted out of there rather fast once you finished your stew." Was he blushing? *Hmm... Erin's pulse raced. She affected him like that?* "Oh, and thank you for paying for mine. You shouldn't have done that."

"My pleasure. I wasn't trying to make a quick getaway. I promised my sister and brother-in-law I'd visit them this afternoon. Didn't want to renege on a promise." A slow grin spread across his face. "Now, that you're here, I'd be delighted if you joined me for supper."

"Oh, that isn't necessary. You don't have to offer—"

He held up his palm to silence her. "I won't take no for an answer. The least I can do is feed you. It's not every day an angel of mercy visits."

"A bit dramatic much?"

"Hardly. This is a new phone. I didn't dole out the additional bucks for the protection plan this time...because I never wash, toss, or lose my phone."

Laughter bubbled past Erin's lips. "Then I guess you owe me big time. What are we eating?"

"It's a surprise. Follow us."

Woof! Woof!

Erin's heart thudded against her ribcage. The guy probably made a mean sandwich. *All right. A harmless supper between new friends and then I'm outta here.*

Chapter Four

What was he thinking? Inviting Erin to supper when he had no earthly clue what he'd even make? However, the chance to redeem himself and start afresh after this morning's bungled attempt prompted him onward. Lunch had gone okay, apart from being a tad wobbly. He wanted to try again. "May I take your jacket?"

"Sure. Thanks."

Erin shrugged out of the lightweight garment and watched him hang it on a wall peg. Blackie bounded ahead of them into the kitchen, but turned in mid-run and barked, as if to say *Come in!*

"That's his way of offering his personal invitation. After you." Mike extended his arm.

A light powdery scent followed Erin as she moved past him, making him fully aware of her presence. She was not a figment of his imagination.

"*Oh, Mike.* Your home is exquisite. I had no idea that you…" Admiration punctuated her words and Erin's voice drifted off as she beheld his abode.

"Owned a cabin in the woods?" he supplied.

"Yes. But it's more than a cabin. It's…*heaven.*" Her gaze bounced from the polished log rafters and high beamed ceiling to the glossy stone floor and its intricate pattern. "You built this?"

"Every square inch. Well, to clarify, my construction crew and I built it, and my sister offered decorating tips.

Mel's kind of a visionary when it comes to designing and that sort of thing."

"I gathered as much when I bought the cottage. She has a knack for reading a space and bringing its personality to life." Erin smiled at him. "I love how the stone in here flows with the oak flooring beyond the kitchen. Your cabin suits you to a T. Wide open floor plan, yet warm and cozy, too. Impressive without being ostentatious."

"Thanks. I enjoy the creative process and working with my hands. Guess that's what led me to this vocation." Her reaction pleased him. He realized it mattered what Erin thought and he wondered why that was so. "I like big, comfy spaces with room to breathe. No chopped-up rooms for me."

"You wouldn't like my cottage then."

"Nah, I didn't mean it like that. Doc Burnside's bungalow is the exception. That stone relic is a charmer. It has an appeal that captivates folks." When Mel and Matt married, selling the cottage had been no easy decision. His sister said it would take a special buyer before she'd be tempted to even part with it. "Your cottage is a major conversation piece around these parts. If Mel hadn't gone and gotten herself hitched, she'd still be there. Truth be told, if it'd been someone other than you who'd made an offer on the place, she probably would've taken it off the market."

"Wonder what it was about me that made her decide *yes*."

"Similar personalities, same drive, close in age. You share a mutual appreciation for old things—vintage and nostalgia and the like. That's how a lot of folks in Ruby feel. She believed you'd fit right in."

"Good to know. Mel's become a close friend since I moved here."

Yeah. Mel had said as much. Like Ida Mae and others, she also hadn't shied away from some matchmaking tendencies, which he'd firmly squelched. Except now, he didn't mind it as much.

"She's said very kind things about you." He'd leave out the parts about her mentioning Erin's marital status. *'Single, and quite the catch, big brother. A real keeper for the one who's worthy of her.'* The love bug had bitten Mel and she thought everyone should be married. Obviously, she quite fancied the notion. Since his sister and Matt had tied the knot, the stars in her eyes had yet to dim. Mike imagined his eyes had mirrored that same glow once. Thankfully, Mel had waited for the right person instead of almost marrying the wrong one.

"I appreciate you sharing that."

"Oh? I...uh..." Had he spoken aloud?

"The things she said. Mel's a real sweetheart. When I moved here last year, she delivered so many homemade goodies to the clinic that I didn't even have to cook that first week. Then, when I bought the cottage and moved in a few weeks ago, same thing." Erin's face warmed. "She's a great friend."

Mike could kick himself. He'd had plenty of opportunities to be Erin's friend, and what had he done? Either given her the brush-off or completely avoided her. Well, he could remedy that here and now.

"I'd like to be your friend, Erin. I know I did a poor job communicating that at lunch. I wish I could have a complete do-over since you arrived in town."

Erin cleared her throat, as if weighing his admission and genuinely considering his offer. What if she said *No, thanks*? He certainly couldn't blame her.

"Do-over granted. I'd like us to be friends." Her mouth curved upward. "No worries at all. I promise not to drag you to the altar. In fact, anything beyond friendship is the last thing on my mind."

"O-kaay."

"Yeah. I think it's best to get that out of the way right now. Eases the awkwardness."

Her laughter, so soft and light, echoed between them like notes on a piano, tweaking those deep places Mike held in reserve. *Oh, boy.* This could be dangerous.

For a moment, Mike simply stared. Then, his forehead creased and a muscle in his jaw twitched. Dark brows knitted together, and his eyes flickered with something unreadable.

Had she hurt his feelings? Mirth that had bubbled up again within Erin's chest dissolved. She'd attempted levity and it had backfired. Why? Talk about mixed signals. Figuring out what made Mike Brewer tick addled her in odd ways. Maybe she was the conundrum. She'd spent the last year fascinated with the man, though, when he'd shown no interest, she'd recognized nothing would come of her one-sided curiosity. However, a firewood delivery and a very thought-provoking lunch, which included Mike's honest admission, raised a certain awareness— again. Something most definitely had shifted between them. In a good way it had seemed. Now?

"I'm glad you set me straight there. Hang on while I remove the pin."

"The pin?"

"Yeah. The one you jabbed in my inflated ego." When a smile inched its way across Mike's face, he gave a chuckle. "So, wha'd'ya say? Shall we shake on this friendship thing?"

Goosebumps danced on Erin's arms as Mike poked out a hand. He wanted to shake on it? Like a business deal? Nevertheless, tentatively, she followed suit. Relief mingled with delight as she met his open palm with her own. When their flesh connected, the warmth of Mike's hand drew butterflies, causing Erin's stomach to flutter. *Relax. He probably shakes a lot of hands. No big deal.* Although the way Mike gently clasped her hand and held it for a few seconds longer than what seemed necessary, certainly didn't feel like any ordinary handshake. This handshake took greetings and agreements to a whole new level. This one had the *wow* factor.

"Friends." Erin disengaged first, allowing her arm to slacken and drop to her side.

Seemingly on cue, Blackie voiced his approval. *Woof!*

"See? Even this fella agrees. He's happy we're friends." Grinning, Mike stepped back and made a sweeping motion with his arm. "Now, how about the ten-cent tour and then I'll whip us up some supper?"

"I'd love that."

"Great. Follow me."

Except as it turned out, the ten-cent tour was more like a one-hundred-dollar adventure. At nearly six-thousand square feet, Mike's cabin boasted beautiful, spacious living areas with a stunning assortment of custom designed cabinetry, bookcases, and built-ins. Beams and woodwork gleamed. Rustic hardware popped.

Floor to ceiling windows sparkled, showcasing glorious views of the hills and hollows reflecting the setting sun.

"Oh, my!" Erin's breath caught in her throat as she regarded the home's resplendent interior.

She loved the reading loft most of all. Positioned intentionally to overlook the outdoor panorama, a chocolate brown sectional with a pair of matching leather recliners lent the space a relaxed air. The perfect niche for daydreaming and lounging with a good book, the loft also boasted several oversized floor pillows.

Judging from the bookcases that graced one of the sloped, wide-beamed walls, it appeared that Mike favored an eclectic mix of titles. Everything from classic westerns to legal thrillers to military history rounded out several shelves. Some shelves dedicated themselves to architecture and design. Other shelves held Bible commentaries, apologetics, and various works on theology—a healthy mix of a well-read individual. Who would have guessed?

Erin reigned in her surprise, lest she seem condescending, but she'd never known a man who shared her similar passion for reading. Granted, her fictional tastes varied from Mike's, and she doubted he'd find her multiple volumes of veterinary medicine especially fascinating, except the fact they both enjoyed books and reading placed them on common ground. A man with an affinity for literature and things of God had to be a quality guy.

Something, though, continued to mystify her. Why build a cabin of this scope for merely one person? If she knew Mike better, she might have asked him.

"I can see those wheels spinning." Mike broke the

silence, addressing the obvious. "When I designed this place...I envisioned the pitter-patter of lots of tiny feet. I'm one of four siblings and I guess I wanted to recreate the scenario one day with a family of my own. Kinda crazy, huh?"

"Not at all." Erin shook her head. "A leap of faith maybe. Not crazy." She trailed her fingertips along one of the bookcases, imagining the picture Mike described. Who had he hoped would be mama to his children? From what little he'd confided at lunch, there'd been someone, and that relationship had ended badly. She longed to offer encouragement, but the words temporarily eluded her. She didn't favor clichés. Anyway, her own baggage had yet to be unpacked. So much of life she didn't pretend to understand.

Finally, Erin spoke again. "My Aunt Bea says when our hopes and dreams align with God's will and timing, He longs to grant the desires of our heart."

"Wise words. Sounds like your aunt is a strong woman of faith."

"Yes, she is. I wouldn't be where I am today without her guidance and prayer." *Careful. You don't really want to have this conversation now.* Erin stepped toward the windows, the last vestiges of golden sunshine bathing the hillside in splashes of color. No wonder Mike loved it here. *Home.* The cabin—its setting—bespoke the word and wrapped one in fantasy and feel-good. "I can understand why you were drawn to build here. It's like hugs and homemade quilts and sugar cookies all rolled into one."

Mike laughed. "I never thought of it quite like that, but yeah. That's a great way to put it. That's exactly how Hilltop Haven makes me feel."

"Hilltop Haven?" Erin turned, a smile forming.

"Uh...my nickname for the ol' girl. Figured I needed something fitting for my little cabin on the hill."

Little cabin? Hilarious.

"Clever. She's worthy of it."

"Thanks. I'm glad you think so." Mike's stomach rumbled, drawing attention to the obvious. "Well, guess that was a dead giveaway. I'm hungry. You?"

"You really don't have to—"

"Invite you to supper. I know." The mirth reached his eyes first. "Can't guarantee it'll be anything fancy, although I can hold my own in the kitchen. My mama insisted on it. Taught her crew well."

"Good for her. Then you're not a frequent flyer down at the Come and Get It?"

"Hey, I'm a sucker for mouth-watering, down-home country cookin' as much as the next guy...or gal, and I do stop in at the diner sometimes, but I wouldn't say I'm a frequent flyer. I enjoy the company as much as I do the grub."

So...maybe Mike wasn't as keen on solitude as she'd gathered. Or at least when loneliness came calling, he appeased that gnawing at the place where everyone who was anyone seemed to gather. The atmosphere at the local diner lent a home away from home appeal, and Ida Mae and Chuck Farrow made sure every patron received special treatment. That's why Erin liked it there. Although she had no family in the immediate area, the Farrows and their staff had welcomed her to their fold as if she were one of Ruby's own. In fact, she'd almost come to believe she belonged there—that she was, indeed, one of them.

"Ladies first." Mike extended his arm, again

encouraging her to go first.

A gentleman. Erin liked that about him. Realizing past hurts had driven his initial aloofness made her want to know more. Who'd caused Mike to shield himself from anything beyond friendship? Did she still live in Ruby?

They descended the loft stairway to the landing below. Briefly, they toured the second floor, which accommodated a lavishly appointed master bedroom suite and three additional bedrooms with adjoining baths. "I guess we did this out of order because I was eager to show you my reading nook. In winter—a builder's slower months—I hibernate there."

"I can see why."

Finally, they wound up where they initially began, on the first floor with its handcrafted furnishings and dreamlike appeal. Erin said nothing of the empty bedrooms and unoccupied space, but her mind raced with the things he'd spoken of earlier. *The pitter-patter of lots of tiny feet.* Yes, this home needed a family. She hoped the Lord saw fit one day to give wings to Mike's dream.

While Erin hadn't thought much of having a family of her own, that didn't mean she couldn't appreciate Mike's yearning. He'd grown up with siblings and a two-parent household. She, on the other hand, had been raised by an aunt with no children of her own. She'd long since shelved the idea of a traditional family, and now, didn't even know what that might look like. Still *ohh*, how she sometimes wondered.

"So...leftovers agree with you then?"

What had he been saying? Erin had missed something. "I'm sorry. Pardon me?"

"I asked if you were a fan of roast beef, taters, and

carrots. Because if you are, I'll reheat and have that whipped up in a flash."

"Perfect. Sounds delicious."

Blackie tagged along, following them into the kitchen. He slurped a few big drinks from his water bowl and then took up residence on his doggie bed in the great room where he could observe all the goings on.

His owner laughed. "You comfy, fella?"

Woof!

"Good deal." Mike started pulling dishes from the fridge, setting them on the kitchen island. He glanced over at Erin. "Does Miranda keep close tabs on you like Blackie does me?"

"Cats are different. More solitary in nature. Though, I have to admit Miranda is unique."

"How so?"

"She enjoys her me time, but she's also very affectionate. I've had her a long while—since college—and when I'm home, we're pretty much attached at the hip."

"You ever take her to the clinic with you?"

"Sometimes. Not on a regular basis. Miranda's well behaved and enjoys visiting, but she's more comfortable in her own home." Erin watched as Mike forked thick slabs of beef from the platter and transferred them to a microwave-safe dish. He spooned several pearl onions to one side, along with carrots and new potatoes to the other. "What about Blackie? Does he accompany you to job sites?"

"Oh, often, he'll ride along as my sidekick. As you're aware, he's a people guy."

"Like you?" It was Erin's turn to laugh.

"How good of you to notice." The corners of Mike's

mouth twitched. "Plates are in that cabinet over there. Would you be ever so kind?"

Amazing. Who would've thought that she and the former Mr. Crabby-Patty would be standing there teasing each other after the past year's icy brushoff? Certainly, not her.

"Of course. Which cabinet would that be?"

"Oh. Sorry. The second one to the right of the sink. That's the dinnerware I reserve for my special guests."

Erin's pulse quickened. Was Mike flirting? Warm brown eyes held hers for the barest of seconds until she refocused on her assigned task. As she opened the cabinet door and reached for two red Fiestaware plates, it struck her how shiny they appeared.

"I've never used them," Mike offered quietly. "I never had cause to...until now."

Chapter Five

"Brace yourself, Mom." Mike seized one of the chocolate chip cookies from the cooling rack and chomped into its gooey sweetness. He savored the bite of heaven for only a moment before swallowing. "I think something unexpected has happened."

The Brewer matriarch's spatula paused over the baking pan where she'd been about to remove the next batch of cookies. Her eyes sparked with awareness. It was more what he hadn't said than what he had.

"And that would be?"

"Something you and Dad have prayed about for the past twelve years."

Hope shone in his mother's face. They both knew what he referred to.

"Praise be." She reached to caress his cheek with her free hand. "A chink of armor's fallen away."

"Yes." Mike placed his palm over his mom's hand, then brought it to his lips and gently kissed it. *Beloved mother of mine. Every fella should be so blessed.*

"Care to share more?"

"Would you mind if I said 'not yet'? I'm still processing it."

"In God's time then."

"Thanks, Mom. I love you."

"And I love you, son."

On Tuesday, three days after the rollercoaster ride with

Mike, Erin sat in her office at the clinic, updating patient progress notes. Officially, the clinic closed at four-thirty, and since today had been a slower one, she'd have things wrapped up by five. She loved her profession, except ever since Saturday, Erin found her thoughts wandering in a new direction. What did Mike do with his evenings? Ramble around alone in his big cabin on the hill? And do what exactly—design homes? Read books? Play fetch with Blackie?

Various images paraded across Erin's mind. Having supper with Mike on Saturday stirred old feelings from the previous twelve months—idealistic notions what it might be like to know the attractive bachelor on a more intimate level.

What did his inner circle of friends look like? From all accounts, the Brewer family was highly regarded. Townsfolk praised their kindness and quiet faith. People appreciated their downhome values and neighborly compassion. Aside from all that, however, who did the Brewers—specifically, the Brewer siblings—spend time with?

Obviously, as a newlywed, Mel's husband garnered much of her attention. She also enjoyed a close-knit relationship with co-workers at The Meadows, the retirement community where she worked. Now her brothers...Gabe, Garrett, and Mike...each one talented and respected professionals in their own right, not to mention single and and quite good-looking, who captured their interest?

Good grief. Erin rolled her eyes heavenward. Who was she kidding? While each one was intriguing and handsome, only one of the Brewer men sent her blood pressure soaring. Although she'd doled out some of the same medicine Mike had dished to her, she couldn't possibly keep it up. Not when the man had sincerely apologized *and* served her a meal fit for a queen. He'd even followed her home in his truck "because it's dark and this mountain has enough twists and turns in the daylight, let alone navigating them when it's pitch black."

Mike had parked in front of her home and then escorted her to the front door as one might after a date. However, dinner at his place hadn't been a date. It had been a spur-of-the-moment invitation in thanks for delivering his cell phone. And yet, Erin detected a distinct undercurrent with his parting words.

"I hope you'll visit me again. No reason necessary."

Erin's cheeks warmed, remembering.

"Must be a doozy of a thought." Vangie, her office manager, leaned against the doorjamb, smiling. "I doubt it's related to your last patient's deworming."

Erin laughed. "Nope. Can't say that it is."

"Well then?"

"Well what?"

"Don't keep me in suspense. I could use a tickle before I head home."

The hitch in Vangie's voice gave her pause. "Everything okay with Mitch and the kids?"

"Oh, yeah. They're terrific. It's our new addition."

Wait. What? Vangie was pregnant? Erin sat up straighter in her chair. "Oh. Congratulations! I didn't know you were expecting."

"Whoa. Are you kidding? Not me. Adding another kiddo to our toddler tribe at this point isn't exactly my idea of peace and tranquility. I meant our new *home addition.*

We're adding a great room and an additional bath to our house. Mike Brewer's heading up the project, and Sam Packard is our cabinetry and finishing guy. Of course, Mitch being a plumber, he'll join the fun and—" Vangie stopped mid-sentence. "Hey. Wait a minute. What's that look?"

"Look?"

"Yeah. The one you just got when I mentioned Mike's name. That look." With two gleeful strides, Vangie plopped down in the chair across from Erin's desk. "*Oh my cupcakes. You* and Mike? In a little, ol' town the size of a hatband, why am I always the last one to know? Why haven't you said something? You're in love! This is sublime."

"No, not Mike and me. You have it all wrong." The warmth in Erin's cheeks fanned out to her entire face. *Wonderful.* She didn't have to look in a mirror to know she'd turned the shade of a ripe garden beet. "The Brewer family has been very kind to me since I moved here. That's as far as it goes, though, between Mike and me. He's...um...a friend."

"Uh-huh. If you say so."

"No, really, Vangie. Mike barely gave me the time of day when I first moved to Ruby."

"Yeah. I remember. I also remember how much it bugged you. What changed?"

"Nothing." Erin updated the last of her progress notes, logged out, and closed her laptop. Vangie leaned forward, waiting. Clearly, she wasn't going to let this go. "We've merely reached a new understanding."

"I wondered. After your lunch date a few days ago, I assumed things were on the uptick."

Oh, no. Was that the latest buzz—that her having lunch with Mike was a *date*? Best set that record straight right now. Though, it appeared the local chitchat had already started. "Mike and I have become friends, but I can assure you that a meal with the man was nothing remotely romantic. I visited the Come and Get It for lunch, and he simply asked if he could join me at my table. That's all there was to it." Barring some inklings. Naturally, no one needed to know that.

Erin stood, stretched, and reached for her jacket, hoping Vangie would take the hint. She liked the mid-thirtyish office manager, a newer friend, who also served as the clinic's receptionist and part-time vet tech, but Erin had no inclination to discuss her love life—or lack of one. Vangie was happily married with three kids and a storybook home, which included the white picket fence and a yard full of apple trees. How could she possibly recall life before seven years of marriage and her blonde-headed brood? Navigating singledom's unpredictable waters wasn't even a blip on Vangie's radar.

Nonetheless, Vangie remained glued to her chair, her face a mix of confidence and delight. "The fact Mike Brewer was even seen in the company of a woman after his twelve-year stint in the Tundra is significant. Trust me."

Erin ran her tongue over her lips and swallowed.

"If you knew what..." The thought faded into the ether, as if Vangie reconsidered her words. She then spoke slowly. "Mike's a fantastic guy. A grand friend. A distinguished citizen. Folks fancy him. But he's also a paradox."

"A paradox?"

"Despite all his fine qualities, Mike's a puzzle. He

doesn't love lightly."

What a strange thing to say. Why would Vangie bookend that comment with such a crazy assertion?

"*Love?* You're reading way too much into this. We ate lunch at the same table. As friends. That's a far cry from what you're implying." She wouldn't mention supper. They'd be here forever. "I'm bushed. Shall we lock up?" Erin poked her arms into her jacket sleeves, closing the conversation and making her intention obvious.

"All right." Vangie stood then. "Only one more thing. Tread carefully, my friend. That spark in your eye and that lunch that might seem happenstance? Eyes are windows to the soul, you know. Furthermore, for Mike Brewer to step over to your table at the diner, plaster his behind in the seat across from you, and eat anything but air, took real determination on his part. Not since Sally Sue Messmer has the guy been so intentional."

That name again. Vangie was the second one to mention it. What on earth had this Sally Sue person done to Mike?

He blamed it on the loaner. Specifically, the coffee mug that Erin had loaned him Saturday morning when he left her place. Why hadn't he thought to return it when she'd delivered his cell phone later that day? *You know why, buddy. It gave you an excuse to do what you're about to do now. See Erin again.* Not only that, rather than drop the mug by the clinic and risk her being with critters—patients—he'd elected to bring the thing to her house. *A real smooth move.*

Mike toed at the gravel with his boot. Summoning confidence, he headed toward the front porch of Erin's cottage before he could rethink his motivation. For a second, he stared. A peephole. No doorbell. He'd forgotten that. Old Doc Burnside never installed one in this vintage beauty. When his sister lived here, Mike always used the back entrance. Ah, well. No matter. He knocked on the door and waited.

Maybe Erin was busy? She could already be eating supper, he supposed. Mike considered leaving, but his feet refused to budge. Light emanated from the picture window, where the curtains were now mostly drawn against the ensuing dusk. From inside, a cat meowed, as if nearby. With a whoosh, the door tugged open, and there stood Erin, wearing navy scrubs and red and white polka dot house slippers. Her blue-green eyes widened in surprise.

"Mike? Hi."

"Hi." He thrust out the stainless-steel mug. "I forgot to give this to you when you were up at the cabin."

"Oh. Thanks." The space between her brows crinkled. "You didn't have to run it by this evening. I have tons of others."

"Yeah, but I thought this one might be your favorite. Besides, I'd wrapped up for the day. You aren't much of a detour."

Erin laughed. "Again, thanks."

You nut. "Oops. How that sounded isn't at all what I meant."

"I know." She stepped aside and motioned for him to come in. "Miranda's microchipped, but I don't want her to slip out."

"Is she strictly an indoor cat?"

"Yes. She has her claws, but she's never been exposed

to the outdoors."

"Ah. I see." Miranda peered at him from the upper berth of her condo. Mike approached the feline slowly, allowing her to get used to the idea of a stranger invading her space. "How does she feel about visitors?"

"I don't get that many, but she's usually pretty chill."

He let the cat sniff his hand, and she promptly nudged it and began purring. "I think she likes me."

"It would appear so." Erin padded toward the kitchen, thermal mug in hand.

Did she expect Mike to follow? He didn't want to assume.

"I probably interrupted your supper."

"No, not really. It's still in the slow cooker. I was going to change clothes first." Her voice carried from the kitchen. A few seconds later, she padded back into the living room. "It's nothing fancy, but care to join me for red beans and rice?"

"Sure. Sounds great. That is...if you have enough." He tried to play it cool. He liked red beans and rice *and* he liked the gal with the strawberry-blonde bob and saucy personality. He could admit that now. Nevertheless, he didn't know what to do with it. What he *wanted* to do with it. Old habits died hard and he had the habit of being alone. Except Erin made him reconsider that. "I hadn't intended to impose or anything."

"Number one, I doubt I could eat an entire slow cooker of red beans and rice. I always make extra for leftovers. Number two, you're not imposing. While I change into jeans, I'll put you to work. Does that ease your conscience?"

Mike bit back a chuckle. "Some. What would you

have me do?"

"Look, King of the Kitchen, no worries. You know your way around a pot roast like you do a blue print. Surely, you can toss a salad?"

"I can do 'er."

"Slice the cornbread?"

"Like a boss."

"Set the table?"

"My forte."

"Pour drinks?"

"With my eyes closed."

Erin placed a hand over her mouth, muffling a giggle.

"I also know how to use a butter knife without hurting myself. As you know, I'm a man of many talents." Mike rubbed his hands together, eager to get started.

"Yes, I'm aware. Now, if you'll excuse me, I'll leave you to your mission, and ditch these scrubs for jeans." She waggled her fingers and turned toward her bedroom. "You'll find everything you need for a salad in the crisper."

Really? Not on the rooftop?

She sashayed away, leaving him with a parting thought. Never had a pair of scrubs looked as terrific on anyone as they did Ruby's newest transplant. Erin could wear a potato sack and still cause heads to turn. Funny thing, though. She didn't even seem to realize it.

Plink. Another chunk dropped off the suit of armor Mike had sported for twelve years. The crazy thing? It didn't terrify him. It liberated him.

As fragile and light as a butterfly's wings, something surprising stirred within and lit on his soul, scattering light to the dim and weary places he'd grown accustomed to. *Rebirth.* A kindling of hope in a heart once broken.

Chapter Six

"I'm impressed." Erin surveyed his handiwork. The grape tomatoes arranged in a happy face atop the butterhead lettuce leaves confirmed it. "That salad is a work of art."

The dimples in Mike's cheeks deepened as he grinned. "Thanks. Presentation is everything."

He'd found bowls, serving plates, and silverware and had set the table nicely. He'd also sliced the small pan of cornbread into nine perfect squares, poured two tumblers of iced tea, and stood waiting for, perhaps, his next directive.

"No one can ever accuse you of being a slowpoke, that's for sure. Thanks for helping."

"Delighted. Thanks for the supper invite. Red beans and rice beat the stuffin' out of a salami sandwich."

"Glad you think so." Erin stepped over to the slow cooker and lifted the lid, delectable scents of sausage, onion, and beans and rice filling the air. She pulled the plug and gave the mixture a stir with a ladle she'd set out earlier. "Will Blackie be okay for a while?"

"Sure. He'll be a mite off-kilter. Nevertheless, he'll rally. I always leave some kibble in his dish, so he'll munch on that until I get home."

Mike had already placed the tea glasses on the table, and without being prompted, he reached for a hot pad and the pan of cornbread, arranging them in the center.

As Erin dished up two generously portioned bowls of red beans and rice, he took them from her and set them at the appointed place settings.

"My, oh my. That's a pretty big serving. Not sure I can eat all that."

Seriously? After what he put away at the Come and Get It, and then again at the cabin? "I can spoon some back out."

"No, thanks. I'll give it a good college try."

Oh. So, he'd been joking. Slowly, she'd begun to read his personality, and she didn't know if this should puzzle or please her. After months of trying to bridge the guy's icy reserve, the recent thaw raised other question marks. Where were they headed? What did Erin hope would come from this new friendship?

So far, books, education, and a career had filled the void of her adult years. At what point had she decided she wanted more? *That would be when I moved here...when this little town drew me in and welcomed me in a way I'd never quite expected.* The novelty of the charming Ozark community, as well as the wonderful people who lived here—those she now called friends—made her want to lay down roots and never move on. If she were honest, Mike played a role in that desire, but she couldn't admit it yet. Past experience taught her to play it safe.

Erin drew back a kitchen chair and motioned for him to follow suit. "There's plenty more in the slow cooker so don't be bashful about seconds."

"Thanks. I'll remember that."

Over supper, they fell into easy conversation. Much like Saturday's meal at the cabin, their time together hit a comfortable stride. When Mike lowered his guard, his gentle nature emerged. A certain vulnerability shone in his eyes. It made Erin recall their lunch at the diner when Mike alluded to past hurts. Somehow, she knew he wasn't the type to communicate the intimate details with just anyone. That he shared the tiny nuggets he had with her took courage. How could she draw him out further?

"So, you like red beans and rice. Pot roast. Stew. Biscuits. Coffee." Erin ticked off the items she knew. "What are your other favorites?"

"Well now..." Mike tapped his fingers against the table, thinking. "I'm a comfort food guy. Steak and potatoes. Fried chicken. Burgers. Apple pie. Those things. I'm not much of a sushi fan, and I don't do liver. No green olives either. I like almost everything else though. How about you?"

"That's easy. I'm crazy over Mexican food. Tacos. Enchiladas. Burritos. Fajitas. You name it. Though, I really just like to eat."

They laughed in unison.

Mike took a bite of cornbread, appearing to savor it. "Mmm... Delicious. You're a great cook."

"Thank you. As a teenager, I helped my aunt in the kitchen. Before that, my mother. Though, that was a long time ago." Emotion squeezed Erin's chest as memories bubbled to the surface. Mama and Daddy had been gone for seventeen years, and yet in some ways, it seemed like only yesterday.

"Mel mentioned you'd lived with your aunt. I remember you call her Aunt Bea, right?"

Erin nodded. "Yes. She raised me after...my parents died in a car accident. I'd just turned twelve." She hadn't intended to talk about this.

"Lord, have mercy. Erin, I'm sorry." Mike reached over and lightly laid his palm across her hand. "I can only imagine how traumatic that must've been. You were so young."

"Daddy was Aunt Bea's brother—his only sibling—so she and I kind of grieved together. We helped each other through a really rough period, and Aunt Bea became like a second mother to me. She never married and didn't have children of her own. I think I kind of filled a void for her."

"I'm sure a tragedy of that nature bonds loved ones together. Was your aunt the one who broke the news...about the accident?"

"No. I was in the accident, too."

Mike's jaw went slack. Envisioning a twelve-year-old Erin in the same vehicle with her parents—where they died—gutted him. How bad were her own injuries? The wreck had to have been horrific. Despite the passage of time, that kind of thing would leave a lifelong imprint on a child. That child, a woman now.

"Again, I'm so very sorry." Erin's hand trembled ever so slightly beneath his, and he gently squeezed it. Why did life steamroll over good folks? He'd asked God that very question a couple times and no answers completely satisfied. "Your recovery process had to have been difficult."

"Physically, no. I survived the entire ordeal with only this." She lifted the index finger of her other hand and pointed to the slight scar above her left eyebrow. "Five sutures. Can you believe it? The rescue team said I was a bonafide miracle. By all accounts, when that buck leaped across the highway into my parents' Suburban, we rolled over twice, pitching us into a steep ravine. It's the kind of crash people don't walk away from. No one should have lived through something like that. But I did."

"No concussion? Broken bones? Anything?"

How was that possible?

"No. Bruises. Additional cuts. A foggy memory, more from the emotional trauma than anything physically. I was in the rear seat, of course, and like my parents, I wore my seatbelt. Being in the front of the vehicle, they took the brunt of the impact. Blunt force trauma and all that. They died at the scene."

God in heaven. She explained more in laymen's terms...like a medical professional might. In rote-like fashion, Erin added some other details.

"We were returning from a week at the lake, where we often vacationed. We loved the Ozarks—the rolling hills and hidden hollows, the unsurpassed beauty, the various forms of wildlife here." She paused and took a sip of iced tea. When she resumed speaking, sorrow punctuated her words. "Aunt Bea debated letting me view Mama's and Daddy's bodies a final time prior to the closed-casket service. In the end, she and the doctors agreed it would be helpful for resolution and closure."

Erin's hand remained warm, but motionless beneath his. Mike had no idea she'd been through her own private hell. To think he'd sidestepped the woman for the past year because he hadn't wanted to give her the wrong idea. *Wrong idea? About what? That you were open to friendly conversation and a stinking cup of coffee? Great job, you jerk. You nailed it. Not.* She'd simply tried to be nice, and perhaps, show interest while he'd continued nursing his own personal wounds, as if he were the only one in the world to ever know sorrow's harsh sting.

Familiar words played like a repetitive melody in Mike's head. *Be considerate of how you treat others. You never know the valley they've trudged or the heartache they've endured.* Pastor Bill's recent message doused him in a cold bucket of truth.

Mike had done a commendable job of serving the community, but deep down, he knew he'd rode the pity party wagon for twelve years at others' expense, specifically his family's. Granted, Mom and Dad and Mel, Garrett, and Gabe understood and forgave. After all, they'd borne witness to the aftermath left in Sally Sue's wake. But Erin? She'd been a helpless bystander. Clueless to events that caused him to turn tail and withdraw at the first flutter of a female eyelash.

Guilt snaked down Mike's spine and clamped down hard. His arms and legs became lead as the weight of Erin's tragedy seeped into his bones. His loss had been an apple compared to her persimmon. There'd been the devastating demise of a miracle yet to be, culminating with his teenage sweetheart publicly ditching him at the altar, and the event formed who he became, certainly. However, though it wrecked him, the experience rocked him in a unique way. One coped differently at eighteen than how one did at twelve. A romantic mismatch could hardly be likened to the sudden and complete severing of parental bonds.

If only he'd known—and done what? Been less of a jerk? He grasped for something, anything, that would salvage the moment.

"Did you choose the field of medicine because of your experience?"

Erin attempted a smile, though it didn't quite work. "Veterinary medicine is a world apart from people doctoring. I chose this path, my path, because of my dad.

He served as the county vet in our area, and my mom assisted as his office manager, lab tech, and wearer of many hats. I helped in the summers when school closed for a few months. I adored working in Daddy's clinic." Her voice grew wistful as she spooned a bite of red beans and rice into her mouth. She chewed, swallowed, and blotted her lips.

"Aunt Bea had to dispense with his practice, of course. At twelve, I hadn't even finished middle school. After Mama and Daddy died, I moved from our small suburb outside of St. Louis to Aunt Bea's larger burb near the city. I knew I wanted to someday return to the Ozarks once I earned my degrees. That probably seems strange, but in a lot of ways this area still holds fond memories."

"Not strange at all. If this is where your family vacationed, you probably feel a deep connection to this region."

Erin's hand noticeably relaxed beneath his. Her shoulders, once taut with tension, loosened. "I can't believe I shared all this. I haven't spoken about the accident in years."

"You and your aunt never discuss it?"

"She didn't move with me—she still lives in the St. Louis area—but yes, we talk about it sometimes. Other than her, and the counselor I saw for a few years during my teens, I've never shared anything about that period...with anyone." Hints of pink rose in Erin's cheeks. "I'm not sure why I did now."

Something wondrous soared across the horizon for Mike. Tiny seeds of hope erupted beneath the dregs of emotional soil, paving the way for possibility. Perhaps, Erin sensed it, too? Perhaps, the last year hadn't been a wash, after all. Maybe, it'd been God's way of preparing them for a new season.

The religious often spoke of such things, though until now, Mike hadn't given it much thought. Not that he didn't believe in such stuff. He'd simply never encountered it. Naturally, the Bible addressed the supernatural working of the Holy Spirit, and the commentaries he owned tackled the subject with great verve, nevertheless, he didn't pretend to understand it. Because of *faith*, he believed it. All things were possible. Though, until recently, the prospect of a new beginning hadn't manifested itself. *Could it be, Lord? Were my days in the valley in preparation for Erin?* She'd expressed interest once. Dare Mike hope for another chance?

"I'm glad you confided in me. I feel like we're on the path to becoming good...friends."

Dummy. He hadn't intended to say *friends*. He wanted to say something else. Except he didn't know what to name it. What did twenty-first century folks call *more than friends*? Talk about out of practice. The few women he'd dated in the past decade were pleasant diversions, but more in the friendly acquaintance category rather than in a friends' classification. How should he let Erin know he'd like to pursue this...this whatever they were?

Erin's mouth tilted upward. She cleared her throat. "Tell me, *friend*, does that path include sharing the last slice of chocolate pie?"

"Homemade?"

"You bet. Is there another kind?"

"With whipped cream? The real deal?"

"Tons."

"Any maraschino cherries?"

"Yep."

"Then I'm in. And me being the gentleman I am, you can have the first bite."

"Thanks. Here's to friendship." Erin raised her tea glass.

"To friendship."

Clink.

Mike's heart tumbled to his knees. *For the love of pickles. I'm a goner.*

For the first time in a long while, he fantasized about what it might be like to kiss someone other than the ghost of his past.

At the door that evening, long after pie and conversation, Mike pinned Erin with a concentrated gaze. "It's been a while, so I'm embarrasingly out of practice at this."

At what? Her heart ratcheted up a notch. They'd known each other for a year, only now, the inexplicable had happened. They'd tiptoed past the periphery of awareness and settled into a comfortable rapport. Given the way they'd started off, she didn't want to assume too much. That could be awkward. "Excuse me?"

"Thanks for the tasty supper tonight. I really enjoyed it." Mike poked his hands in his jeans pockets, as if needing to do something with them. "Three meals together in five days. It's been rather nice not to eat alone."

"I agree. Blackie and Miranda aren't exactly the best conversationalists, are they?" Erin's wit drew a grin.

"No, they aren't. Barks and meows are a language all their own."

She understood now. Or maybe she did. Just how long had it been since Mike asked a woman out? Maybe as long as it had been for her to agree to a date? Then they were both in trouble.

Before she could probe the particulars too much, he sucked in a deep breath along with what?—a dose of courage, exhaled, and finally posed the question. "I'm wondering if... Would you like to do it again sometime? Officially? The Come and Get It has a lot of fine qualities. So does Pennies from Heaven, Charla Packard's bakery and deli. There are also some nice restaurants in Sapphire, twenty minutes down the road. Or would you prefer a movie? Or bowling? Or I'm open to other suggestions."

He stood waiting, his handsome face a composite of nervousness and wonder. The shy schoolboy resemblance struck a chord of empathy with Erin. She understood feeling unsure of one's footing. Not only did the fear of rejection play a role in today's dating dynamic, but when past hurts were involved, as in Mike's case—as well as her own—that generated its own set of quandaries. Stepping into the public eye as a couple guaranteed idle chatter and certain expectations. The fine citizens of Ruby didn't mean any harm, but people here could start a tale and write the book as gospel before the day ended. Did Mike want that kind of attention? While known as a genial sort around town, he also had a private side. The side, Erin would bet, he allowed few people to see.

Maybe a slow, gentle approach would be best. It'd save awkwardness later if nothing came from this. *This* being what exactly? Appeal? Attraction? Romantic intentions?

Erin met his gaze, careful to hold her interest in check. She knew something about a fragile heart, too, and until she knew more of Mike's story, she'd reserve a portion of hers. "How would you feel about leaf peeping?"

"About...what?"

"Leaf peeping. You know. It's a term for viewing fall foliage and—"

"Yes, I'm aware of what it is." Mike scrunched his brows. "That's...your idea of a date?"

"Sure. This is the optimum time of year for it in the Ozarks."

"I know. It's just that... Well, what exactly did you have in mind? A drive? A walk? A hike?"

Clearly, Erin's suggestion baffled him. She had to admit, it must seem somewhat offbeat. "Surprise me."

"You're serious?"

"Something low key might be fun."

"That's one word for it." Mike chuckled. "Okay. I'll give it some thought. Are you free this Saturday? Say about ten?"

"Sounds perfect."

Mike withdrew his hand from his pocket and extended it toward her. "It's a date."

When she met his hand to shake it, Erin noticed a slight quiver. Did the word *date* rattle him or was it something else?

Chapter Seven

"Are you going to make me drag it out of you or do you plan to share before we close up shop for the day?" Vangie tucked a few stray tendrils behind her ear and then finished wiping the exam table with sanitizer. She stood waiting as Erin's fingers flitted across the computer keyboard.

"Hold on a sec." Erin liked to complete her progress notes on her furry patients within minutes of examining them. A well-oiled machine left no room for a rusty operation. Or so Daddy used to claim. She added a final thought on Buffy, the Farrows's newly acquired beagle, and logged out of the system. "Now, what was it you asked?"

"Look, the entire day has passed, and you haven't spilled the beans yet."

"Spilled the beans?" Oh, dear. Had tales already taken wing? "About?"

"What do you mean *about*?" Vangie tossed her an exasperated eye-roll. "Word has it that Mike Brewer's Silverado was seen parked at your house for a while last night. Like for a *long* while."

Oh, boy. Which neighbor should she thank for that?

"Easy, Vang. Don't wanna drool all over that table you disinfected."

"Enlighten me and I won't have to."

Despite her mild annoyance, Erin laughed. She filled Vangie in with a few of the particulars, purposely omitting her and Mike's upcoming date. No sense in adding more fuel to the rumor bonfire.

"My, oh my. This gets better all the time. Mike's such a nice guy. No wonder he's had a little more pep in his step the last week or so. Mitch has even noticed it, and trust me, my husband isn't necessarily a sentimental kind of fella."

"Easy, my starry-eyed friend. Don't read too much into this. Mike and I had supper, not a romantic encounter." Erin made her way toward the door. "I may have found him attractive when I first moved here—in fact, I probably should have curbed that a bit more—but I won't make a fool out of myself twice. Where this goes from here, I'm not sure. The trajectory's up to Mike."

"Blah. Blah. Blah. Up to Mike, my eye. That's *so* yesterday. If you sense the landscape's evolved, then you should lean into it. Proceed thoughtfully, yes, but avail yourself to open doors when God presents them. *Ooh!* I love it."

Vangie's animated appeal almost encouraged Erin. Sure, she believed God created opportunities and opened doors. She also believed in the reality before her. The reality being Mike came with baggage and so did she.

"I'm gonna venture out on a limb here." Erin said carefully. "Not to seem irreverent, but while I believe God crafts certain circumstances, I also think He gives us free will. Because of this, sometimes, we mess up what He intends."

"I agree. Except, since God is omniscient, nothing takes Him by surprise. Everything that happens plays a role in the bigger picture—even our missteps He allows us to make in order to redirect us."

Erin released a breath. She didn't know enough

about such things to enter into a theological debate. "Well, if I get a sense of what's ahead, I'll be sure and clue you in. Deal?"

"Deal." Vangie hit the light switch as they strode out into the hall together. "Don't be surprised, though, if what's ahead is right in front of you."

Like Sally Sue Somebody had once been for Mike? Look how that turned out. Only Erin didn't say that.

Saturday's silent, rosy dawn kissed the eastern horizon as Mike watched from his second floor bedroom window. For a weekend, he'd awakened earlier than usual, chalking it up to excitement and jitters.

Now, as the first vestiges of daylight danced across the morning sky, he did something he hadn't in years. He padded over to the closet and reached for the plastic bin on the upper shelf. Slowly, he tugged on the bin, freeing it from old clothing he'd been meaning to donate. With fingers poised to lift the lid, he paused. Maybe he better sit down for this.

"I probably should grab a cup of Joe, too. Huh, boy?" Mike gave Blackie a pat as the Lab hopped on the bed and joined him. "Already take your morning constitutional? Hope you flipped on the Bunn on your way back up."

Woof! Woof! Blackie's tail beat a rat-a-tat-tat on Mike's unmade bed.

He didn't know what made him want to search for the note he'd stashed away so long ago. Perhaps, he needed to reassure himself that part of his life had indeed come and gone. He'd truly moved on. Granted, until recently, he hadn't done a very good job of it, but now, the cusp of something new appeared within reach. Mike sensed it. He merely needed to find the note and toss it, shred it, or burn it, once and for all closing the book on that difficult chapter of his youth.

Resolutely, he popped open the lid. The plastic bin contained various odds and ends, old birthday cards, and mementoes from the past. He'd never considered himself a sentimentalist, but when he'd built the cabin, the container came with him.

After a moment, he spied the missive. There, tucked beneath various memorabilia and cards, the faded, folded paper lay. A note he hadn't read since what was to be his wedding day twelve years ago stuck out like a piece of coal among the stash. Mike's gut wrenched.

Eighteen at the time, he'd been a kid high on love, smitten with his high school crush. One dumb lapse in judgment and it set the course for consequences and heartache. His marriage to Sally Sue hadn't happened, a blessing in disguise, though the emotional fallout rocked him for years even as he'd entered college and gained his footing in the world.

When the Messmers moved out of the area a few months later, Sally Sue left, too. Life meandered on as townsfolk went about their business and rarely spoke about the past. Around him, at least. Most folks assumed common sense or cold feet got the best of the childhood sweethearts who were too young for marriage but too old to spank. Folks were kind enough to let that be that. Only Mom and Dad, and eventually, his siblings, knew the whole story. Rather than chastise with moral lectures and "I told you so," his parents came alongside in love.

"Son, sometimes trials that are due to our own making are hard lessons. And hard lessons—painful lessons—are

the best ones. We're not likely to repeat the same mistakes." Dad had draped his arm over Mike's quaking shoulders as they'd had a man-to-man in the church that day after all the guests had gone home. "*I know it hurts like the devil right now, but one day, the pain will ease and you'll move forward. When you're ready, when God orchestrates it, He'll send the life partner that's meant to be.*"

Mom had joined them, eyes shimmering with tears. "*Dad's right, love. Don't doubt it for a minute.*"

At least they hadn't pulled the *You're so young. You have your whole life ahead of you...*routine. Bless them. No kid wanted to hear that. As true as it might be, a kid's reality hinged on the present.

Except the years flitted by, and with them, Mike's belief that marriage would happen. Now at thirty, he held out little hope for the life partner Dad spoke about, much less, a family of his own. He'd learned to steel himself against the inevitable. He took life as it came, carving out a well-respected niche in the beloved town of his youth, dating about as often as the groundhog saw his shadow. No amount of ribbing from Garrett and Gabe could prod him otherwise. Mike wasn't interested. *Until Erin.*

Slowly, he released the breath he'd been holding. Why had he held onto this stupid piece of paper? What purpose had it served? Sally Sue never returned. Not that he expected her to. Her words made her intentions clear.

His eyes scanned *Mike* on the outer portion of the note. He unfolded the missive and began to read.

I'm sorry. I can't do it. I can't marry you. I don't know why we ever let it get this far. We're so different. You're an old soul. I don't want to be tied down to someone who acts so old. I want to have fun the way teenagers are supposed to.

I guess after we found out I was pregnant, we got caught up in the fantasy and feel-good of what marriage could be. But the thing is...dating is one thing. Marriage is another. I don't love you. Not the way I'm supposed to. I mean, come on. We're eighteen! I'm sad about the baby, but I want to start over. I want to blow this one-horse town. You're suited to rural life. Not that there's anything wrong with that. It's simply not what I want anymore.

Sally Sue never intended to marry him. One couldn't scrawl out a note like this five minutes before a wedding. The penmanship was purposeful. Measured. Written with neat precision and fancy curlicues. He'd bet money she'd penned it well in advance of their planned nuptials. *Why?* Why not simply cancel the event rather than carry out the farce until the very last minute?

I know. I'm terrible. But I like presents. What can I say? I think I'll keep some of them. You can have the boring stuff...like the slow cookers and such. You should go ahead and attend the reception. The good church ladies do make some delish fried chicken and potato salad. I may have them send the wedding cake over to my parents' house though. Buttercream frosting is my favorite.

Had Mike known this girl at all? *Have mercy.*

As a starry-eyed teenager, he'd sat at the Messmer's dinner table for many a meal. Arch and Violet Messmer were fine people. But their daughter?

"Spoiled to the core, that one."

"Did you get a load of that new Mustang?"

"And she drives it like a bat fleeing Hades."

"Arch and Vi best take that girl in hand or she'll leave

chaos in her wake.”

In school, Mike had dismissed the idle talk about town. Of course, later, he realized he'd seen evidence of Sally Sue's true nature. But love blinded folks. Especially young boys, ripe with hormones and pent-up passion.

He couldn't stomach reading the last paragraph. Instead, Mike refolded the note and shoved it back into the container, returning the container to the closet shelf. One day, he'd burn that stinking note. Today, however, wouldn't be that day. Today, he had a date with Erin.

“What do you think, Miranda?” Erin struck a pose. “Blue jeans and sweater suitable attire for this low key rendezvous?”

Miranda opened one eye and yawned.

“That's what I love about you, my sweet. You're refreshingly honest.”

And you're a crazy cat lady.

Well, so what? Everyone she knew talked to their fur babies. Granted, as a veterinarian, she'd expect no less. When one was single, one resorted to whomever was available. Talking to oneself, a pet, a door, whatever— anything was fair game when a person lived alone.

Mike arrived promptly at ten, also wearing blue jeans, and a navy henley with sleeves pushed to mid-arm, accentuating his muscular frame.

“Hi.”

“Hi. Come in.”

His eyes held hints of laughter and mischief, and Erin couldn't help but notice the faint scent of his spicy aftershave as he stepped through the doorway.

“Those are fine for now, but do you have some hiking

boots we can toss in the truck?" He pointed toward her sneakers.

"Oh. Sure. Hang on and I'll grab them." Hiking boots? Erin guessed their leaf peeping included a hike, after all. Mike probably knew all the best places around the area. "Do I need anything else?"

"It's a bit on the cool side this morning. Maybe a jacket? I have water bottles and other things in the truck."

Other things? What else could they possibly need? If Erin had known Mike planned a hike, she would have made sandwiches or at least gathered snacks.

"There are gorgeous colors around the cabin this time of year, but I thought it might be fun to explore a little farther from town," Mike mentioned as they drove.

"Sounds like a plan. I'm sure there's a lot around this region I haven't seen yet."

"Me, too. That's the cool thing about the Ozarks. There's so much country to appreciate even for those of us who've lived here our entire lives. There are tons of hidden gems. Lots of hills and hollows. Woods. Caves. Springs. Lakes. It's a nature-lovers' paradise."

Yes, Erin remembered. That's why her parents had loved this area.

They drove about fifteen miles out of town, deeper into the winding hills and up the mountainous inclines where woods thickened and earth met sky in a seamless blending of color and clouds.

Erin drew in a breath as nature's palette blazed before her. Red maples, sweet gums, sycamores, birches, sumac, and sassafras charmed and enchanted with their autumnal beauty, cementing their place of prominence in this region so pure and unfettered by manmade trappings.

"I know. Stunning, isn't it?" Mike veered to the right, up another steep rise where pavement became pebbles. "Not a lot of city folks venture into this neck of the woods. They don't even realize that places like this still exist. We're glad for that."

Glad, Erin guessed, because natural beauty this unspoiled had become a rarity in many places. The mindset being *if we build it, they will come.* Never mind what must be razed in the name of progress. If big business and money-driven corporations envisioned financial gain, dollar signs drove their bottom line. They didn't give one hoot about heritage, culture, or preservation.

Erin had seen it happen too many times in the St. Louis burbs. Communities that held fast to the notion that some things were worth preserving eventually got left in the dust, as industries only devised different plans and schemes to get what they wanted. In some instances, however, their methods worked. Their logic? Promise the moon and toss a bigger money bone to the holdouts and see if they nibbled. In some cases, they did. After a while, the bone tasted mighty good to stagnated communities, and sooner or later, they fell prey to glowing promises of recovery and revitalization.

Only when the luster dimmed did people realize they'd been misled—that what was in their best interest was a fallacy. By then, when all the i's had been dotted and t's crossed, deals were done. The time for good judgment and critical thinking had passed.

To be fair, some areas, indeed, saw an economic boom, but many did not. In towns that prospered, the pockets that were lined the thickest were the big industries, not the communities that sold them their gravy trains.

"Who owns this acreage—all this land?" Erin asked as Mike slowed the vehicle.

"This is a public access road we're on now. Though, much of the land around here is owned by various individuals, thus the "Private Property" and "No Hunting" signs."

"Wow. I'm surprised big money hasn't discovered this place. I hope it never does."

"Well, it'd take a lot of cash in some cases. I don't figure anyone around here will ever belly up to the bar and drink what they're offering. At least, I pray not." Mike cut the engine at a wide juncture in the road. "I keep my ear to the ground for anyone interested in selling. So far, folks are keeping a level head. Word has it that no one has the itch to deal."

"What would *you* do with the land?"

Considering the amount of property Mike already owned with the cabin, what would he do with more? He wouldn't develop this acreage for homes, would he?

"I'd hold onto it. Prevent the suits from buying it. The only thing I'd ever consider building on one of these nearby hills would be a lodge—a small, secluded place to offer a little R & R to those needing a respite. There'd be a screening process for guests. Profit wouldn't be my sole concern. My mission would be more about a soul-satisfying hiatus rather than providing another tourist trap."

"I love that idea. Even so, isn't that how it starts? Someone builds something, and others get the same idea. Pretty soon, the big boys are knocking on people's doors, dangling all the tasty carrots."

Mike rubbed his chin, as if weighing Erin's words. "I agree, but we're a different lot around these parts. We understand the trade-offs of commercialism. There have been too many financial fiascos in nearby tourist meccas that led to the rack and ruin of a lot of prime land. We don't want that."

"That works as long as everyone's on the same page. As you know, people can be fickle. They may say they'd never do this or that, but when pressed to the wall, wants and desires shift."

"True. Guess there are no guarantees. I just don't think any of our locals have it in 'em to sell out. Unless it's to another good 'ol boy from the area. One they well know and trust."

"Someone like you, for instance?"

His mouth angled upward. "Yes, ma'am. Someone like me. If *or* when I ever decide to approach one of the owners, or *if* I see the property listed. Now, ready to do some leaf peeping?"

"Isn't that what we've been doing?" Erin laughed.

"Nah. We've barely begun to take in the fall foliage here."

"We won't be trespassing, will we?"

"No way. I have permission from Garrett."

"Garrett? Your brother?"

Mike nodded.

Really? Erin couldn't keep from laughing again. "How much of this land does he own?"

"Enough. As far as the eye can see and then some. Mom and Dad raised us with excellent business heads. When Dander started hinting about selling off some of the acreage a few years ago, Garrett approached him."

"Dander Evans? The barber?"

"I hear an echo." Humor padded his reply. "That's right. Dander Evans the barber. He lives in town, but his parents used to live out this way. When they passed, he inherited their land. Same thing happened with Horace Sapp, one of our deputies. Around here, rather than sell out to big business, it's kind of an unwritten rule that folks will title their property to family first or offer it to locals. Just the way we do things."

"What does Garrett plan to do with the land?"

"Dunno. We've mulled over some possibilities."

"Like the one you mentioned—the lodge?"

"Yes." Mike reached into the pickup cab's rear seat for his jacket and backpack. He also grabbed Erin's hiking boots. "Here. Time to ditch those sneakers and lace up. Adventure awaits."

For being a reserved kind of guy during the past year, all the info Mike shared made Erin's head spin. She liked this new side of him. The side, relaxed and free, that tempted her to throw caution to the wind and confide her wants, dreams, and desires, as well. Not her private heartache, though. No, not yet.

Chapter Eight

What was it about Erin that made Mike want to yammer like a blathering fool? He'd spent the past year trying his best to pay the woman no heed, and within a week of playing good Samaritan with a wood delivery, suddenly, his tongue flapped as free as a bedsheet hanging on the clothesline in a southwest breeze.

Buddy, you've as much as admitted it already. When Erin came to town, she smacked you silly. This redheaded, green-eyed gal whomped you upside the head three ways from crazy. What'd you do? Snubbed her. All because you wanted to play it safe. You idiot. He hoped his face wasn't some girly shade of pink.

Mike held the passenger side door open and stretched out a hand. "Remember, use the step bar."

"Thanks. This is a big rig. Practical for what you do, huh?"

"Yeah. In my line of work, I never know what I might haul."

For instance, today, a small cooler. Monday, probably a new load of lumber and building materials for Mitch's home improvement project. A rick of wood sometime next week for an elderly church member. This sturdy gal came in handy for a variety of things, including hillside jaunts and leaf peeping with pretty women. Well, one pretty woman. He'd never brought a date here before. Wouldn't have occurred to him. Erin made him tap into his creativity bank, and wonder of wonders, he liked it.

She grasped his hand and stepped down, her eyes

connecting with his. "How far will we hike?"

"Maybe a mile. Not far. You game?"

"Yep. Oh—will we have cell coverage?"

"Should. It might be spotty in some places for a tiny bit."

Surely, she wasn't one of those frenzied types who stayed chained to social media or couldn't live a moment without checking her e-mail. At least, she didn't strike him as that sort.

"I ask in case my service needs to reach me. Thankfully, the weekends aren't usually busy, but since I don't go into the clinic on Saturdays or Sundays, I want to be available in the event of an emergency."

Mike mentally thumped himself. He should have thought of that. Of course, that would be a consideration. "Understood. Not to worry. We won't wander too far off the beaten path. Just far enough so we can do some proper leaf peeping and so I can show you something."

"Super. Lead on."

Erin let go of his hand, and he attempted to cover his disappointment by adjusting his backpack. It didn't weigh much, and it only took him a minute to secure the shoulder straps.

"What did you bring in that thing anyway?" Erin tipped her head, indicating the backpack.

"Sustenance. Odds and ends. A first aid kit."

"Whoa. A first aid kit? Good thinking. I'm impressed."

"That's my middle name. Mister Impressive."

"I'll try not to twist my ankle or anything."

"Awesome. Don't set your foot down on a copperhead either, please."

"Wait. Are you kidding? You're kidding me, right?"

"Mostly." He winked at her. "They're not too active this time of year. Just watch your step."

"I certainly will. I may be a veterinarian, but I don't do snakes. Not if I can help it."

Poor gal. He shouldn't tease her. "I'm more concerned about getting smacked by a tree limb or accidentally tripping than I am about running into snakes. I keep some bandages, antiseptic, and a few other things in the kit for that reason."

"Thanks for clarifying that."

Erin matched his pace, oohing and ahhing over the rainbow of colors. Every once in a while, she whipped out her phone and snapped pictures. After they'd walked a while, they stopped to remove their jackets and Mike offered to grab some shots of her. "I'll take them with my phone and send them to yours. I'm sure your aunt would enjoy seeing you living the dream."

"Ha! She would, indeed. I'm not great with selfies."

"How's this?" Erin hopped on an old tree stump and stretched out her arms wide like Kate Winslet in the old movie *Titanic*.

Using the orange and scarlet leaves of the surrounding trees as a backdrop, he focused on Erin, framing her dead center. Next, Mike grabbed some shots of her holding handfuls of fallen leaves, and then letting them rain through her fingers like water. He even snapped a few candid shots of her gazing off into the distance, as if deep in thought. He didn't know what that was about, but his pulse quickened as a slight breeze blew strands of red hair around her face, creating a vision of angelic beauty. He almost had to pinch himself to make sure she was real. She said something then, but he'd been too engrossed to hear it.

"I'm sorry?"

"My number." Erin rattled it off again.

This time, Mike added her to his contacts and sent her the pictures. All of them but one. The one with the curtain of hair framing her face, her smile as radiant as the noonday sun. Eyes full of wonder. Her body language, relaxed and unassuming.

Before he knew what she intended, she whipped her phone around and started snapping pictures of him.

"Hey! No fair. I wasn't prepared. I didn't get to ham it up like you did."

"That's okay. These are great."

Her laughter echoed through the trees, bouncing off branches, lighting on the hollow places of Mike's heart and seeping through the cracks and crevices, where once there'd only been pain.

As they approached a slight clearing, the sun broke fully through the cloudbank, illuminating the surrounding acreage in vibrant shafts of glorious, warm light. Nearby, treetops glowed beneath the bright sunshine, their canopies of changing leaves as if on fire.

By then, they'd hiked about a mile, the "hike" seeming more like a gentle walk really, except uphill. If they'd been older and not as physically fit, the exercise might have taxed them, but today, Erin found their rambling exhilarating. It reminded her of her adolescence, when she and her parents would tramp into the woods at the lake, appreciating each other and the wonders of God's creation.

Thinking of those times brought a bittersweet

longing, and Erin thought, also, of Aunt Bea, whom she should call soon. Knowing where her mind could wander, she refocused on the moment at hand.

They traipsed onward several more steps until the clearing widened, and unadulterated splendor unfurled before them. Tree leaves of every color—scarlet, lemon, umber, and orange—dotted the valley below with seemingly marvelous precision as if placed there by human hands, though more likely, by way of divine appointment and natural propagation. When the breeze blew, dew-laden treetops glistened like diamonds, causing their colorful crowns to shimmer with all the grandeur of royalty awaiting review. Too stunned to speak, Erin could only gape.

"Exquisite, isn't it? This is why I wanted to come early. Timing's everything." Mike touched the small of her back, his palm lingering there, as they stood side by side reveling in nature's transformation. "Nothing like watching the earth awaken at the direction of God's hand. When it's not cloudy, daybreak is best, but today's considerably outstanding I'd say."

"Oh, Mike. It's splendid." Without thinking about it, Erin leaned into him. "As mesmerizing as the view from your cabin. Thank you for bringing me here."

The hand that rested on the small of her back fluttered briefly. Gingerly, his arm encircled her waist. "You're welcome. I'd hoped you'd feel that way."

His touch disarmed her. It crept into the very marrow of her bones, lodging there, taking up space. She'd never felt such an immediate connection with another human being.

Oh, she certainly found Mike attractive. Had since

moving to Ruby. But when he hadn't shown similar interest, she'd shoved the ridiculous thoughts from her mind. Until recently. Until the past week, when the landscape changed. Mike seemed...ready? Ready to explore new possibilities, it seemed.

For now, they treaded slowly, each reveling in the other's presence. More so than a physical reaction, an emotional bond drew them—a tug so strong—the sliver of distance between them seemed magnetically charged.

They spent several moments rooted there, Erin's thoughts wandering, her emotions all over the map. So much heart and heritage and culture inherent to the Ozarks lived and breathed here. In this spot. In Mike and others like him. She may very well be a born-and-bred city girl, but from the time she was a kid, this region enthralled her. Deep down, she'd always known she'd return to the area her parents loved so. Would they be surprised? Probably not.

Before they hiked back down the hillside, Mike slipped off his backpack and reached for items inside. He unrolled a blanket, stretching it across a patch of soft earth, cushioned with fallen leaves and fading grass.

"Only the best for you," he said, waving his arm like he'd just produced a magic carpet. "There's more." Mike took out packages of trail mix and two vitamin waters and handed Erin one of each. "I made the trail mix myself. Cashews, chocolate chips, dried apricots, raisins, and pretzel sticks. You're not allergic to nuts, are you? I should have checked."

He continued to surprise her. Was this the same guy who, only a year ago, would have walked the opposite direction if he ran into her on the street? Surely not. Erin stifled a snort. Snorting would definitely kill the moment.

"No, not allergic to nuts, and this is incredible. Thank you."

"You're very welcome. Enjoy." They munched and sipped and talked. When they finished the snacks, Mike gathered the trash, stuffed it in his backpack, and extended a hand. "Ready to head back down? More surprises await."

More surprises? This date got better every minute.

As they neared town, the sun choked out remaining clouds, turning the sky ocean blue. The sort of blue that made one believe in daydreams and miracles. They might have passed a handful of vehicles as Mike veered toward the familiar bend in the road that led home.

They drove in companionable silence for a while—not the uncomfortable kind that made one want to say something only to fill the stillness—but the kind that bespoke peace and contentment. Erin's presence calmed him in a way he didn't understand. Funny, given the fact he'd spent the past year avoiding the woman at every turn. If only he could recoup the wasted effort he'd spent shunning her, who knows where they might be now? But all he could do was focus on the present—grabbing hold of whatever lay before them as they tiptoed forward. Both the thought and challenge caused his gut to stir with awareness.

After a while, Erin scooted around in the seat to face him. "This surprise. Is it at your cabin?"

"Near there." He didn't want to give it away until they arrived.

They meandered on another five minutes, winding

around the hillside and the lane that led to Hilltop Haven. At his property line, Mike eased over where blacktop met gravel.

"Are we taking another hike?"

"Could be." He enjoyed the hint of mystery. "Nah. Not really. It's only a short walk from here. Are you up to it?"

"Of course. I'm not a lightweight, you know."

"Yes, I know. Sorry."

He parked beside a cluster of trees, near the familiar path he'd cleared last spring. Before they set out, Mike reached for the cooler in the truck bed.

"Why don't you use the wheels on that thing?" Erin asked. "Wouldn't that be simpler?"

"Would be if the terrain were a bit smoother. It's not heavy though and we're not headed far. Up that gentle rise, then to your right." Mike inclined his head, pointing Erin in the direction they'd be going.

"Let me guess. We're having a picnic."

"The cooler gave it away, huh?"

Her laughter echoed through the trees as she marched forward. "I love picnics. If you'd told me earlier what you had planned, I would've made potato salad or fried chicken or cookies or something."

"As I recall, you said 'surprise me.' Did you not?"

"I did. Thank you. You've succeed—" Her voice fell away at the same time she saw it.

"You were saying?"

He wished he'd thought to record the moment. This would be another memory worth saving. Awe. Wonder. Reverence. Indeed, surprise—all the emotions one might expect—played across Erin's beautiful face. Mike set the cooler down, enjoying her reaction.

"Does anyone else know this is here?"

"A few people, I'm sure, but it's one of those things that we locals hold close to our vest."

"Oh, Mike...this place. It's extraordinary." Her eyes lit on the gurgling spring—the slight, but persistent rush of water—that trickled from the mouth of the cave entrance and wound around the hillside, bubbling over rock and earth, before finally ebbing into the deep woods. "It looks like one side of the entrance is completely dry, whereas the other side sees all the action. How far does the cave extend?"

"I'm not quite sure. While the overhang is fairly narrow, once inside, the area broadens to about eight feet across, but the cave itself only stretches back to about fifteen feet before tapering off to a mere crack in the main wall. This underground spring seems to originate beneath a portion of the cave floor there. Come on, I'll show you."

He reached for Erin's hand and together they made their way over damp brush and stones. Mike guided her to the right side of the cave entrance where it was dry and where they'd be least likely to get their boots wet.

"Would you like to go inside?"

"Oh! Can we?"

"Certainly, we can. I own this property. I just wanted to make sure you weren't claustrophobic or had a problem with maybe a sluggish bat or two."

Erin's eyes widened. "Bats? Ooh. Neat. I hadn't thought of that."

"So, you do bats, but not snakes, huh?"

"Not really, but bats are kind of cool. One might even consider them cute."

Wonders never ceased. Then again, Erin Shaye

obviously possessed a fondness for critters. After all, being a vet, she must have an affinity for wildlife in addition to small animals and pets.

A rush of cool air met them as they made their way beneath the overhang and entered the cave. Mike hadn't ventured here in a while and paused for a moment to simply absorb the beauty of the various stalactites that hung from the backend of the cave's ceiling. Normally, too dark to see early in the day, by now, shafts of bright sunlight bathed the room in golden splendor, revealing walls white with mineral deposits and limestone. Across from them, a thin stream of water bubbled forth beneath clefts and fissures in the cave floor and made its way over various shaped flowstones and rock.

"I used to come here to think." Mike explained. "As an eighteen-year-old reeling from emotional whiplash, this place brought solace and a sense of peace. When Dander listed this portion of his property a few years back, I knew this is where I wanted to build. Well, farther up on the hillside anyway. Better view and easier to clear. Here, I'd have had to disturb more of the natural habitat, and I didn't want that."

Erin cocked her head, studying him with an intensity so strong he nearly gasped. It was as if she knew his thoughts before he verbalized them. Impossible, and yet, again, her keen awareness immobilized him.

"So...you built Hilltop Haven on higher ground, away from others, yet still accessible to the ebb and flow of daily living. Interesting."

"*Wow.* You drilled that down quicker'n a dentist prepping for oral surgery."

"Yeah, sorry. Forgive me if I'm too direct. It's a

tendency of mine."

"Not a problem. I'm that way myself." Mike glanced down at their palms, still linked. When he lifted his gaze, he admitted honestly, "I'm struck how we seem to read each other, is all. We're in sync without explanation or pretense."

"Maybe it's because I empathize. I understand emotional whiplash. I may not know your story yet, but I totally get your reasoning and the desire to carve out a quiet space away from it all. I did that for a time, too."

"You mean when your parents died?"

"No." Erin shook her head. "I was only twelve then. I didn't have the where-with-all or the maturity yet to carve out anything for myself. Years of therapy, along with the love and care of a very special aunt, helped me navigate the road to healing. Mostly, anyway. I was speaking of something else. Another time."

"Another time? Tell me. Please?" Mike squeezed her hand. He wanted to know. What else had she endured that made her who she was? What had wounded her spirit? Who'd hurt her?

"I almost married someone."

Almost. Married. Someone? Just like me.

"What happened?"

"Fifteen minutes before the wedding was scheduled to start, I discovered Phillip wasn't the person I thought he was. I'll spare you the details, but suffice it to say, he went his way, and I went mine."

The louse! A muscle ticked in Mike's jaw. What were the odds? "The guy ditched you at the altar?"

"No. I ditched him."

Chapter Nine

The space between Mike's eyebrows creased as his mouth drew into a frown. "Pardon me?"

Why did I tell him? Erin's heart began to race. She hadn't intended to share this intimate part of her past yet. A college sweetheart and the one-year time frame following her college graduation before veterinary school, now a distant blip on the radar, but a significant event, nevertheless.

She hardly ever thought of Phillip Buckley anymore—the good-looking pre-med standout whom she dated for two years and almost married—but something about Mike's broken heart, perhaps, opened her own in ways she hadn't expected.

"I...um... It was a long time ago." Erin didn't have the desire to revisit the intimate details surrounding that season in her life. She'd treaded carefully in recent years, and now she'd entered a new era. She liked what she and Mike had begun to build. "I think I'd rather not go there today, if you don't mind."

Mike's eyes darted briefly toward the ground, and then back to her. He released her hand and nodded. "Understood. Maybe another time?"

The obvious disconnect startled Erin. Had she hurt him? Irritated him? His voice registered a certain detachment that hadn't been there earlier. In fact, his reaction mirrored some of their initial encounters prior to the intimate rapport they'd recently established. Did Mike have a problem with her admission? Without knowing the facts, had he already judged her as a *love 'em and leave 'em* kind of woman?

Erin rolled her shoulders. "The past is the past, but yes, maybe another time."

She'd like to rattle a few of the skeletons in his closet, too. He'd certainly alluded to a few. Everyone had a history.

Mike attempted small talk as he toted the cooler over to a slight clearing strewn with pine needles and fallen leaves. He set down the cooler and unfurled the same blanket they'd used earlier for snacks.

"Hungry?"

"I am."

Leaves rustled overhead in the slight breeze as sunlight danced through the swaying tree limbs. Again, the perfect spot to rest or indulge in an afternoon picnic, it afforded stunning views of nature's fall palette, as well as the picturesque town of Ruby. Erin understood why Mike purchased this sliver of paradise and why he loved this land so. October in the Ozarks imprinted itself upon one's soul—its centuries-old beauty an absolute feast for human eyes.

"Remarkable, isn't it?"

"Oh, Mike...it's surreal. To realize that places on earth like this exist is mind-boggling."

She wanted to circle back to his abrupt change in demeanor earlier, but he'd opened the cooler and had started removing its contents.

"I brought a variety of things. Sub sandwiches with everything—Italian salami, ham, turkey, lettuce, pickles—you name it. Three-bean salad. Fruit salad. Brownies. Apple pie. Sodas. There's a plastic bag tucked in the corner of the cooler here with some paper plates and disposable silverware."

He'd thought of everything. She'd never known a man to put so much effort into a picnic, and Erin's heart swelled at his thoughtfulness.

"Sounds scrumptious. You must have bought out the market."

"No, ma'am. Only what I needed. I had the paper products and plasticware on hand. I made the rest."

"You made all this?" Erin couldn't contain her surprise. "Even the pie?"

Mike's laughter rumbled between them. "Even the pie. Remember, I told you my mama made sure all of us boys knew how to turn a pan." The gleam in his eyes replaced the prior hint of reserve. "Lest my offerings dazzle you too much, gotta be honest. There's nothing hard about making sub sandwiches or a few salads. Oh, and while I'm being really forthright, the brownies are a box mix. But I did add extra butterscotch morsels and I dusted confectioner's sugar over the tops."

"It's perfect. All of it."

Erin didn't know why tears suddenly pricked the corners of her eyes. Perhaps it had to do with past meanderings. Other than Aunt Bea, this was the first time in years she'd allowed herself to get close to anyone. In the beginning, she'd been drawn to Mike, but his previous aloofness had tempered any romantic fantasies. The matter of an impromptu wood delivery had been the catalyst in causing her mind to roam again.

Careful. Don't blow this out of proportion. It's a picnic. Not a proposal. Though Erin had hoped for more, Mike's intent wobbled all over the map. Acknowledging sparks and fanning the flame were two different things. The odd vibes she'd gotten a few moments ago tiptoed around the perimeter of her better judgment, issuing a note of caution. She wouldn't play second best to another woman ever again—in the flesh or as a memory. If referencing her stint to the altar tipped the apple cart, obviously, Mike had trust issues. She'd bet her DVM degree he had Sally Sue Messmer to thank for that.

Would it be inappropriate to ask Vangie to elaborate?

"I wouldn't say that exactly."

"What?"

"What you said a minute ago. About the picnic being perfect." Mike handed her a paper plate and eating utensils. "That's a mighty fine compliment. 'Perfect' is rarely what it seems."

Hmm. What was she supposed to draw from that? That he appreciated the praise but took exception with her word choice? How odd.

Except...what niggled at her the most was the hidden meaning behind his comment. Almost as if he were trying to tell her something.

He couldn't help it. Erin's disclosure rattled him in ways he didn't want to admit. She'd done the same thing to a fiancé that Sally Sue had done to him. *Lord, have mercy.* Of all the things she could have told him, that one completely blindsided him. It'd taken all he had to regroup and focus on the Erin he knew. Or...was getting to know.

As they ate, Mike attempted to push past the unpleasant thoughts that teased his subconscious. He didn't know the circumstances under which Erin had canceled her wedding. She certainly didn't impress him as

CYNTHIA HERRON | **91**

the self-centered human being he'd long ago realized his former fiancée was. In fact, she'd alluded to 'Phillip' somebody not being the person he'd made himself out to be. That in itself waved a red flag. If she ditched the guy at the altar, obviously, she had good reason. He wished Erin trusted him enough to elaborate.

"On a scale of one to ten, how'd I do today?" Mike asked, breaking the silence. "Leaf Peeping 101. Was it a win?"

Erin swallowed the bite of sandwich she'd been chewing. "Most definitely a win. An eleven plus. So much more than I could have dreamed. I captured some really great shots to send to my aunt. Thank you so much for today."

"My pleasure. Thank *you*. I'd love to do this again—I mean see you again."

"I'd like that, as well."

Aw, man. That little dollop of mustard at the corner of her mouth. Dare he? *Nope. It's too soon.* Besides, a kiss would probably only smear it. Instead, he leaned forward and wiped it away with a napkin.

"Mustard," he explained.

"Thanks. Can't have that."

The slight upturn of her mouth made the lunch in his belly shift. Why had he snubbed this woman for the past year? Again, shame and embarrassment squeezed his chest. This was the first time in over a decade he didn't want to mess up an opportunity with a woman. Before Erin, his limited dating life included safe gals. Women who had great qualities in their own right, but qualities that weren't necessarily suited to him. And vice versa, of course. Not that he lingered around them long enough to know them on anything beyond a polite basis only. Occasional dating assuaged the loneliness that crept upon him from time to time. It never completely dulled the inexpressible ache that set his mind to wandering. Except now...being with Erin lately had eased the sting.

Mike quelled the bunny trail. Once more, the silent pause had grown obvious and Erin regarded him with...what exactly? Curiosity? Apprehension? Worry? Most likely, she knew he wanted to resume their prior conversation, but she'd made it clear her near trip to the altar was off limits.

"Erin, I...I'm sorry if I overstepped earlier."

"Overstepped?"

"Insinuating I wish you'd share your past. I have no right to pry."

"It's not that." She cast her gaze downward. "I sense there's a lot going on with you that affects how you perceive life—how close you're willing to let others get to you."

Yep. He couldn't disagree there. He'd told her as much at the diner the other day.

"You're right. Sorry about that. It's hardly fair of me to ask personal questions when I have issues of my own."

Erin glanced up, her eyes, sympathetic. "No. It isn't that either. Well, not entirely anyway." She set down the remainder of her sandwich. "My wedding day—or what was to be my wedding day—poked a pin in the balloon."

"I'm sorry?"

"It burst the fantasy. Everything I'd imagined romance, love, and marriage to be vanished in an instant. It took years to get over Phillip's deception, and even longer to put it behind me. I swore off relationships for a long while after my attempt down the aisle."

Anger squeezed Mike's throat. The thought of anyone hurting Erin made him want to punch something. Or at the very least, shove a pie in the no-account's face. "What did your fiancé do?"

"Phillip slept with my best friend. 'A momentary lack of judgment' as my best friend called it. Apparently, Phillip made advances toward Patty a few weeks before our wedding date, and Patty succumbed to his charms. She told me in the church dressing room fifteen minutes before I was to walk down the aisle. She hoped to ease her conscience, I guess. That, and I think she really wanted me to see Phillip for the loser he was." Erin pinched the bridge of her nose. "I didn't blame Patty as much as I did Phillip...or maybe even myself. I'd heard talk about Phillip's wandering eye, but I didn't want to believe it. We'd grown up together. Attended the same church. Wanted the same things. Etcetera."

Mike couldn't help but ask. "Your friend *or* so-called 'friend,' Patty? Did she and Phillip end up together after you broke things off?"

"Ha!" It sounded more like a squawk than a laugh. "Patty had a fiancé, too. He must have forgiven her because they married six months later. I never spoke to her again. Haven't in seven or so years."

Lord, have mercy. Choices and the aftermath. The tragedy of human failings.

"Phillip? What became of that good-for-nothing?"

"He's a trauma surgeon in St. Louis. With two failed marriages, three kids, and probably a partridge in a pear tree."

"*Wow.* Heartbreaker and healer. The ultimate

dichotomy. What a combination." Mike shook his head. "I'm sorry he and your friend hurt you. I shouldn't have pressed."

"You didn't. I offered."

True. Kind of. But Mike wished with everything in him that he hadn't gone down this path. What started off as a great day had quickly gone south. There were still so many questions he wanted to ask though. Things he wanted to say and share himself, but the words gathered on his tongue and refused to stir. How could he salvage what he'd hoped to be the start of something new? He couldn't undo his lack of foresight. From here, he could only stumble forward.

"Thank you for telling me." He skimmed her cheek with his fingertips. "You've overcome a lot."

"Thanks, but I'm not unique. Everyone deals with hardship and disappointment at some time or other."

"Yes, but some folks suffer way more than others." And doggone it all if the good-hearted souls' misery seemed to outweigh the stinkers' trials. "I apologize for adding a measure of grief to your anguish. You have every right to kick me in the shins."

Erin smiled at that. "Don't give me any ideas."

"Okay. Scratch that. Let's just say I'm glad you didn't hightail it back to St. Louis. I'm also glad you gave me another chance."

"Me too. Ruby's a great fit. I'm glad I moved here."

Ruby's a great fit. Not *You're the reason I'm staying.* Mike shook off the negative inclinations. From this moment on, he'd do whatever it took to redeem himself. He owed it to Erin. He owed it to himself. A debacle on the way to the altar did not a failure make. If anything, the collapse of Erin's planned nuptials, as well as his own, groomed them for something better. God's best, in fact.

Now, where on earth had that come from? Mike hadn't credited God with much of anything in recent years. It occurred to him that attending Sunday worship was a whole lot different than *active worship*. Somewhere along the way, he'd lost sight of that fact.

Erin made him think new thoughts. Consider new possibilities. A kernel of hope took root, softening areas previously hardened by lies and deception, priming the fertile expanse around his heart.

Whatever they'd both endured in the past, a new season now beckoned. Mike could hardly fathom it. Everything his parents had hoped for him, including the fresh start he'd once dreamed about, now lay at the doorstep of the present, summoning him inside. Only one question remained. How would Erin react when he revealed *his* secrets? All of them?

He tamped down the mental taunts and centered his thoughts on the woman who sat across from him. He didn't really know how to start, but from the beginning might be a good idea.

Mike inhaled sharply. Exhaled, and began. "For years, I insulated myself from the fallout that often goes with broken relationships. Rather than put my heart and head on the line again, I dated casually, but never anyone with serious intent." He chomped a bite of his sandwich and then took a swig of soda. Erin's brows drew together, then relaxed. Was she weighing his implication?

"I know I referenced it the other day at the diner, but when you moved here last year, something clicked for me. Corny as it sounds, you stole my breath." He set down his paper plate, no longer hungry. If he didn't get this off his chest, nerves would get the best of him and he might never have another opportunity to tell Erin how he felt.

"Yeah, I admit I handled those feelings badly. Steeling myself against another possible disappointment before even getting to know you probably seems stupid."

"Mike, what happened? What rocked your world so hard that made you afraid to try again?"

"That's the kicker. A similar situation to yours."

"You...almost married someone?"

"Yes. Sally Sue Messmer. My high school sweetheart."

"You called off the wedding?"

"No. She did. I stood at the altar during a rousing round of Mendelssohn's Wedding March while the church pianist played her ever-lovin' heart out to three hundred wedding guests. To her credit, Sally Sue left me a Dear John note in the bridal room." The moment flitted across his mind as if it had happened yesterday. "Long story short, my fiancée suddenly—or maybe not so suddenly—realized she didn't want a future with me."

"I don't understand." Erin frowned. "Why?"

Mike wished he didn't have to say it, that he could couch it another way. "I didn't measure up. Didn't fit her version of the ideal husband. That, and the fact she'd miscarried our baby so there was really no point in marrying me anymore."

The last portion of Sally Sue's note referenced other things, but no point in going there now. What purpose would it serve?

Chapter Ten

Erin sucked in her breath. *No wonder.* No wonder Mike had reacted the way he had. He and Sally Sue had created the miracle of life together. They'd shared the ultimate bond. Then...they'd lost the baby, and eventually, Mike lost the young woman he loved. Devastating for anyone, but at eighteen, especially heart-wrenching.

Oh my. How could he *not* want to know the circumstances surrounding Erin's failed wedding day? In his mind, abandoning someone at the altar equaled heartache and humiliation, and he was right. Except, in her case, if Erin hadn't ditched Phillip—and had actually married him—the marriage would have been disastrous. After learning additional facts about Phillip's philandering ways, she had no doubt that his pattern of unfaithfulness would have continued.

So...her experience and Mike's... Parallel heartaches in reverse. Except Mike had suffered his loss on the cusp of adulthood, when young love—first love—cut to the bone and forever colored future perspectives. How tragic for him.

Erin touched his arm. "I'm so sorry. We both bear scars, don't we?"

"Yes. Yes, we do." Mike sighed, covering her hand with his. "I know I should have moved on. It was a long time ago. You endured trauma as a child, and to compound that, later, from one you trusted. My experience can't even compare to everything you've survived."

"It's different. Not less than. Besides, people process things differently."

"Thanks for saying that. I appreciate it."

"It's true. Trust me. Any therapist would tell you the same thing."

Mike lifted her hand to his lips where he feathered the lightest of kisses. "I can't believe someone else hasn't garnered your heart."

"He has." The words escaped before Erin realized it, yet, she wasn't sorry. They weren't children. Might as well give her thoughts wings.

"Me?"

"You."

The sides of Mike's mouth inched upward. "Well, glory be." He leaned in close, as if he might kiss her, but he simply smiled the hugest of smiles. "That makes me so happy. Happier than I've been in a very long time."

"Me, too."

They finished lunch, a comfortable silence hovering over the afternoon. She and Mike simply absorbed each other's presence, feeling no need to fill time and space with idle chatter. They simply savored the quiet—the newness unfolding. Later, they circled back to Mike's cabin for hot chocolate and a movie, an apropos end to their date, and something Erin could never remember doing with Phillip. Too high-strung to sit for more than a few moments, he always had to be doing something or going somewhere. Movies weren't his thing.

"I never imagined a woman liking *A Man Called Peter*." Mike said as the closing credits rolled. "It's not typical date fare, is it?"

"Really? I loved it! It had all the elements—warmth,

humor, faith, wisdom...romance. I remember Aunt Bea talking about this old movie. It became one of her very favorites. Peter Marshall's wife, Catherine Marshall, also wrote the book. Of course, you know who she is, right?"

"Mmm-hmm. Best-selling author of *Christy*, in addition to many other books. Catherine Marshall is one of my mom's favorite authors, too."

"I'm so glad we watched *A Man Called Peter*. It makes me want to read the book again."

Mike grinned, drawing her up from the sofa. "Who knew we shared so many mutual interests—movies, picnics, hiking, pets."

Plus false starts. But Erin didn't say that. Instead, she nodded. "New beginnings."

"I like the sound of that."

"Let's relish it for a while." She leaned into his chest, delighting in the strength of his arms around her. He brushed a kiss along her cheek, his lips pausing momentarily, as if he contemplated more.

"You make me think about things I haven't in a while."

"Oh?"

"Whoops. That's not what I meant."

"Hmm..." She knew what he meant, though, for him to try to articulate it, thrilled her.

"Wait. It's not what you're thinking." Mike lifted her chin with his fingers. In his eyes, she found tenderness, and sincerity so raw it nearly broke her. "You're a very attractive woman, Erin, but what I'm trying to say is that...because of you, I see life through a new lens. You make me consider things I'd placed on a shelf."

"Like what?" Erin prompted.

"Possibilities. What it might be like to be with someone who could truly like—maybe even love—me for me. I know thirties aren't ancient, but I'm too old to beat around the bush. Playing cat and mouse with someone who isn't invested in a mature relationship isn't for me. I'm no longer that naïve eighteen-year-old kid, full of wide-eyed wonder and rosy imaginings."

He hesitated a moment. "Loving someone fully, with one's entire being, goes beyond the depth and breadth of heartstrings and hormones. It's the reality of day-to-day life and what that encompasses, as well as a deep, abiding commitment to build upon the foundation that's already been laid."

"I completely agree. Sometimes, life fools us, and it's hard to separate fact from fiction. Circumstances erode our confidence in others. That's when we try to make sense of a poor judgment call, and we pray for supernatural discernment." Like Erin had with her former fiancé. Then again with Mike.

At times, it seemed like God wasn't listening. Like her pleas for God's direction had frittered away with the wind. Then finally, a year later, when she'd all but given up on the youngest Brewer brother, God presented an unexpected twist. Was Mike saying he realized it, too?

"I almost see those wheels turning..." he teased.

"Not almost. They are. I'm curious what turned the tide? What made you want to take this—us—to the next level?"

"Fair question. I think it was when you called me out for my rude behavior after that wood delivery. I realized how much I'd hurt you during the past twelve months, and that wasn't my intention at all. As I've said, in my poor attempt to insulate myself and keep you at arm's length, I alienated you further. I never intended that. Didn't want that. I nearly drove myself crazy thinking what a rat I'd been to the only woman who'd begun to matter. I wish I could undo all the times you smiled at me on the street, in the market, or at church, and I slighted you. That wasn't who I am. You flipped my world upside down, and because of the risk involved, I reacted badly. Again, please forgive me."

"I've told you I do. We needn't revisit this."

"I guess I continue to say it because I really am sorry, and I'd like us to move forward with a clean slate with nothing left unsaid. Also...what I'm feeling for you is...more than camaraderie. I don't want to mess this up."

The poignancy in his voice startled Erin. She drew back, facing him, righting herself on the sofa. "Mike Brewer, the only way you can mess 'this' up is if you grow fur and turn into a werewolf. Even then, I'm sure we could work out something."

"I think they made a movie about that. Didn't the girl choose the vampire?"

"Yeah. I always thought the werewolf got the raw end of the deal."

"No worries either way. Only in make-believe land do such things exist, and since I'm a real, live, flesh-and-bone guy, I'm not likely to grow fur or fangs."

"See? Nothing to mess up then. Besides, you're not going anywhere, and neither am I."

"Oh." Mike's mouth eased into a smile. "So, you're staying the night?"

"What do you think? Great try though—and bonus points for flirting." Erin didn't know he had it in him. He *was* kidding, right?

"Thanks. You may have guessed that I never really mastered the art of flirting. You make me rethink that."

Seriously? He thought he lacked in that area? Erin's cheeks flushed with heat. For the past year, she'd fantasized what it would be like for Mike to notice her. Not only that, but that his feelings for her would evolve and deepen, as hers had for him.

"I don't think it's a problem."

"Which? Mastering the art or the actual flirting?"

She glanced heavenward, then with a laugh, fixed her gaze on him. "You've developed a funny bone, too. Are you sure you're the same guy I've known for the past year?"

"Yes, ma'am. Same guy. Only better. Because of you."

Happiness splintered into a million slivers, filling parched chasms and crannies within Erin's fabric. She shoved doubts and misgivings aside, refusing to give credence to "It's too soon." After all, she and Mike had known each other for a year. Well, at least known each other from social gatherings and church. Now, they knew each other's stories. They'd reached a new place. Like with any building process, they simply had to shore up the foundation and frame of a work under construction. Certainly, an architect would agree. *Right, God?*

Mike hadn't kissed her yet. One couldn't count Erin's hand or cheek. Not that those kisses weren't pleasant. They were. But he longed to trail his lips along hers and communicate everything his heart wanted to say. He shouldn't have to analyze it. What held him back?

Have mercy, he'd never courted a woman before. Not really. The few dates he'd had over the years could hardly count. As for Sally Sue, they'd fallen into dating—a comfortable routine as two immature teens—as high schoolers so often pick up. Embarrasingly, even as their physical relationship escalated, he'd never felt the need to woo her. She'd always seemed contented with the way things progressed. Until...they didn't.

Shame zigzagged along the fringes of Mike's memory. He'd known better. His folks raised him better. Regardless of his feelings for the girl he loved, or thought he loved, he should have acted more responsibly. Sex outside of marriage didn't build a lasting foundation. In their case, it had life-altering consequences. Forever.

I'm sorry, Lord. Once again, he internally uttered the words, like he had a million times before. Maybe one day, he'd believe the Lord forgave him...and maybe one day, he'd forgive himself.

As he and Erin drove back toward town that evening, Mike sought her hand and held it. The sun limped along the horizon, as they pulled into Erin's drive, nine hours together seeming hardly but a few. Today they'd shared intimate pieces of themselves, and they both knew they'd crossed the discernable line between friendship and something more.

Had there ever been a better day? Granted, there'd been some great ones. He ticked off a few of his favorites. Family get-togethers. Special holidays. Mel's wedding. Adopting Blackie. For far too long, though, there'd been many lapses. Fair-to-middlin' days where one day blended into the next. Now today? Today ranked as one of *the* best in a very long time. If days like this were gold, he'd be a wealthy man.

As Mike walked Erin to the front porch of her cottage, he rested his palm on the small of her back. They paused at the door, where he cleared his throat. "I enjoyed our time together. Thank you."

"You beat me to the punch. Thank *you*. You made everything perfect. You knew the best spots to see the fall foliage. You showed me beautiful places I'd never been before. I loved our picnic. Our conversations. The movie. Everything. All of it."

"Simple things."

"Perfect things." Erin reached inside her crossbody bag for her house key. "Would you like to come in for a few moments?"

Did birds fly?

"Sure. I'd love to."

The soft scent of vanilla and something floral wafted on the evening breeze as Mike trailed in after her, and he resisted the urge to draw her into his arms. He'd noticed the scent earlier, along with other things—the ring of Erin's laughter, her small, upturned nose, the tilt of her mouth when she smiled—and the images embedded themselves within his brain.

More than her physical attributes, the essence of who Erin was captivated him. Her spunk and resolve complemented a tender heart and generous spirit. She tapped into his deepest reserves, drawing emotions he hadn't allowed himself to feel in years. In short, she made him as giddy as a schoolboy. Yet, it differed from his fiancée fiasco. This burgeoning sensation—the admiration, respect, and ache he felt for Erin—opened his eyes to what God intended. Foundation, first. Everything else, second. A relationship matured and prospered when placing honor above self. Wasn't that what Dad had always said?

Buddy, you best remember that when you say

goodnight to Erin. You're older and wiser than you were at eighteen. Heaven, help him, he wouldn't repeat the same mistakes twice.

"We had hot chocolate with the movie, but I could make more. Or would you like a soda?"

"No, thanks. Actually...I probably should say goodnight."

Erin frowned. "What is it? What's wrong?"

"Not a thing. For once, everything's right." Mike stepped toward her, within a hair's breadth, capturing her cheeks within his palms. "Before I go, at the risk of sounding incredibly old fashioned, I'm wondering...may I kiss you?"

"I like old fashioned. Thanks for asking first." Erin's face bloomed with color as she tipped her chin upward.

Oh, Lord. Does she know how incredibly gorgeous she is? He'd almost forgotten how to do this. Shockingly proper by today's standards, Mike hadn't kissed many women since Sally Sue. In the few times he'd dated after that debacle, he and his date might have shared a simple, perfunctory peck at the end of the evening and that'd been that. He'd had no inclination to revisit potential disasters with the wrong person. Work became his friend, date, and marriage partner. Except when Erin entered the picture. Suddenly, work didn't fulfill him the way it once had. Now, other things churned in his head. Dare he even name them? Nope. Not yet.

Time stopped as Mike slowly lowered his head and touched his lips to hers. Soft. Sweet. Heaven. *I knew it would be like this. She tastes even better than I imagined. Like Mom's homemade apple pie drizzled in ooey, gooey caramel, still warm from the oven.* The analogy almost made his stomach growl. *Great, dude. You're shaking?*

Relax. It's a kiss. Not the Olympics.

Might as well be. He'd never wanted to go for gold so badly in his life.

When she yielded fully to his kiss, his thoughts scattered, yet he held himself in check. *Just a few seconds longer...* He allowed his lips to linger on hers, his mind doing handsprings over the river and through the woods, as if caught in a cartoon with his backside ablaze. What a way to go!

Mike gave himself a mental shake and drew back, resting his chin along her forehead. "Yes, ma'am. Like I said, everything's right. Right as rain. Because it's so, I want to keep it that way. Obviously, we have chemistry."

"You noticed that, huh?"

Her fingertips lightly stroked the back of his neck, distracting him.

"Very funny. I'd have to be a stick figure not to notice. The thing is...I'm falling..." He stopped short of saying it. Regrouped. "I care enough about you, what we're becoming, that I don't want to risk missteps."

"Interesting. When you and the Chamber welcomed me to Ruby last year, I wondered if that flush in your cheeks smacked of bother or boredom."

"Oh, you bothered me all right. More than I wanted to admit."

He mentally bounced back to the day the strawberry-blonde firecracker of a gal, with a fondness for critters and polka dots, opened shop, appearing every bit the confident professional come to set their world on fire. When Mike thrust the chamber's fruit basket into Erin's arms, he'd practically tripped over his words. *On behalf of our magnificent little community, Welcome to Ruby. We're pleased you're here.*

"Is that why you turned tail and all but ran down the cobblestone walkway when I said *Thank you, Mr. Brewer. I love it here. I look forward to getting to know you better?*" A smile teased the corners of Erin's pretty mouth.

"Aww, man." Mike scrunched his eyes closed, embarrassment creeping down his spine. "Sorry about that. I don't know how I could've acted like such a dimwit."

"At least now I better understand your...uh...reservations." Erin gently pried his eyelids open with her fingers. "Have to admit, initially, your indifference offended me. Then...I thought there must be more going on with you than met the eye, and I decided I wouldn't let it bother me. Until it did."

"That's when you gave me a piece of your mind."

"Yep."

"I deserved it," Mike admitted. "Your scolding made me realize a fantastic woman would slip through my fingers if I didn't man up. Hey, bunny trail. Could I, perhaps, persuade you to make some more of those cinnamon love knots sometime?"

Amusement flickered in Erin's eyes. "Maybe. I always make extra batches around the holidays and give as gifts."

"I have to wait that long?"

"Good things come to those who wait, remember?"

"I know."

Boy, did he know. He'd waited a lifetime for the anchor around his heart to lift. For God to release old memories and craft new ones. He'd waited for someone like Erin and hadn't even realized it until he'd almost botched the obvious.

Miranda jumped down from her kitty condo then and wound herself around Mike's legs, sidetracking his reverie. She purred happily as he reached down to stroke her side.

"She likes you."

"I like her, too. She's a great cat."

"Shh. She doesn't know she's a cat. She thinks she's a princess."

"I get it. Blackie doesn't realize either that he isn't human."

He could chitchat all night with Erin. Of course, a few kisses sprinkled in here and there would be nice, too.

"Tell me."

"Tell you what?"

"Where your mind just went."

Oh, mercy. How'd she know? The way they'd started to read each other tugged his emotions in all sorts of ways. This woman melted his insides like cow butter on a stack of hotcakes. Would it be crazy to take Erin in his arms and break out in a tango smackdab in the middle of her living room?

Yeah. Two problems with that. One, he didn't know the tango from a jumping jack, and two, the square footage of this space didn't lend itself to dancing. That settled that. Still, if it hadn't been for his pocket vibrating, he might have attempted it.

He didn't want to answer the ill-timed diversion, but his cell continued to vibrate. "Sorry. I don't have anything hanging fire tonight, so I doubt it's an emergency."

"It's okay. Really. Go ahead and check."

Mike nodded. "Thanks."

If he hadn't silenced the volume, he would have known the ringtone in a heartbeat. Elvis's *All Shook Up* belonged to only one cell phone contact.

Chapter Eleven

Joy eclipsed everything else that Sunday morning after their date. While Pastor Bill's sermon filled Erin with hope and renewal, admittedly, Mike's mother calling him last night superseded the good preacher's closing remarks. Not that Erin didn't appreciate the laundry list of announcements. She did. However, at the moment, socials and showers fluttered past—along with coordinating dates of said events—as she anticipated Sunday dinner with the Brewer family.

How wonderful of Mike's parents to invite her to their home today. A sweet couple and pillars of the community, Jake and Billie Gail went out of their way to welcome newcomers in their midst. Erin first met them a year ago when they'd attended Open House at the clinic. Now, she saw them every week since their entire crew usually lined the fourth church pew from the front.

"The gang's looking forward to it." Mike chuckled after ending the call with his mom. "Oh, and be forewarned. Mom's a hugger. Hope that doesn't bother you?"

"The 'gang' as in *all* of them? Your mom and dad, Gabe, Garrett, Mel and her husband Matt?"

"Yes'm. It's a tradition. We always have Sunday dinner together. We play games, watch old movies and the like. Sounds kinda prehistoric, I know, but it's what we do."

Erin's eyes had welled with tears. "Not prehistoric at all. I always pictured family get-togethers like this."

"*Whoa.* Hey, what's this? Darlin', please don't cry."

Mike gently brushed an escaping tear. "My folks are big teddy bears. Gabe and Garrett are full of mischief and mayhem, but they mean no harm. Little sis—well, you already know Mel—is sugar and sass. Matt, that husband of hers is a super cool guy—a geriatric social worker who's also an accomplished painter with an eye on his own studio someday. We're regular people. We won't bite."

"It's not that." Erin's voice wobbled. "After Mama and Daddy died, it was just Aunt Bea and me. I never knew what it was like to enjoy bigger family events. I dreamed about them, though."

Another intimate piece of herself she'd shared with Mike last night. Blessedly, he hadn't made a big deal of it. If he had, she might have totally broken down.

He'd simply taken her in his arms again and whispered, "Dreams are God's version of miracles in the making. You're my dream *and* my miracle."

Erin turned to Mike now as they drove toward his parents' place. "I wish your mother would have let me bring something. I don't feel right coming empty-handed."

"Relax. Mom'll have enough to feed a circus, trust me." Mike squeezed her hand. "She usually likes to show off her rump...er...rump roast and all the fixings. Though, I have it on good authority that today she's serving Italian. Probably homemade lasagna and garlic bread. Veggies. Salad. About a dozen pies. You know. Usual fare."

Oh, golly. Usual fare? Butterflies lit on Erin's shoulders. How could he be so blasé about it? His mother had probably worked into the wee hours of the morning preparing such a sumptuous feast. She should have at least brought...what? Flowers, maybe? Nora and Ned's Market sometimes carried floral arrangements. With it being late fall, Erin doubted they stocked any. They possibly had mums?

Wait a minute. An idea sprang to mind. "Do we have time to take a five- minute detour?"

"Sure. Where to?"

"My clinic. I'll be quick."

Mike stole a glance in her direction. "Everything all right?"

"Yes. I thought of a hostess gift."

"A hostess gift? That isn't necessary. Really." However, Mike hung a left at the next stop sign. "I must tell you that my parents probably have no need for flea and tick treatment. They haven't had any house pets in years."

"I think they'll enjoy this."

Five minutes later, they pulled up in front of Erin's veterinary clinic. Another minute and they were on their way again.

"Seriously?" Mike shook his head and snorted, his laughter filling the cab of the pickup.

What? Didn't everyone want a wall calendar with cute baby animals? One of her suppliers had sent an entire box of them.

"I know the new year is still a few months away, but maybe your mom and dad might like one of these early."

"That's very thoughtful. The cover reminds me of Blackie."

Eight Lab puppies and one baby piglet with matching red bows snuggled together on a Christmas themed patchwork quilt. The caption? *Proper nutrition and exercise help us grow strong...but never underestimate the power of a great nap!*

"Compliments of my pharmaceutical rep."

In the lower-right hand corner was Erin's name and clinic number. Below that, the medication logo used for...what else? Flea and tick treatment.

Mike laughed again. "They'll love it. Everyone needs a handy, dandy wall calendar."

"You think?"

"Sure. Best host and hostess gift ever."

"Glad you like it. You'll get yours at Blackie's upcoming checkup. All my patients' kith and kin get one. Merry Christmas."

"Gee, thanks. I couldn't ask for more." Mike raised Erin's hand to his lips where he feathered the softest of kisses. "Strike that. I could, except I'm driving."

"Flirt."

"See what you do to me?"

Bright October sunshine streamed across the dashboard as they turned down the Brewer family's graveled lane. Erin took a deep breath. Released it. Dinner at Mike's parents' home earmarked an important page in the new chapter that was Mike's life. Hers, too. She didn't have to ask if he'd brought another woman here since Sally Sue. Nor did they have to dissect what this meant. The implication silenced further need for discussion.

Let the circus begin. Mom and Dad, Garrett, Gabe, and Mel and Matt had beat them there from church and stood prattling away on the wrap-around porch of Mike's childhood home. Judging from Dad's animated expression and the others' snickers, most likely, he regaled them with one of his infamous jokes or fishing tales. Never let it be said that Jake Brewer lacked for stories. A genial fellow about town, his father's wit and wisdom charmed young and old alike.

As he and Erin parked alongside the century-old maple tree he'd climbed as a boy, affection for his family coursed through him. With all the exuberance of a kid on Christmas morn, Mom waved and hurried toward them. No sooner than they'd stepped down from the pickup did his mother meet Erin on the passenger side, arms raised in pre-hug mode.

"Welcome, Erin! We're delighted you could join us." She dithered for only a second before asking, "How do you feel about hugs? Personally, I like them. I'm a hugger. Mike may have told you, but I know some people don't have an affinity for hugs. That's okay."

Erin giggled. Good sign.

"I absolutely love hugs, Mrs. Brewer. Hug away."

No need to say it twice. His mother threw her arms around Erin and squeezed. "Now, enough with that 'Mrs. Brewer' business. Makes me feel old. It's simply 'Billie Gail'."

"Certainly. Oh, this is for you." Erin handed the calendar to his mother before it, too, got a good hug.

"Why, thank you, dear. Look at those sweet pups and piglet. I'll replace our old wall calendar in the kitchen with this one when it's time."

"Goodness, sugar, let the girl breathe," Mike's father called. "'Sides, it isn't like we've just met the young lady. We attend the same church. Saw Erin only fifteen minutes ago."

A fact. His family also knew something had shifted between him and Erin. What Ruby's grapevine hadn't spread, his family gathered. Mike Brewer wasn't one to bring a woman home. Not that he wanted to downplay the fact. Dad didn't want to call attention to it. It was his father's way of respecting his privacy. He knew Mike would share more in time.

Now, his brothers were a different story. Their guffaws and throat clearing suggested they wouldn't let him off the hook so easily. The guys' way of showing they cared.

To prove the point, Garrett elbowed Gabe in the ribs and shot Mike an all-knowing glance. "Meant to tell ya, little brother, you've been cleanin' up awfully well these days. Dress slacks for Sunday services instead of jeans. Collared shirts. No hint of a five'o'clock shadow. Mighty spiffy."

"Yeah," Gabe piped up. "We bet your socks even match. Good job, man."

Mike's brothers shelved some of their dad's diplomacy, bantering back and forth as he and Erin climbed the front porch steps. Their goodnatured ribbing took brotherly love to a new level and reinforced what Mike already knew. They loved him. When crushed by the weight of the wedding that never happened, young as they all were, Garrett and Gabe had propped him back up on his feet with equal doses of truth and compassion.

"Good riddance to her." Garrett had plunked down beside Mike at his parents' breakfast table on a particularly dreadful day way back when and offered his blunt assessment. "I'm sorry you're hurting, bro, but we saw through Sally Sue like a lace curtain. That gal cares about one person and one person only. Her fancy, fickle self."

Gabe wandered into the room then and joined them

at the table. "What Garrett says is true. We realize neither of you is perfect. You guys crossed boundaries. Still, you wanted to do the honorable thing in marrying the girl you loved. But gotta say it. She played you like a fiddle and had no intention of going through with that wedding. Mom and Dad suspected it. We knew it. Mel knew it. Now, you know it."

"One day," Garrett jumped back in, "Someone's gonna come along who'll knock your socks off. You guys will complement each other like taters and gravy."

"How're you so sure?" Mike demanded, forcing back a sob.

Garrett slapped his thigh. "Because God's got your back, man. And your brothers—Gabe and I—are already praying for your future bride."

"*You-hoooo.* Earth to Mike." Mel's voice snapped him back to the present. "I said I hope you and Erin are hungry. I helped Mom make two heaping-helping pans of lasagna in addition to other goodies."

"Oh. Yes. That sounds amazing, Sis. Taters and gravy are my fave."

"Not potatoes and gravy, silly. Didn't you hear me? La-saaaan-yuh. Along with garlic bread slathered in butter. Seven layer salad. Green beans almondine. Fruit and brownie trifles. Cherry Amish sugar cookies. Need I go on?"

"*Wow.* Thank you. Like I said, that sounds amazing."

Shoo-wee. Good save. He'd hardly missed a beat.

As the eight of them trailed inside the house, Garrett whispered under his breath to Mike, "Taters and gravy, huh?"

Overhearing, Erin's lips curved upward. "It's its own

wonderful category. Italian food is also phenomenal."

Mike stuffed down the quip that danced on his tongue. Someday, he'd share the inside scoop. Today he'd savor the knowledge that he'd meant what he said the first time.

"So, Erin, how are you liking the cottage? Adjusting okay?" Mel's husband, Matt deposited another spoonful of seven layer salad on his salad plate. "I remember how much Mel enjoyed the place. The cottage is unique—it has its own personality."

He aptly described it. Since moving from the back room of her clinic to her newly purchased cottage, not one minute detail about the home had escaped Erin. Mike's sister had retained its character and strutural integrity, while also making a few improvements along the way.

"I love the cottage. I really like what Mel did with it."

"It'll always hold a special place in my heart," Mel acknowledged. "If I hadn't fallen in love with Matt and married him, I'd still be living there."

Matt leaned over and brushed a kiss along his wife's cheek. "I'm a blessed man and I know it."

"Ahh. Young love." Billie Gail gazed at her daughter and son-in-law from across the table. "It's good to see a couple appreciate one another. Makes my heart go pitter-patter."

"Nah, sugar, that's your oven timer." Jake Brewer grinned, rising. "You set it for that extra batch of garlic bread you put in a few minutes ago. I'll get it."

"Oh! Thank you. I almost forgot. Good thing I set a reminder."

When the Brewer patriarch exited the dining room,

Gabe switched his half-eaten plate with his dad's. No one blinked an eye except Billie Gail who shook her head and raised her eyes toward heaven.

"You kids and your hijinks. Why Gabriel, you're the elementary school principal. Don't you ever tire of playing tricks on your father?"

"No, ma'am." Gabe swiveled his dad's plate to where the green beans were nestled at the three o'clock position. "Ten bucks says he doesn't even notice."

Mike snorted. He eyed Garrett and they reached across the dining room table to high-five one another in a show of solidarity. "We're in. Except let's make it twenty. Baby needs a new pair of shoes...er...bag of kibble."

"I'm in!" Mel nodded. "Except I say Daddy *will* notice. You can pony up the cash now or later. Matt, honey? Mom? Erin?"

Mel's husband raised his palms. "Hey, leave me out of this one."

"He'll notice," the Brewer matriarch nodded. "But I don't condone gambling. Losers have to clean up the kitchen. No money changes hands in this household."

Mel shifted her gaze to Erin. "How about it, girlfriend? What do you say? You in?"

"I don't think it would be fair of me to guess. I'm visiting."

"Playing it safe, huh?"

"You bet."

The group stifled their laughter as Jake Brewer entered the room with a basket of garlic bread.

"Piping hot, fresh from the oven. Who wants more?"

"I believe I'll take some, Dad." Mike commented.

"Me, too." A chorus of echos erupted from the table.

Mike's father handed him the basket. "Might as well pass that around, son. Sounds like everyone wants some. Oh, on second thought—hand that back to me. Erin's our guest today. Let's let her have first crack at it.'"

"Thank you, Mr. Brewer."

"Delighted, Erin. Feel free to call me 'Jake.' Or something less formal."

Erin accepted the basket of bread, the delicious aroma of garlic buttery goodness making her mouth water all over again. On the other hand, a giggle worked its way up from her stomach to her chest as Mike's father seated himself at the table.

Everyone resumed eating, no one uttering a peep, as Jake proceeded to finish off Gabe's mound of lasagna, followed by a hearty swig of iced tea. "Pastor Bill preached a mighty fine sermon this morning."

He didn't detect anything? Erin stabbed a couple of green beans, managing to hold her laughter at bay. How long could she do it?

"Yes, indeed," Jake continued. "I've always fancied what we refer to as the 'love chapter' in first Corinthians. Chapter Thirteen. The entire passage is excellent, but verses four through seven—where the apostle Paul, in his letter to Corinth, references love and its meaning—really lays it out."

Heads bobbed in agreement. Mike and his brothers grabbed second helpings. Mel snagged her mother's eye, waiting.

"Let's see if I can recall how it's worded in Scripture. Pastor Bill uses the King James translation in which *love* is referred to as *charity*. *'Charity suffereth long, and is kind; charity envieth not; charity vaunteth not itself, is not puffed up, doth not behave itself unseemly, seeketh not her own, is not easily provoked, thinketh no evil; rejoiceth not in iniquity, but rejoiceth in the truth, beareth all things, believeth all things, hopeth all things, endureth all things. Charity never faileth...'* and so on. I once memorized the entire thing."

Jake forked a generous bite of salad. *Gabe's salad.* Paused. "Yep. It's a good passage to consider. A lot of folks often incorporate it in their wedding ceremonies." In went the bite of salad. He chewed slowly. Deliberately. Directed his gaze at each son, one by one. Then he observed his daughter. Wife. Son-in-law. Erin. *"'Rejoiceth in truth.'* I like that. Truth's a noble quality."

His mouth twitched. His lips inched upward.

He knows.

"Now, where'd that bread basket make it to?"

"Right here, Daddy." Mel started the basket back around the table. "Would you like more lasagna? There's another entire pan in the kitchen. I'll get it this time."

"Thank you, princess. You and your mother prepared this mouthwatering feast. I believe Gabe would be happy to get it for us. Wouldn't you, son?"

"Yes, sir. I would. Anyone else need anything? Drink refills? More ice?"

His family shook their heads no.

He'd almost made it to the doorway when his father remarked, "You know, all my children are great eaters. No complaint there. But only one of them lines their green beans up like little soldiers straight in a row before eating them. Have since you were about four and learning to count."

Slowly, Gabe turned around. He laughed so hard that

his eyes teared. "Busted. Mike, Garrett—I guess we get kitchen duty."

Jake began laughing, too. "You should know by now your old pop pays attention to detail. Mike over there finishes his vegetables first. Gets 'em out of the way. Garrett eats his last. Your sister eats her veggies however the mood strikes her. First, last, or with her meal. Just as long as they aren't touching the main entrée. Now, your mother? She stacks her vegetables as high as Mount Everest."

Snickers broke out among the group and a glorious warmth spread through Erin. *This is what it's like. What having a family means.* The joking and jesting. The silliness. The camaraderie. Good days, and probably not so good days.

Big, bold, laugh-out-loud love emanated from each person seated at the Brewer table, their bond, apparent and unbreakable.

She wanted this. She wanted it with Mike.

Chapter Twelve

By mid-week, except for his mother and sister, Mike had spent more time with Erin than any other female in twelve years. She was the first one on his mind when he awoke in the morning and the last one he thought of when his head hit the pillow at night. If he were honest, she never left his mind throughout the day. *Whoa.* Did he have it bad.

"Hey, that's a new look for you, man. I like it." Mitchell Bench smacked him on the back as he entered the Bench's newly framed great room. "Way to accessorize your toolbelt."

"Huh?"

Mitch pointed. "That. I take it that smooshed mess inside your hammer pouch used to be a biscuit and jelly?"

"Oh." Yeah. He wondered where that went. He knew he'd wrapped it in a napkin and stuffed it somewhere.

"Plus the boots. They really take your contractor's gear to a whole new level."

Mike glanced down. As usual, he wore his work boots. Except this morning, he'd managed to lace up one brown and one *black* steel toed boot. Two separate boots from two separate pair he periodically interchanged and kept by the mudroom door. *Holy cats.* How'd he done that?

"I...uh...must have had my mind on other things."

"Yeah, guy. It happens. Is her name Erin?"

Oh, boy. The local grapevine had bloomed again. Heat crawled up the back of Mike's neck, warming even his earlobes. He mentally checked himself, attempting to will away the embarrassment. Didn't work.

A biscuit in his toolbelt. Mismatched boots. What other dumb thing had he done? Quickly, he retraced his steps. He'd washed his face. Combed his hair. Dressed. Nothing else seemed amiss. Unless one counted the bag of dog treats stuffed in his shirt pocket. For the love of pickles, he hadn't grabbed the package of licorice whips off the counter? *Sheesh.* Had Mitch noticed?

Yep. The gleam in his friend's eye confirmed the worst.

"If you say anything, I'll lash you three ways from Sunday with these things."

"No worries, buddy. I have your back. So do a couple dozen of the good church ladies, your barber shop cronies, and the Come and Get It regulars. Oh, and quite possibly the local bowling league. Probably even our men's group."

"*Aaack.*" Mike groaned. "You're kidding."

"What'd you expect? The way you've been keeping time with Doc Shaye, you might as well plaster your intentions on a billboard. You know how it is here. This town hands you a hanky before you sneeze."

"Vangie say something, did she?"

"Shame on you." Mitch slurped his coffee and set down the mug. "Yeah."

They laughed. He wondered what else Vangie had said. Had Erin confided any deep secrets? Shared her thoughts regarding him? She wasn't the type of woman to reveal confidences, however, she must have some close women friends with whom she talked.

Men and women differed that way. Men weren't apt to go as deep with their buddies. Women, on the other hand, were all about feelings and intimacies. Though,

Mike did have his brothers and dad, and he considered them his closest confidantes.

A thought struck him as he set to work on Mitch's and Vangie's new home addition. He'd disclosed more to Erin in the past few weeks than he ever had to anyone, including his own family. That in itself spoke volumes. She'd been the only one he'd ever wanted to share with completely. He felt no need to whitewash the truth or put up façades. Like he'd told her, beating around the bush served no purpose. Good thing, because he'd shared most of the important stuff. If blunt, raw honesty hadn't scared her away yet, why not go for broke? Erin would either love him...or not.

Normally, Wednesdays were the clinic's slow days. That was when Erin typically scheduled less pressing appointments and closed shop an hour earlier. Today, however, had been the exception. That afternoon, Tilly Andrews—dining hall manager at The Meadows Retirement Community—bolted in unnanounced carrying her French bulldog, Herbie. Herbie, it seemed, had scarfed down a small dollop of chocolate mousse when Tilly had turned her back only for a few minutes to "You know...take care of business." When she'd returned, Herbie's muzzle was covered in the evidence and only a bare plate remained.

"I don't know what got into the little rascal. He's never done anything like this before. Will he be all right, Doc? I know chocolate is very bad for dogs. I can't bear it if something happens to my Herbie."

As if on cue, Herbie hiccupped. As a rule, chocolate and pets didn't mix. In fact, the outcome sometimes proved dire if the matter wasn't addressed expeditiously. In Herbie's case, the small amount he'd eaten shouldn't affect him since he wasn't exhibiting symptoms. Still, to be safe, Erin addressed the situation by inducing vomiting. She and Vangie monitored Herbie's vital signs the remainder of the afternoon, and by six that evening, Herbie appeared no worse for wear. The little guy yipped and yapped and wagged his behind as if he'd made new best friends.

"Continue to observe Herbie tonight and call my emergency number if you need me. I believe he's going to be fine, but I'd still like to see him again tomorrow morning."

"Oh, thank you! I don't know what I'd do if anything happened to my baby boy." Tilly's eyes moistened. "After Herb passed two years ago, his namesake Herbie here became my constant companion. Between him and the grands, they keep me going." She hugged Erin close, her tears gathering steam.

The poor woman. Erin tried her best to reassure her. "Tilly, I'm so happy to help. Herbie ate a very small amount of the mousse and we dealt with the issue. His vital signs are normal. and I really believe there's no harm done."

"Well, thank you again. I owe you the moon, Doc."

"The pleasure is mine." Erin gave Herbie one last pat and sent the two of them on their way.

After they left, Erin insisted that Vangie head home to her family. She'd already stayed well beyond her normal working hours.

"Are you sure you wouldn't like me to help you wrap up the odds and ends here? I texted Mitch earlier about our walk-in emergency and he totally understood. In fact, that guy of mine already fed the kiddos and had their bath water running."

"What a great fella. And yes, I'm absolutely sure. You go home and relax with your family. I appreciate you staying as long as you did. You're tremendous."

"Delighted. We make a great team."

"We certainly do." Erin squeezed her friend's hand. "I'm thankful to have you as my sidekick."

"I'm thankful you hired me. Don't you stay too late either. Leave the less important stuff until morning and we'll sort it out then." Before she ventured off into the night, Vangie turned. "I almost forgot to tell you. Mitch said Mike may drop by."

Erin paused in mid-yawn. "Here?"

"Not sure. Here or maybe your house."

"How would Mitch know?"

"Guess Mike mentioned it. He worked at our place most of the day. I thought I told you we were in the midst of a remodel?"

Yes, Vangie had told her. Odd that Mike wouldn't have texted. While tiny slivers of delight danced down her spine, exhaustion from the longer work day crept into Erin's bones. Exhaustion often followed the adrenaline rush from a crisis averted.

"Thanks. I'm sure we'll catch up at some point."

"Okay then. Guess I'm outta here. G'night."

"Goodnight. See you tomorrow."

Erin finished charting and straightened her desk. She left the clinic about twenty minutes later, satisfied that she'd completed most of the busy work, and relieved that barring another emergency, tomorrow would be a light day.

When she arrived home, Miranda greeted her at the doorway, purring, and immediately rubbed against her legs.

"I know. I'm late." Erin stroked Miranda's head. "Did you eat your kibble? Let me change out of these scrubs and I'll dish up the good stuff in a minute."

Miranda meowed, as if to say "hurry up already."

I'm such a pushover.

Erin threw on a pair of old jeans and a sweatshirt, fed Miranda, and was poking about her fridge to find something for herself when a couple raps sounded at her door. Rarely did visitors call after dark. She knew before checking that it would be Mike. Still, she peered through the small peephole.

There he stood, a grin plastered to his handsome face, shocks of brown hair askew, as if he'd run his hands through it in an attempt to corral it into submission but hadn't quite made it. In his arms, he held an insulated container of some sort, and a round, plastic tub sat perched on top of that.

He brought supper? Erin's stomach growled her appreciation.

She tugged open the door. "Hi."

"Hi. I understand some sort of emergency came up this afternoon. Thought you might rather relax and not have to cook." Mike held out his offerings. "Homemade chicken pot pie in this one. Fried okra in the tub. If you can take these, I'll run back to the pickup for the chocolate chess pie."

"Oh, my goodness. That sounds scrumptious. You made all this?"

"I'd like to impress you by saying I whipped it up after

I finished for the day, but I can't fib. I ordered tonight's special from the diner. Ida Mae threw in the pie at no charge. Said to enjoy it."

An entire pie? This town. These people. That's why this Ozarks community endeared itself to her. They took kindness and compassion to a whole new level. While certainly not perfect, townsfolk here looked after their own, as well as transplants they welcomed into their fold. Most would give you the shirt off their backs...or a homemade pie with a twelve-dollar price tag. Erin would make it up to Ida Mae someday.

"How sweet!" Erin carried the dishes to the kitchen while Mike retrieved the pie.

She assumed he'd follow her inside once he got the pie, but a minute later, he tapped at her back door, holding the boxed dessert. "I thought I'd come around here so I could peel off my work boots. Didn't want to tromp through your house on your clean floors in 'em."

"Oh. That's very considerate. I..." Her words trailed into the ether as she reached for the pie and then watched him unlace and remove his boots. One brown and one black. One, a little newer, and one, obviously, a bit more worn. He stood them outside on the Welcome mat and traipsed past her in his stocking feet.

Slowly, Erin closed the back door. She tried to curtail the unladylike snort but failed. "Are you going to enlighten me, or do you want me to guess?"

Mike shrugged. "What can I say? Brain fog, I guess."

"You wore two separate shoes, boots, all day?"

"Yes'm. I already got one ribbing from Mitch—a few more if you count Ida Mae and Chuck and their crew—so go ahead. I can take it."

Erin burst out laughing. "Oh, shoot. Everyone's done that before. No big deal. You must've had other things on your mind."

"That's what I told Mitch."

"What'd he say?"

"Funny you should ask."

"So. I give you brain fog, huh?" Erin's eyes lit with mischief.

Mike's blood pressure ratcheted up a notch. He desperately wanted to lean across the dinner table and kiss the daylights out of her, but refrained. A gentleman never lost his head. Maybe his heart, but never his head.

"Yeah. Yeah, you do. I'm not too proud to admit it. Like I said, I'm not into games. You make me crazy, Erin Shaye."

She rolled a bite of pie around on her tongue, savoring it, and studied him for a second.

Aw, man. What's she thinking? Probably that I'm already there. Crazier than a loon.

"What did you do before I came along? Before I made you crazy?"

Good question.

"Worked mostly. Loved on my family. Prayed a lot. Hoped. Dreamed. Almost caved to indiscretions, a time or two." Though she seemed unfazed, he wanted to elaborate. "I've never been a love 'em and leave 'em sort of guy...but after Sally Sue...in my early twenties, I'm ashamed to admit the weight of loneliness sucker punched me. It was a time of self-reflection and will power. That's why I didn't date much or even want to...until you."

"That's a lot of honesty right there."

"I know. You make me want to share everything. The good...and the raw."

Erin licked the pie off her lips, her fingers stilling over the fork she'd set down. "I want to be honest with you, too. Phillip and I dated for a long while before he asked me to marry him. We were young adults. Not children."

Was she trying to say what he thought she was?

"You slept together?"

"No. I'm a virgin. But we shared intimacies beyond hugging and kissing. Beyond what was biblically correct."

Mike's heart skipped a beat. *A virgin?* Erin had been engaged and waited for marriage? A marriage that didn't happen. She'd remained pure and he'd...

Heat seared his cheeks, shame coloring his reply. "Obviously, I failed in that department."

"Mike..." Erin placed her hand on his. "We choose differently. We learn. We grow. We can't go back, but we can make wiser choices. I know that sounds corny and clichéd in the twenty-first century, but it's true. After Phillip, I decided I'd never test those boundaries again. I finished veterinary school and kept my nose to the grindstone...until you."

Mercy. Like a lightning bolt between the eyes, Mike grasped what she was saying. "We need to be careful then. Because not only do I want to date you, I...I'm falling in love with you. That's the thing. It'd be all too easy to overlook the past. Throw good judgment out the window and all that."

"I know," Erin agreed. She toyed with the edge of her placemat. Drummed her fingernails against the tabletop. Paused. "I want to tell you something. What I feel for you is different from what I felt for Phillip. I dated the man for two years, and come to find out, I barely knew him at all. What I thought I knew, I discovered was a façade. Lies. Honestly, I used to beat myself up for being such a bad judge of character."

"Great acting. I know something about that. Sally Sue fooled me, as well."

"Then you understand. It's the very reason I poured myself into my passion—my veterinary career—and as you confided, why you did the same with your work. Once burned makes returning to the fire about as appealing as walking barefoot on hot coals."

The creases between Erin's brows eased and she continued. "I've known you for a year, and in only the few weeks' time we've grown close, I've shared more of my authentic self with you than I ever did with my former fiancé. On one hand, I wonder if we're rushing things. On the other hand, this feels...right. How God meant for our relationship to unfold."

Yeah. He liked the way she put that. She summed up everything he'd been thinking, except in a more eloquent fashion. Something about the inflection in her voice, though, caused him to sit up a little straighter.

Then it hit him.

Was Erin slamming on the brakes?

Chapter Thirteen

"I'm detecting an undercurrent here."

The timbre of Mike's voice startled her. He'd misunderstood.

"I only meant the pace of our relationship might seem abrupt to others. It doesn't bother me. Does it you?"

"*Whew.* You scared me. No, it doesn't. Not in the least." He clasped Erin's hand, lacing his fingers through hers. "Granted, here, we approach life differently than in the city. We're prone to a slower stride, sure, but that doesn't mean we dawdle when love's on the line. I guess to be fair, some folks—like the Farrows—may take the scenic route, but others fast track it to the altar quicker'n a water moccasin slithering through the creek. We're not a one-size-fits-all bunch. We're unique."

"So, your parents aren't concerned about the momentum of our—to coin the term everyone else around here seems to use—courtship?"

Mike chuckled. "Darlin', Mom and Dad would like nothing better than to see all their kids married off and happy. As long as it's to the person God has in mind, they don't give two chicken wings about momentum."

His Ozarkian vernacular cracked her up. Aunt Bea would absolutely adore Mike. The Ozarks that existed in her aunt's mind, and no doubt in others' minds, was still very much the same region portrayed in the classic novel *Shepherd of the Hills.* Only when living here did one fully realize the stereotypes that still existed. Of course, some locals—like Mike and his family—partially fit the bill with their dialect and expressions, but it also belied their sensitivity and intellect.

"I'm glad your parents feel that way. Aunt Bea wants the same for me."

"I'm sure I'll charm her." Mike leaned forward and grazed her lips with a kiss. "When we meet, I'll make sure my boots match."

"That would be good. Don't want to get off on the wrong foot."

"Very funny."

His mouth moved over hers then, leaving no doubt how much he appreciated her quip. If she hadn't been so immersed in the kiss, Erin might have given additional license to the question that tickled her brain. For now, it remained on the periphery of her subconscious.

What had become of Mike's first love?

For over a decade—twelve years to be exact—the past had bedeviled Mike. Moving forward with Erin freed him from chains of yesterday, reigniting dreams for the future. Like a kid awaiting Christmas, each day drew him closer to a new chapter in his life.

Colors seemed sharper. The world, more vivid. For once, he considered paths he'd relegated to the back burner.

He'd done well as a builder, earning a solid reputation as one of the best in the area. His youth served him well. Where other contractors had age and experience on their side, Mike was known as a visionary who thought out of the box. He used his talents and skills beyond the norm, often exceeding homeowners' expectations.

As he plopped his behind down on a bar stool at the

Come and Get It later in the week, Mike mulled over his accomplishments and pondered other pursuits. The conversation he'd had with Erin on their hike in the woods, about possibly building a small lodge one day, played in his head.

It would be a secluded, beautiful respite with no more than ten or fifteen guest rooms—a quiet, restorative hideaway ensconced in the Ozarks' hills and hollers—where guests would come to recoup from the busyness of life, a unique gem in the vein of his own Hilltop Haven.

Since his own spread wouldn't be quite enough acreage to expand his vision, there'd be the issue of land. Specifically, would any of the locals be willing to divvy up their property? He'd heard Dander might. Maybe there were others. Then there were rezoning rules and regs he'd need to address. Ones that wouldn't pose risks to the environment or landscape. Also, who would oversee his concept? Who'd manage the inn or whatever he chose to call it? Mike had a great business head, but he knew nothing of running such an operation.

"Penny for your thoughts, young fella."

Mike's head snapped up as Edwin Ramsey, local oldster and friend to all, scaled the stool next to him. The fellow had to be in his late seventies now. *Lord, please don't let the guy topple off.* But although Edwin motivated rather slowly, his movements were sure and deliberate. Once perched, he folded his flannel-clad arms atop the counter and relaxed his thick-soled shoes against the chrome footrest.

"Howdy do, friend." Mike reached over to pump Edwin's hand. "To be honest, you caught me daydreaming."

Edwin stroked his chin and nodded. "Nothin' wrong a'tall with that. Daydreaming sharpens our desires. 'Course, sometimes, we need to act on our fancies."

Why did Mike get the feeling that Edwin was referring to Erin? Did the entire town know their business? Dumb question. Certainly, Ruby and her cadre of characters knew he and the pretty vet were keeping time. Rather than vex him, the notion made Mike grin.

"You're right. In this case, I was contemplating something I've had in the back of my mind for a while now."

"Doc Shaye? You thinkin' on marrying up?"

"You do get straight to the point, don't you, Edwin?"

Edwin gave a raspy chuckle. "Yep. Comes with age. I tend to say what's on my mind. It's either that or forget what I was gonna say entirely. Then you and I would be sitting here exchanging niceties instead of meaningful conversation."

"You have something there." Mike toyed with the edges of the laminated menu. He could confide in Edwin. Church deacon, solid citizen, and lifelong Ruby native, he probably knew all the town secrets and then some. Edwin kept a confidence the way a vault stored treasures. Locked and safe. "Honestly, it wasn't only Erin who occupied my thoughts just now. I was actually deliberating a business venture. Something I've contemplated for a while."

"Hmm. A new path?"

"Not exactly. More like in addition to. I have an idea—a low key approach—that would benefit visitors to the area, as well as provide county revenue. Because of its smaller scale, my plan wouldn't transform us into some kind of tourist trap. It'd be more of a refuge to folks wanting some peace and quiet for a spell—those weary of heart and mind who want to get away from it all, yet also be close enough to nearby towns like Ruby when they want to shop or sightsee."

"You'll need land for this endeavor." Edwin cut to the chase. "How much do you think?"

"Probably about forty acres. I don't want to carve up the mountainside. Enough for a small two-story inn with about fifteen rooms and parking. Some space for a gazebo. Acreage to commune with God and nature."

"That's not asking for much."

Mike caught the gleam in Edwin's eye. "Grandiose, huh?"

"That's another word for ambitious. I like that word better."

Ida Mae sidled up to the counter then. "What'll you two dumplings have? The morning special is *This Little Piggy Went to Market*. It includes a boatload of vittles, so you best be hungry."

"You still with us, Miss Ida Mae? Heavenly days, I thought you'd birthed those buttercups by now." Edwin flipped over his coffee cup, indicating he'd start with that first.

Mike followed his lead.

"No, sirree." Ida Mae filled their cups, fanning herself with her free hand. "I still have about six weeks to go. You may not see me around here as much, though. I'm planning on standing down soon."

"You said that weeks ago, love." Chuck hollered from the serving window.

"Yeah, I know. But I really mean it this time. My feet are killin' me and my belly's as big as Texas. Time for this old girl to kick back and relax for a while. Now, what'll you boys have?"

"Cheese grits and toast for me, please, ma'am."

"You got it, Edwin. For you?" She directed her gaze at Mike, as if knowing full well what he'd answer, but asked anyway.

"I believe I'll have the morning special, Ida Mae. I'm hungrier than usual."

"No wonder. Happens every time."

"Pardon?"

"Lovesickness. Increased appetite is a sign. Take it from one who knows."

"Doesn't pregnancy cause it, too? Increased appetite, I mean?"

"Well, my land o' Goshen, Michael. We know *that* doesn't apply to you."

Titters from nearby patrons echoed throughout the diner. Was there anyone in Ruby who didn't know his business?

She called out their order to Chuck and moseyed away, giggling, to fill other customers' coffee cups. Halfway across the diner, she turned, and added, "If it's more land you want, I understand Clinton Farley listed some."

Sheesh. She'd overheard them? Mike's next train of thought made him scratch his head. Clinton Farley? The octogenarian and reformed grouch that resided at The Meadows Retirement Community with Edwin?

Edwin clapped him on the back. "I was just about to mention that. Since Clinton has no living heirs, he's itching to sell his piece of the mountain. To the one who'll meet his asking price, that is. With the sale, he says he wants to fund an art studio on The Meadows' grounds.

CYNTHIA HERRON | 137

You may recall, he used to paint some. Quite talented, in fact. Oh, and I imagine once he and Miss Minerva marry, they'll want to move into one of the married couples' units. You know women and their fondness for redecorating—making something their own. In other words, my buddy Clinton will use his new resources wisely."

Great day in the morning. Had this development really just fallen into his lap? Mike's head swam. He couldn't wait to tell Erin.

When Erin pulled into her driveway that evening, Mike waited beside his pickup at the woodpile. Surely, he hadn't made another wood delivery? She'd barely touched the stack he'd delivered only weeks ago.

His grin magnified the dimples in his cheeks and Erin's heart raced like a schoolgirl's. Warmth stole up her entire body as he righted himself from his reclined position against the truck gate and began walking toward her.

"Hi."

"Hi, yourself. You wrapped up early over at Vangie's and Mitch's?"

"I did. Drywall crew comes tomorrow. Their new great room will be ready for the holidays."

"That's what Vangie's hoping for. They want to do a big Christmas party this year."

Mike's grin fanned across his face as he leaned toward Erin and feathered a kiss along her jawline. "You give new definition to *stunning* in those polka dot scrubs you're wearing. Don't think I've seen those before."

"Polka dots are my favorite. They're new. The scrubs, that is."

"They look great on you."

His kiss, chaste by today's standards, heightened her awareness of him. They'd fallen into such an easy, relaxed pattern when being together that Mike's feigned indifference of her almost a year ago seemed like a foreign concept. If she'd only known then how she affected him, she might have made a bigger fool of herself than she had. Good thing God eased them into this relationship. For whatever reason, the timing a year ago wasn't right. Maybe Mike's heart had to adjust to loving someone new. Maybe hers did, too.

A jolt of surprise shot up Erin's spine. Did they love one another? She'd thought she loved Phillip. Yet, she hadn't worn the heartbreak over their breakup like a second skin the way Mike had with Sally Sue. Maybe she'd been able to move past it easier because of Phillip's unfaithfulness. Regardless, what she felt for Mike was far stronger—more mature—than anything she ever had for her former fiancé.

"Would you like to join me for a bite of supper? I have leftovers I could warm up." Erin unlocked her back door and Mike followed her inside. "Hope you like spaghetti."

"One of my favorites, but I didn't expect to drop by unannounced and have you fix supper. It's still early. We could grab sandwiches from Pennies from Heaven, Charla Packard's place, or we could run down to the diner?"

"Don't be silly. Reheating leftovers isn't a problem. I'll change clothes while you set the table."

"Are you sure? I promise not to make this a habit."

"I'm absolutely sure. You brought supper last time, remember?"

Besides, Erin rather liked this habit. She enjoyed sharing meals with Mike. Eating together, versus alone, pleasantly capped off the day. Even Miranda had taken a liking to the change of pace, and when Erin returned to the kitchen, she found the feline purring contentedly on Mike's lap.

He'd set the table and placed the dish of spaghetti in the microwave to warm it. Miranda barely glanced up as she entered the room.

"I think I'm her new favorite person."

"Fickle girl." Erin sighed, reaching in the cabinet for glasses. "At bedtime she will have changed her tune and she'll be ready to cuddle up with me in her usual spot."

"Which is?"

"Curled up against my chest. Then by morning, she's sprawled on the pillow next to mine with her motor running in high gear. If I lie there one minute past my alarm, she taps me on the head with her paw, reminding me breakfast is overdue."

"Seriously?"

"Yep. Seriously. Cats are pretty regimented. As you can see, I have an automatic feeder over there, but for some reason, Miranda doesn't want to eat without me. Talk about habits." Erin shook her head in mock upset. "I've tried reconditioning, but eventually, we fall back into the same routine. I know. Bad form for a vet. Don't tell anyone, okay?"

"Who? Me? Never!" He gasped with fake indignation. Chuckled. "Blackie and I are right there with you. The goofball never turns down a meal, but his preference is to eat when I do. For instance, when I'm not there, he'll scarf down his kibble if he gets hungry, but the second I hit the door, he tears off toward the pantry where I keep the good stuff. I also supplement with the better refrigerated kind.

Spoiled? You betcha. Oh—and sleeping arrangements? I can identify with that. My guy gives new meaning to bed hog. Don't know what he'd do if someone else ever tried to claim his spot."

"Me either with Miranda."

Erin's eyes connected with Mike's as the implication grew like a balloon filling with air.

"Guess we'll cross that bridge—or bedpost—whenever the situation arises." Then, as if he realized the even bigger inference, he clamped his mouth shut. Raised his gaze toward the ceiling, and after a second, redirected his attention back to Erin. "That didn't come out right."

"Don't worry. I'm not easily embarrassed. I know what you meant."

Mike gently lifted Miranda from his lap and stood. "Good. Because, despite the fact we communicate really easily, sometimes, I get foolishly tongue-tied around you. It's like my thoughts go haywire between my brain to my mouth. I speak without thinking or I don't say things correctly."

"It's, okay. You're not being graded."

"That's a relief." Mike motioned, as if to wipe his brow. "Here, let me help you fill those glasses, and then I want to share an exciting development. That's actually why I dropped by this evening."

He shifted gears so quickly, Erin blinked. Whatever the news, it must be important. The kiss she'd hoped he might give her flitted away with iced tea and wishful thinking.

Chapter Fourteen

Smooth. Real smooth transition there, bud.

Mike mentally grabbed a two by four and conked himself over the head with it. In an effort to dispel bedtime rituals and sleeping innuendoes, he'd taken a serious moment between them and flashed the spotlight on himself.

"Hey, I'm sorry." The microwave beeped, indicating the cycle had ended. The spaghetti could wait. So could iced tea glasses and the initial offer he'd drawn up with his real estate agent regarding Clinton Farley's parcel of land. "In an effort to do and say the right thing when we're together, I don't always. Occasionally, I miss cues or respond awkwardly. Chalk it up to being too far removed from the dating scene. Or maybe I'm afraid you'll..."

Erin settled her palm against his cheek. *Lord, have mercy.* Her touch was so tender...so soft...he almost had to shake himself to refrain from completely losing control with her. He would never venture into that territory with a woman again unless it was as husband and wife. God willing. He'd vowed as much a long time ago.

"You're afraid I'll what?"

"It's stupid."

"No. Tell me. You're afraid I'll what?" she pressed.

"Disappear."

"Disappear? But I won't. Why would you think that?"

"Because, as I'm sure you know, we don't always think logically when we've experienced trauma. I think of how long I waited for someone and how I all but gave up.

Then here you've been under my nose for a whole blame year, and I almost blew my last chance with you. Sometimes, I think you're too good to be true. That we're merely a fantasy of everything I'd ever hoped for."

"No. We aren't a fantasy. Do fantasies kiss like this?" Erin raised on her tiptoes to demonstrate. The brush of her lips against his, a kiss so soft and yet so potent, nearly wrecked his resolve. She drew back, her eyes glistening with tears, and said, "We are here. In this together. We're real people with past hurts who once loved the wrong human beings. Naturally, previous choices are going to color our life lens. Except now, we're moving forward with each other for the right reasons because we're with the right people."

If Cupid were real, Mike would have sworn her arrow nailed its target with spot on precision. His chest swelled with the knowledge of it.

"That's an excellent way to put it. You're an absolute wordsmith."

"Thank you. I mean what I said. Now, tell me. What's your exciting news?"

Erin hadn't imagined he'd move so quickly on the land deal. As Mike filled her in, he grew more animated by the minute when he spoke of future plans.

"Clinton won't sell to just anyone. Like I said before, we don't operate that way around here. He wants to ensure the land is preserved as much as it can be, and when we rezone it, it'll be as I specified. There would be the possibility of a small lodge or inn, but no flashy hotel or vacation mecca. Marshall Realty is going to reword the offer with everything outlined to a T. Clinton's asking price is steep, but I expected that. It's a deterrent. Only folks with serious intent will come forward."

"You stand a good chance then."

"I do. I can't imagine anyone else matching my offer. I'm meeting his price tag and then some. I don't know Clinton well—he used to be kind of an old sourpuss until the Lord changed his tune—but he's forthright and honest, and he has the community's betterment in mind."

Mike's enthusiasm mirrored his personal ideals. Hard-working and goal oriented, he also had this area's best interest at heart. She well remembered that day in the woods when he'd first shared his vision with her. Now, it seemed as though the seeds of his dreams were sprouting to fruition. Joy bubbled up within Erin, touching every nerve ending, settling along invisible margins dormant too long.

A few nights later when she and Aunt Bea sat down to FaceTime, giddiness rang in her voice as she spoke of the man who'd irrevocably wound himself around her heart.

"I can't wait for you to meet him. Did I mention he loves animals?"

"Yes. Several times." Aunt Bea flashed her a smile, nodding. "His Lab, Blackie, is the king of his castle, as Miranda is the queen of hers. Have the two been introduced yet?"

"Not yet. Maybe soon."

"Well, darling, Mike and his family sound very special. I may make a trip down your way soon, and perhaps, I can meet them."

"Oh, that would be great, Aunt Bea. Now that I'm moved, you'll no longer sleep on the spare cot in the back room of the clinic. The cottage is compact, but so cute and cozy. You can have the bedroom and I'll sleep on my new sleeper sofa."

"Nonsense. I won't have you kicked out of your own room. The sofa will suit me fine, and maybe we'll have a movie night where we watch old flicks and munch popcorn and catch up on everything there is to know about Ruby."

"I'd really like that, Aunt Bea. I've missed you." Tears sprang to Erin's eyes as they wound down the conversation.

"One last thing, darling. Your new life—what you've become and how you've triumphed over adversity—would make your mother and father so proud. Never doubt for a moment how delighted your old maid aunt is. I love you, doll."

"Thank you. I love you back. I'll remind you that sixty is not old."

"Good try. These silver strands do not lie." Her aunt pointed to her newly-styled coif, a touch shorter than Erin's bob. "However, I'm contemplating making some changes in the future."

"Ooh. What?"

"We'll discuss this when I visit. Would around Thanksgiving be all right?"

"All right? That'll be perfect! That's only about three weeks away. I'll look forward to you coming."

"Me, too, darling."

They said their good-byes, and Erin drifted off to sleep that evening, dreaming of Aunt Bea, who'd raised, nurtured, and loved her as her own, and the town that had adopted her with equal verve.

Predictably, a warm and cuddly Miranda snuggled up

to her chest, purring, and Erin's dreams shifted to another—the flesh and blood person who held her heart.

"That's a lot to take on. Most of your career has involved residential construction. What makes you want to pursue a project of this magnitude?"

Despite his joker tendencies, Mike's brother Garrett possessed great business acumen. He saw beyond the obvious and honed in on potential. More than that, however, he weighed the pursuit as a whole. The venture had to have heart. Financials mattered, but without passion, one's concept would be dead in the water. Garrett should know. He hadn't built Sticks and Stones on a whim and a wish. Because of his drive and God-given talent, his handmade furniture business had boomed. He fancied what he did, and it showed.

"Building homes and new additions have been my bread and butter for the past seven or so years. Love it. Nothing like seeing homeowners' faces light up as each phase advances their ultimate dream. As you know, though, I've always wanted to create something in a similar, yet different, vein. My vision for the lodge is a way to do that—to use my gifts to continue carving out a living, yes, and to also give back to folks who need a little extra nurturing in a quiet place akin to paradise."

Garrett nodded. "A refuge."

"Something like that."

"Where folks can come to relax and regroup. Bounce back from what ails 'em."

"Yeah. And on a practical, business note, lodge guests would also bring revenue to local businesses in Ruby."

"Okay. Let me play devil's advocate for a minute. You

have no experience in this arena. Building a lodge and operating it are two very different things."

"You're right."

"There are motels and hotels farther on down the road in larger towns. You'll have competition."

"Maybe."

"Your proposal is a major undertaking. It'll demand time. Lots of it. You ready for that? Is Erin?"

Mike chewed on Garrett's points.

"To your first statement, I'm a fast learner. Plus, I'll hire capable, experienced staff to manage the place. As for nearby lodging available, my endeavor will offer a very distinctive feel. We'll extend personal touches and present a unique spin that'll become our hallmark. In the way Sticks and Stones differs from our friend Sam Packard's N2Wood carpentry business, my lodge or inn will command its own niche. In other words, each of us is gifted with individual talents. You design handcrafted furniture, whereas Sam builds some of that, but his specialty is cabinetry and the like. There's plenty of pie for everyone to have a piece."

"And the time factor?"

"Winter is typically my slow period for new home builds. My crew knows to expect that. I'll simply redirect my efforts."

Garrett hiked an eyebrow. "What about Erin? You've got a good thing going, brother. We're talking a major time investment here. Some dreams will keep. Others won't."

"I understand. Erin and I are on the same page. I've spoken with her about this."

What was with the weird look? Didn't Garrett realize how much Erin meant to him? Naturally, he wouldn't do anything to jeopardize his relationship with her.

His sibling clapped him on the back, as if refocusing. "All right then. You have my full support."

"The lodge will need furniture. Lots of it."

"I'm your man." Garrett jabbed him in the ribs. "I'm already counting the dollar signs."

"Ha! I knew it."

The brothers howled, teasing one another as siblings so often do, their banter, lively and good-natured. If Gabe had joined them today, he'd share their fun. Instead, this weekend was Ruby Elementary's fall carnival, and as school principal, he'd been tasked with various duties. About now, he should be manning the dunk tank. Or sitting in it. *Brrr....* What a chilly morn to volunteer for that. Though, all for a great cause. Carnival money would help fund additional books for the school library.

"When's Jerry presenting the new land offer?"

"Soon. I'll let you know when Clinton accepts it and we'll celebrate. Maybe a fall cookout?"

"Pretty sure of yourself, huh?"

"I'm having Jerry make an offer he can't resist. Trust me."

"Sounds good. I'll buy the steaks."

They continued their trek into the woods, along the southern side of the mountain. Crisp, morning air filled their lungs, as scents of pine and cedar carried on the breeze. As they rambled over the leaf strewn path, Mike recalled when he'd wandered here with Erin, the memory coaxing a smile. Had she slept in on this magnificent fall Saturday or had she risen early to make cinnamon love knots? He could practically taste them...and her.

"A good thought, huh?" Garrett slowed his stride.

"Yep. Mighty good."

His gazed traveled from Mike to the clearing that

opened before them, where Garrett's parcel of land met Clinton's, giving way to unfiltered splendor.

"God's bounty. What a blessing to live here in the Ozarks."

"And own a sliver of it," Mike added. "Say, what do you plan to do with your sliver—your acreage?"

His brother rolled his shoulders. "Dunno. Sit on it for a season, I expect. One day, I hope to do what you did."

"Build your own cabin in the sky?"

"Yeah. When that special someone comes along. My tiny house on the corner of Elderberry and Vine won't cut it if I want to raise a family one day."

"I know a builder who'll help you out when you're ready."

"I'd be mighty obliged, brother."

They swiveled around and faced east, as flickers of golden sunshine pranced across the fertile valley below. In the distance, the town of their heritage and birth awakened, and vehicles tootled along the highways and byways of Ruby, meandering down tree-lined streets toward errands, shopping, and whatnot.

Tucked in there somewhere, on a gentle rise overlooking the community Mike called home, Erin's cottage stood sentinel. If someone had told him a few years ago that his future bride would hail from there, Mike would've deemed him nuts. Why would he believe such a thing?

When old Doc Burnside bequeathed the tiny jewel to Mel, she vowed she'd never sell it. Then love found Mike's little sis and she'd married Matt. Had love found Erin, as well? That he referenced *future bride* in his mind bolstered what Mike hoped.

Chapter Fifteen

They'd eased into a comfortable rhythm. During the day, Erin and Mike went about their daily tasks. Where they once worked beyond their normal hours—not that a veterinarian or building contractor's hours were ever actually normal—they now committed to a schedule and stuck to it. As evening drew close, they set aside "just one more thing" and the busyness of work they enjoyed for the opportunity to be together and nurture something they treasured more. Each other.

On Monday afternoon, Erin's last patient scampered in, his somewhat flustered owner shadowing him. "I'm sorry we're a few minutes late for his well exam. I do have a good reason."

How could she be upset with these two?

Blackie's tail whipped from side to side in a friendly show of affection as he nudged Erin's hand to be petted.

"You're forgiven. Busy day?"

"No more than usual, but something came up a few minutes ago that garnered my attention." Mike closed the exam room door. A corner of his mouth lifted. "Jerry presented my offer to Clinton."

"Oh! He's accepted it?"

"Not yet. He has forty-eight hours to respond. It's in the bag. How could it not be? With the cash I'm offering, it's enough to finance Clinton's fondest dreams and then some."

"I hope so."

"It's a very generous offer. Plus, we've outlined my

intentions for the land so there's no secrets or hidden agendas. Clinton knows my family, what stock I come from. The same honor that ran deep in our ancestors' veins runs in mine."

"He's aware of your vision. The lodge?"

"Yes, ma'am. We've stipulated no ostentatious tourist trap. Nothing obliterating the views or compromising the land. No neon signs or gaudy billboards. Limited asphalt. A dozen other things, I'm certain, we'll both agree upon."

The excitement in Mike's voice ricocheted off the walls and fueled Erin's enthusiasm.

"A dream realized."

"One of them." His eyes twinkled as he clasped Erin's hand. Blackie doused their linked palms in slobbery kisses offering his nod of approval. "Whoa there, boy. Let Erin do her thing and then maybe we can coax her into celebrating with us."

"I'd like that."

Erin gathered some patient information and history from Mike. She then observed Blackie's gait, carriage, and breathing. In between doggie kisses, she checked his heart and belly sounds, which were normal. His eyes were clear with no discharge or redness.

"Also, Blackie's coat is nice and shiny with no dandruff or bald patches. Weight is good and his gums and teeth are healthy. Last thing we'll do is trim a few nails and update this fella's vaccines, and you'll be set."

Afterward, Erin pronounced Blackie fit as a fiddle. "He's one well-loved pooch. Great job, Dad."

Woof! Woof! Blackie voiced his agreement and heeled at Mike's feet like a good boy, though his rump trembled with glee.

"Thanks, Erin. I really appreciate the time you spent with us, and again, I apologize for being a tad late."

"Considering the reason, I totally understand. Please let me know if you hear something."

"Of course. Say, why don't I shuttle this guy on home and then pick you up in an hour for an early supper?"

"That sounds great, but I hate for you to run all the way back into town after a long day's work."

"It's only a few miles. Besides, it's my pleasure. You're the best part of my day." Mike reached for her hand, weaving his fingers through hers. "Don't you know that by now?"

That seemed to be their pattern. Her cottage, his cabin, the diner, or occasionally, sandwiches and dessert at Pennies from Heaven. Erin enjoyed their budding intimacy and sensed where they were headed. *I love Mike.* The sparks she'd held in check for the past year, now burned like a hundred matchsticks on the verge of a bonfire. *I know he loves me, too.*

The hurt and loss they'd endured because of others' choices now seemed a distant memory. She and Mike had entered a new phase of life. One in which the future never looked brighter or more promising. Would it be crazy to break out in an off-key rendition of the *Hallelujah Chorus*? How about fling her arms around the man she loved and kiss those outrageous dimples? Totally professional, right?

So much for silly musings. Erin would save the emotional display for another time when more than a mere door separated the exam room from Vangie's office.

When he arrived at her door an hour later, Erin had traded

her scrubs for blue jeans and a sweatshirt. Nothing fancy, and yet, she undid him in all sorts of perfect ways.

"How is it that you always look spectacular?" Mike hadn't realized he'd spoken aloud until the sound of Erin's laughter jolted him into awareness. Maybe he should clarify. "No matter what you wear, you're always beautiful."

"Thanks. I think."

"Oops. That came out wrong."

"I understand what you meant." She tugged the front door closed and they turned to walk toward his pickup. "I'm me. Plain and simple. I often choose comfort and practicality over manufactured veneer. Makes life a whole lot easier."

"Well, let me tell you, Miss Plain and Simple, a lot of women could take a page from your handbook. You wear comfort and practicality finer than royalty headed to tea time."

"I doubt royalty wears jeans and a Kansas City Chiefs sweatshirt to tea time."

"That's my point. The Royals probably sip their afternoon tea in their fancy duds and tiaras while secretly pondering such silliness. Trouble is it's always been done that way. It'd be poor form to breach tradition."

"Phooey. I'm all about tradition, but give me comfy clothes any day."

"Another reason I love you." Yep. That time Mike realized he spoke the words out loud. He didn't care. Emotions he'd held at bay for weeks plucked at his heartstrings. "It's true, you know. I'm not falling in love with you any longer, Erin Shaye. I'm already there."

No going back now.

They paused at the passenger side of the truck. Erin wound her arms around his neck and studied him for the longest time before countering, "That's really good to know. I feel the same way."

"Any bets on how long it'll take to make it across town if I kiss you just now?"

"Do we really care?"

"Darlin', I like the way you think."

Good thing they'd already discussed boundaries because, if they hadn't, he'd be mighty tempted to forgo supper and hurry back inside Erin's cottage and...do what? *Bud, don't let your mind go there.* Heaven, help him, he'd not venture down that rabbit hole.

Instead, he ended the kiss much sooner than he would have liked, drawing away before the frying pan could inch him closer to the fire. He wouldn't make the same mistakes he'd made in his youth. The next time he made love to a woman, she would be his wife.

"Maybe we should decide where we're going to eat?"

Erin cradled his cheek within her palm, her touch so tender, it almost moved him to tears. Grown men didn't bawl. What was wrong with him? He took a second to regroup.

"I think you're right."

They opted for Pennies from Heaven, the cozy bakery and deli owned by Charla Packard, at the far end of Main Street. Small, with a vintage vibe similar to the Come and Get It Diner, Pennies from Heaven specialized in delectable, homemade sweet treats, as well as a unique selection of sandwiches. Mondays were half price dessert days. Not that he was a cheapskate. He'd buy out the entire dessert case if Erin wanted it. She only had to say the word and all the pastries, pies, cookies, and cakes were hers. He had it that bad for this woman.

They placed their order for two Reubens, already deciding on chocolate pound cake for afterward, and seated themselves at one of the six tables overlooking Main Street. Outside, street lamps illuminated nearby store fronts and sidewalks where autumn themed flags flanked various junctures and rustled in the evening breeze. A few people milled about, but most ambled toward their cars, eager to get home to supper tables and families.

At one time, Mike would been one of those people still milling about until town rolled up the sidewalks at six. That, or he'd be on a job site surveying his subcontractors' progress. Except for Blackie, there'd been no particular rush to hotfoot it home. How life had changed. Since Erin, he'd made a conscious effort to restructure his work hours and alter his schedule. He couldn't wait to see her at the end of the day. Couldn't wait to hold her. Often, he caught himself counting down the minutes until he wrapped up obligations and appointments. His profession fulfilled him. He enjoyed what he did. Erin completed him.

Garrett's reminder of his workload increasing with his proposed business venture wouldn't interfere with what he'd found with Erin. Would it? *Nah.* Years of heartache and lonesomeness schooled him well. No way would he jeopardize what he and Erin had. She understood and appreciated his goals and dreams because she'd worked just as hard to obtain hers. She'd established her own veterinary practice by the sweat of her brow. It wasn't like he was shifting careers. He simply wanted to step up his game with something new.

Something that would benefit others.

"My Aunt Bea is visiting in a few weeks." Erin's voice roused him from his thoughts. "She can't wait to meet you."

"I'd like that. What's she like?"

"Well, I've already told you how she raised me after my parents' accident and how we attended grief counseling and support groups. Aunt Bea became like a second mother to me. We were close before, but when Mama and Daddy died, that reinforced our bond even more. She became my legal guardian and I moved into her cute Craftsman in the St. Louis suburbs. She immediately redecorated the spare bedroom upstairs in all my favorite colors and pre-teen desires. As we adjusted to our 'new normal,' we also adjusted to each other. Aunt Bea didn't try to take the place of my mother, but she filled the void with tons of love, and when necessary, gentle discipline. She's such a sweetheart. I love her. Everyone does."

"Your aunt never married?"

"No. I think she had her share of admirers in her younger years, but never anyone she wanted to settle down with. I always wondered if maybe she put her life on hold when a child permanently entered the picture. She assured me that wasn't the case, though I do sometimes think about that. She gave up a lot for me."

A wistfulness washed over Erin, clouding her attractive features. Again, Mike tried to imagine what it must have been like to lose so much at twelve years old and then deal with subsequent guilt over upending her aunt's life, however erroneous her thinking. The kid Erin must've beat herself up over her perceived intrusion. Adult Erin realized the depth of her aunt's willingness, yet the sacrifice wore on her even after all these years. When it came to love and loss, one's thoughts weren't always rational. He should know.

"Something tells me your aunt, special soul that she is, wouldn't change a thing. You didn't prevent her from finding love. You helped her discover it in a new way."

"Thank you. That's kind of you to say."

Mike reached across the table and linked his hand with hers. "I believe it."

"I want to. I'm trying. You see, Aunt Bea is a very youthful sixty. Beautiful inside and out. Energetic and vivacious. Great health. Loves adventure. Likes meeting people and making new friends. She's a retired teacher with so many additional talents yet to unearth. Now, I've moved away...and it pains me to think of her sitting alone in that house, darling though it may be, directionless and without goals."

"Maybe God's redefining her goals. Steering her toward new territory. Have you discussed this with her?"

"Not yet. I plan to when she comes at Thanksgiving. She did allude to changes of some sort."

"See? Hopes, plans, and dreams can shift in a heartbeat."

Erin squeezed his hand. "You encourager, you."

"That's me. Mister Encouragement. Another distinguished moniker of mine. One of many."

The real secret? Erin encouraged *him*. From strained courtesies to genuine conversation, they'd come a long way. Their relationship had continued to blossom, and he no longer identified as the same guy he'd been a year ago. Erin had made him take a deeper look inside. He didn't want to return again to living life on the fringe with work being his sole source of satisfaction and enjoyment. Work didn't warm his bed at night. It didn't make him ponder life's finer points. Like, for instance, how marrying the right person—the one God intended—could cause the planets to realign and the world to change orbit. *Marry?* Yeah. Marry. Marriage. To Erin. The thought didn't seem as outlandish as it once might have.

Goosebumps jitterbugged down his spine. For the first time in a long while, Mike's path forward crystalized. His career burst with promise. With his prospective land deal, a new objective formed, and his biggest cheerleader sat across from him, fully on board with the natural order of things. Why sweat the one matter that nagged his conscience? Adding an additional goal to his work queue shouldn't affect where he and Erin went from here. She understood and appreciated ambition, especially when the end result benefitted others. Naturally, worthwhile ventures necessitated sacrifice. At least during the initial planning stages. Mike would never allow work to take precedence over the woman he loved. No way.

Conflicting emotions fled as the teenage server delivered their mile high Reubens accompanied by dessert plates, which held thick, fat slices of chocolate pound cake drizzled in a vanilla glaze and cherry topping.

"Wow. Would you look at that." Erin ran her tongue over her lips, eyeing the food. "I'm really tempted to start with dessert first."

"Me, too."

Though, it might embarrass her if he jumped across the table and started kissing that luscious mouth of hers. He doubted the other patrons would mind. Who knew? They might even enjoy it.

This town might be small, but what Ruby lacked in big city options, it made up for in down-home distinction. Both the Come and Get It Diner and Pennies from Heaven knew their customers' palates like the ladies' sewing circle knew their way around a good toddy. They understood *"A merry heart doeth good like a medicine..."* and elevated it to a whole new level. Except Erin was pretty sure The Sewing Bees took some liberty with *"But a broken spirit drieth the bones..."* when imbibing for medicinal purposes. Not that she would know. That secondhand snippet came via Tilly Andrews.

"Absolutely sublime. Though, I'm certain there were a thousand calories in this meal." She set down her fork and sighed. Not a crumb left on her plate.

Mike had scooted his dishes away, a grin forming. Did she have cake crumbs on her lips? Food in her teeth?

"I agree. Pretty sublime, all right. Same with the food."

Erin's pulse ping-ponged inside her wrists. A heady sensation zipped from her head to her toes, leaving a trail of warmth in its wake. For a guy who once sheltered his emotions behind a stone pillar façade, this new and improved Mike continued to surprise her. She liked it.

"You've become an outrageous flirt."

"Yes, ma'am. See what you do to me?" He drained his soda, placed several bills on the table for a tip, and extended his hand. "Ready?"

"Yes. Thanks for the delicious supper and dessert and for playing chauffeur tonight. I feel properly spoiled."

"I want to spoil you forever."

The warmth in her bones grew into a steam bath. Was

he insinuating what she thought he was? *It's too soon. Too soon. Too soon.* But logic flew out the window when love dashed in. Besides, he hadn't proposed. He'd simply insinuated. Anyway, *too soon* was a relative term when God had obviously set them on this path.

Mike placed a palm on the small of her back as they moved toward the door. They stepped out into the brisk evening, the sidewalks now almost empty. At the passenger side of the pickup, he turned toward her fully and started to embrace her.

"You can't possibly know how much I—" His phone chimed with a unique ringtone. Instead of going for the kiss, he hesitated. "That's Jerry."

"Oh, my goodness. Clinton's accepted your offer! By all means, take the call."

Chapter Sixteen

Mike hit the speaker. "Hey, friend. Where are we celebrating? Your place or mine?"

"Neither. Yet." Jerry sighed audibly. "There's been a bit of a hitch."

"A hitch? Let's not play Ring Around the Rosie, Jer. What kind of hitch?"

"Mike, I'm sorry. Clinton's had another bid on the property. For substantially more than yours."

His jaw dropped. The supper in Mike's belly turned to lead. Another offer? Only a smattering of people, besides himself, could pony up that much cash, and the ones he could immediately tick off in his brain, hadn't expressed the slightest interest in Clinton Farley's land deal. *Lord, have mercy.*

"He's considering selling to an outsider?"

That didn't fit Clinton's personality at all. Before his come-to-Jesus meeting in the past year, Clinton had been known as a difficult sort. However, according to Mel who worked at The Meadows, the old fella had made a complete one-hundred and eighty-degree turn. He'd chucked his sourpuss tendencies and evolved into a gentler individual and a softer, kinder soul.

He'd taken up painting again, made friends, and even asked Minerva Walters, a flamboyant widow and fellow resident at the retirement community, to marry him. In short, the guy had developed a new lease on life. Thus, his decision to sell off his land and fund the art studio he'd hinted at building on The Meadows' property.

Erin touched his arm, concern and confusion evident in her face. Mike tried forcing a smile, but his mouth tasted like cotton and refused to cooperate.

"Normally, as you know, I'm not at liberty to discuss the potential buyer, but in this case, I'm afraid I don't know anything about the other party."

"How's that? Why not?"

"I'm not their real estate agent, Mike. They're using a big shot realty team from the northern part of the state. Don't mind telling you though—it's all pretty tight-lipped."

"Okay, Jer. Shoot it to me straight. What's the deal? How much more money are we talking?"

"One hundred and fifty thousand."

"*Dollars?*"

"Well, it sure isn't cans of creamed corn, son."

"Just so I'm clear. That's in addition to the three hundred thousand dollar asking price?"

"Yep."

"For the love of pickles, that's ludicrous! Who'd offer that kind of money?"

Mike let a curse word slip under his breath. He normally didn't use foul language. *Sorry, Lord.*

It had to be some big entity. They were going to waltz in, rezone the land, and slap up condos or a high rise. *Holy cats.* Had Clinton Farley lost his ever-lovin' mind? Had he allowed the dollar signs to blind him? Maybe senility had finally gotten the best of him. Couldn't he comprehend the other party's objective?

Ire played tiddlywinks with Mike's emotions. Someone had come along and effectively pulled the wool over an old man's eyes. What other explanation could there be?

"Now, it isn't a done deal yet." Jerry's voice brightened. "There are a lot of unknowns here. While we don't know who the other party is, or their goal, we do know a couple things. Clinton hasn't countered back. I mean, with the offer they made, from their perspective, it's a slam dunk. If the forty-eight-hour window that he wants to consider the offer expires, the party could walk, yes, but apparently, money isn't an issue. They may very well draw up a more lucrative offer. In other words, they want that land."

"Another consideration..." he continued, "This is a new listing. It'll take a bit for the bigger boys—investors and developers—to come calling. There's still a little wiggle room. However, with this kind of property, word will eventually get out. We've seen it in nearby communities, such as Branson. Developers have flocked to the Ozarks for decades. It's a hotbed of prime development opportunities within a gem of an area. Some have positioned themselves well and experienced tremendous success...and others have built what they swore would be God's cherry on top of a success sundae only to sit there and rot."

Mike swallowed, digesting Jerry's words. "So, we wait."

"I'm afraid so, buddy."

"Maybe if I appeal to Clinton personally?"

"I know we're a close-knit bunch around these parts, but look—how do I say this delicately?"

"You don't have to. I know. It's a matter of ethics and professionalism."

"There is another option." Jerry cleared his throat. "We could always counter with a higher bid."

He didn't want to do that. He didn't want to risk Hilltop Haven, his business, dip further into his own coffers, or incur deep debt to buy land for a pipe dream. Jerry knew that.

When Mike didn't answer, Jerry continued. "Keep your chin up. Remember, your original offer is still on the table. At least for another forty-eight hours—make that about forty-four or so."

Right. Mike's heart sunk. Their offer was dead in the water and they both knew it. Since Clinton hadn't immediately bit, that could only mean one thing. Big money was edging them out. The death of a dream didn't bother him as much as the prospect of city boys tearing up the mountainside and these centuries-old hills and hollers in the name of tourism and the profitable pot of gold it spawned.

Lord Almighty.

Last night, what began on a high note, ultimately, ended with a dull thud. Erin couldn't help but replay the evening in her head, from the fantastic sandwich and pound cake at Pennies from Heaven to the dreadful finale with Jerry Marshall's phone call. What a blow.

The devastation on Mike's face, as Jerry explained the latest twist, made it difficult to concentrate. She went from appointment to appointment today, hoping that some unforeseen miracle had transpired, giving Mike the upper hand. When she heard nothing, she told herself no news was good news, but what it actually meant resonated in slow, measured waves. Certainly, Clinton would go with the highball offer. He'd be absolutely foolish not to. *All that money.*

Erin closed her laptop and switched off the lights in her office. The faint scent of pet friendly cleaning solvents tickled her nose, and once again, she noted Vangie's dedication and hard work. Her friend and office manager met her at the back door of the clinic, and they walked out together.

"Five canines, four felines, a rabbit, and a hamster...and a partridge in a pear treeeeee." Vangie belted out the last part in a high pitched, sing-songy voice, laughing. "Just think if you specialized in large critters and livestock. We could be singing an entirely different tune."

"You're right. I'm a sucker for most animals, but I think I'm called to treat God's smaller creatures."

"You certainly have a way with them. Mike Brewer's Lab, Blackie, is quite smitten with you. When they were in yesterday, I thought he was going to lick you to the moon and back. The dog. Not the man."

"Glad you clarified that." Erin winked, amused more by Vangie's perceived wit than by her actual assessment. "I'm fond of him, too. The dog. Not the man."

Vangie's eyes went round. "Not the man? But I th—"

"No. I'm *more than fond* of the man."

"Ohh. How much more?"

"Lots."

They shared a knowing look, but before her friend could press for details, Erin waggled her fingers. "See you tomorrow."

"Hey! Wait. You can't leave me hanging like this." Vangie tapped her shoulder, her expression a mix of curiosity and delight. "I've heard rumors, but you know I'm not one to pay them much mind. So, the buzz is true?"

"I don't know. What buzz are you referring to?" Erin opened her driver's side door and slid into the seat while Vangie practically salivated.

"The *buzz* is that the youngest Brewer fella and the single, unattached veterinarian are a match made in Ruby heaven. Again, I don't put much stock in rumors, but Dander Evans dropped that juicy morsel inside a full barber shop the other day. Mitch happened to be in the chair at the time. Naturally, Mitch told me who's now telling you. Who you tell is up to...well...you."

"Thanks. It's always good to keep abreast of such things, especially when the tales involve one's self." Erin gave a final wave and closed the door.

As she drove away, Vangie smirked and fist-pumped the air, undoubtedly certain that Dander pegged the love match correctly, and equally pleased that she'd weighed in on the pairing. For not putting much stock in rumors, she could have fooled Erin.

Anyway, the whole town relished a romance, including a possible love connection, so Erin couldn't be cross. She found their interest sweet. Mike probably did, too. After all, he'd known this bunch his entire life. They might joke about wedding bells, but considering the fiasco of his youth, they meant well. He deserved the fairy-tale ending that never happened—except with someone else.

Nearing the stop sign, Erin's stomach growled. Though she and Mike hadn't planned anything this evening, she'd hoped he would call or text. Maybe he'd gotten hung up at Vangie's and Mitch's or another job site. She'd begun to look forward to meeting him after work, and not hearing anything at all, especially after last night, raised concern.

She started to text him while stopped but thought better of it. She had another idea. Why not visit the diner and order two meals to go? Tuesdays were fried chicken night. What red-blooded American male didn't like fried chicken? He probably hadn't eaten supper yet. She could text him from the Come and Get It and have him meet her at home. Likely, the disappointment and upset over the land deal still weighed on Mike. Fried chicken and a quiet evening together might very well draw him out of his funk.

So immersed in her thoughts, Erin almost didn't notice the sleek, red sports car that zipped up from behind until the driver honked, veered left, and passed her on the city street near a residential area of picket-fenced houses.

What made him stop at the diner? Mike intended to go home after finishing up at Mitch's, but he'd hoped Jerry might touch base, informing him of any news. Probably stupid. Then again, the unexpected could happen. It could. He wanted to be in town to celebrate with Erin should they hear something positive. It'd been a little over the twenty-four hour mark since presenting the offer to Clinton. Less than twenty-four more to go. They were still in the window.

Uh-huh. And pigs fly.

Mike sunk into the booth, resting his chin on folded hands, and surveyed the menu. Closed it. The fried chicken special sounded good. Smelled good, too. Except he didn't want to eat without Erin. He'd grown used to her company. Maybe too used to it. Had he taken that for granted?

The clinic must be closed by now. For a second, he considered texting her to invite her to supper, but it seemed too last minute. Like an afterthought. He never wanted her to feel that way, and yet, it seemed that most of their time together centered on spur-of-the-moment meals. Not that he didn't enjoy those. He simply wanted more with Erin than a few hours at suppertime. Shoot, he wanted to spend his whole life with her. He wanted to marry the woman. He'd mulled it over since last night. If he were honest, he'd chewed on it for a while. He'd spent so long denying his feelings for Erin that now he'd admitted them, the well overflowed. He couldn't go back to who he once was. Exisiting didn't equate to living, and certainly, not to loving.

Land deal or not, God knew best. Obviously, Mike couldn't have the whole enchilada. In a perfect world, maybe. But in reality, bad things happened. He'd get over it. He'd rather have Erin forever, and all the time in the world to spend with her, than a pie-in-the-sky dream which entailed long hours and leg work. He only hoped the party who'd outbid him had some scruples. The thought of a tacky tourist venue or some other ugly cash cow blotting out the unadulterated views and natural beauty of these old Ozarks hills and hollows set his skin to crawling.

Absentmindely, he shook his head. Enough of this. Imagining the worst would get him nowhere.

Resolving to plan better regarding his time with Erin, Mike opened the menu again. Maybe he'd order two fried chicken specials after all. He'd get them to go and surprise her. She probably hadn't eaten yet because she always changed from her scrubs when she got home for the evening.

Okay. Chicken it would be. Now, what for dessert? What kind of pie would she like? Would Erin rather have apple, cherry, or peach? How about chocolate? Everyone raved about the chocolate and he could personally testify why. Its flaky, buttery crust could make the angels sing.

He continued scanning the menu as the cow bell chimed over the front door of the diner. A familiar sound when patrons entered or exited, folks had grown accustomed to the clatter and usually continued eating and visiting. Clatter or no clatter, not much got between hungry folks and their grub. He didn't bother to glance up.

But something shifted in the room. Glasses clinked against tables, as if set down in haste. Silverware stilled. The hushing of voices grabbed Mike's attention and he lifted his gaze. His stomach lurched. For a second, he couldn't breathe. *No.* He must be seeing things.

There she stood—rosy cheeked and smiling—with long, golden tresses cascading over svelte shoulders, falling almost to her waist, framing a memorable, heart-shaped face with delicate features. She sported form fitting, designer jeans, a fire engine red sweater the same shade as her lipstick, and high heeled leather boots that reached her knees and matched the leather handbag in her hand. From head to toe, she exuded confidence and poise. No longer the girl of their youth, the woman's natural beauty, nevertheless, transcended polished elegance.

Time stopped as twelve years flitted away and past and present met. Their gazes locked, and like a movie reel playing in slow motion, Sally Sue strolled toward the booth he'd taken at the back of the diner.

"It's been a long time."

For a Tuesday, the Come and Get It teemed with action. The fried chicken special usually brought people out in droves, and tonight was no exception. Vehicles occupied every parking space at the recently paved lot and every spare corner of grass.

Immediately, Erin noticed *the car.* The fancy red number that blew past her a while ago in a no passing lane. Naturally, it would be the one vehicle taking up two spaces midway from the front door of the diner. *Missouri license plates.* But not from around here. No respectable Ruby citizen would be so crass as to flaunt their privilege and power in a such a rude way. They'd do their best to shimmy between the yellow lines, leaving plenty of room for a neighbor to park. Of course, no one in Ruby drove a BMW. This out-of-towner had plenty of ego, but no class.

On a happier note, Erin also spotted Mike's Silverado positioned beside a tall oak with fluttering leaves at the very back end of the parking lot. Knowing he was here kickstarted her heart into a frenzied rhythm worthy of a starry-eyed teen attending her first prom. It fleetingly crossed her mind why he hadn't touched base with supper plans, but maybe something came up. More likely, his mood had cast a cloud over his day and he didn't want to be a wet blanket.

She understood wet blankets. For months, after her parents' deaths, not much could draw Erin out of her self-imposed bubble. She didn't want to burden her friends with the life-changing loss of her mother and father, though, that was a double edged sword.

On one hand, mere adolescents themselves, they couldn't possibly understand what she'd experienced. On the other hand, when Erin did take part in a sleepover or fun event, guilt wracked her terribly.

Likely, Mike was still trying to wrap his mind around being outbid on the land of his heritage. That he could, in no way, compete with the other party, must sting so badly. The death of a dream killed any chance at hope.

Two completely different wet blanket scenarios, yet both shared a common thread. Neither wanted to be the ice water on someone else's day.

Erin didn't care. Let the ice water flow. Surely, Mike realized by now, that sharing in each other's ups and downs were what bound them together. If he'd had a bad day or heard some additional distressing news, she hoped she could encourage him. He didn't have to shoulder the setback alone.

She steered her SUV onto a patch of earth near Mike's pickup and parked without disturbing too much of the grass. Two things came to mind as she organized her thoughts. One, she really hoped the Come and Get It hadn't run out of fried chicken. Two, if they had, she'd kidnap Mike and spirit him away to her cottage. Surely, between the two of them, they could slap some fried chicken together...or have a good time trying.

In all seriousness, what would she say to him? How would she boost his spirits? Erin vacillated several minutes between upbeat idioms and frank truth spun in a positive way. Finally, when her stomach growled with hunger, she decided to wing it. Skillful eloquence would only come off as stilted and rehearsed. Mike deserved better. He deserved her honest assesment. It didn't look good, granted, but no ink had dried on the contract. God could still swing things in his favor.

Buoyed by that thought, Erin was about to slip from her vehicle when the chirp of her cell phone waylaid her mission. She couldn't very well ignore her answering service. It might be an emergency.

Chapter Seventeen

She slid in the vinyl seat across from him, her long hair swaying like a pendulum as she moved. "You look well."

You look well? Yeah. About as well as whiskey in a teacup. *Merciful Father.* What was he supposed to say to that?

Sally Sue deposited her handbag in the space next to her and rested her arms across the red Formica tabletop. "I understand you followed your passion. You're a builder—a contractor?" The corners of her mouth lifted.

Funny. He knew nothing of what she'd become or what she'd done with her life. Though, whatever her path, she'd obviously elevated her station beyond what her parents could afford. Arch and Violet Messmer were cream of the crop folks. Hard-working folks. From what Mike remembered, they had some financial means, but they weren't especially wealthy. What he detected now mirrored affluence and privilege.

When Sally Sue left Ruby after the wedding that never was, he'd lost touch with her family's whereabouts. There'd been some vague talk over the years, but nothing of any significance. The speculation of a new love interest had floated about, but soon, that idle tittle-tattle dried up like cow patties beneath a July sun. Mike didn't have much use for social media, and he hadn't been inclined to search out details like a lovelorn loser.

The silence grew too long and he forced out the words. "That's right. I'm a home builder."

"I guess that shouldn't surprise me. Shop was always

your favorite class in high school. Do they even offer that anymore?"

So. The girl—woman—he'd almost married, the one who'd dumped him the day of the wedding and the one he hadn't seen in twelve years, now sat across from him attempting to engage him in casual conversation?

"I wouldn't know what the school curriculum is, Sally Sue."

"Really? Isn't your brother Gabe the school principal now?"

"Of the elementary school."

"Oh."

He didn't have to glance around the diner to know that all eyes in the room fixated on them. Patrons may have resumed eating but chewing and swallowing didn't prevent folks from watching delicious story fodder unfold. Knowing Ruby as he did, it probably made 'em hungrier. Not that he could blame them. Everyone knew their history.

Except for the muscle in his jaw that started to tick, Mike remained motionless. He'd sometimes wondered what it would be like to run into Sally Sue again. In the years following their wedding day disaster, weirdly, he used to fantasize about it. Now he didn't need to imagine. He knew. The numbness in his chest confirmed it. The love he once had—or thought he had—for his high school flame had burned itself out.

"What brings you back?"

"You haven't heard?" Her golden eyebrows wrinkled. "In the town that knows when a toilet flushes, I assumed word would travel."

"And what would that be?"

"Seriously? You really have no idea?"

Why in blazes would he?

Sally Sue drummed her manicured fingernails against the tabletop, acknowledging his clueless state with a manufactured cough. Her smile widened, presumably, ecstatic that she could personally share the news.

"Why, I've just bought myself a mountain. Or I'm about to. A slice of it, anyway. The deal's all but clinched."

Lord, have mercy. Mike's gut twisted. *No.* She couldn't be the one. No way could Sally Sue be the other potential buyer for Clinton's property. Not in this lifetime.

"Pardon me?"

"Wow. You *are* oblivious." Sally Sue paused and relaxed against the back of the booth. "My last name is no longer Messmer. It hasn't been for six years."

Why should he care? What kind of stupid game was she playing?

"It's Ribeck," she continued. "You may have heard of Ribeck Industries?"

For Pete's sake. The electronic parts manufacturer? A Missouri-based company with additional facilities in several other states and some overseas.

"Yes, I've heard of them."

"Sheldon Ribeck, the company president is—was— my husband. Unfortunately, he suffered a heart attack during a business trip last year."

"My condolences."

"Thank you. He was only thirty-six. A traumatic loss, but I've managed."

Quite well, it seemed. Not that Mike had any right to doubt her. He didn't even know the woman anymore. Had he ever?

Zook Mercer, the jovial high school teen Ida Mae recently hired, set down two ice waters. The boy's royal blue braces gleamed beneath the newly installed LED light fixtures. "Good evening, folks. 'Course you know tonight's our fried chicken special. Would you like more time to look at the menu? May I start you off with a basket of biscuits?"

"No, thanks. We're not eating," Mike quickly answered.

"I am." Sally Sue shifted her attention to the young man, flashing a humongous smile. "I'll start with a sweet tea, please, while I glance over the menu because I haven't yet."

Confusion cantered across Zook's face as he tapped the order pad against his other palm. His gaze traveled from Sally Sue to Mike and back to Sally Sue when Mike offered nothing further.

"Sure thing, miss. I'll have that right out to you." The boy bounced away, retreating to the drink station near the counter.

Enough of this. Whatever Sally Sue's intent or angle, Mike wasn't biting. She could stay and drink all the sweet tea she wanted. He had no intention of sitting here, carrying on a conversation with the woman like they were besties. He started to rise, but Sally Sue reached across the table and touched his hand.

"I think you might be interested in what I have to say."

"Why is that?" Mike plunked his rear back down.

"When Shel died, Sid—his brother—assumed the role of president, but I maintain controlling interest of the company. In addition, my former husband left me well provided for in the event something unforeseen happened, which, sadly, it did. He never realized he had a heart abnormality. I didn't either, of course. Anyway, I've decided to invest capital in a new adventure. Something completely different and much more stimulating than little ol' electronic parts."

All right. She had his full attention now.

"What would that be?"

"A posh resort. An extravagant hotel with all the high-end amenities where the upper crust can come and relax in the Ozarks' nirvana while soaking up all the feels here."

Lord in heaven. His worst fear. She didn't have to lay out the specifics. He knew from the gleam in Sally Sue's eyes what she had in mind. The hairs on the back of Mike's neck bristled.

"Why here? Near Ruby?"

"Why not?" Sally Sue shrugged. "I don't intend to live here. It's an investment—a moneymaker—not my idea of a vacay. To others, it's the ideal escape."

Zook arrived with her iced tea and she thanked him. She ordered a chef salad, stating, "Everything but tomatoes. I hate tomatoes. Oh, and place the ranch dressing on the side, please. I prefer to drizzle it on myself. That's all."

"You got it." Zook grinned, completely smitten with the woman twelve years his senior, not at all deterred by her dismissive air.

When he meandered away, Sally Sue resumed her line of thought. "I have an entire team at my disposal to handle everything. Hotel Ribeck will be unlike anything this area has ever seen. I call the shots. My people handle the details. It'll be a grand, glorious utopia worthy of the elite who vacation here."

In the distance, the cow bell chimed again, though Mike couldn't tear his gaze away from Sally Sue. What in blazes had gotten into her? "You intend to turn Clinton's property—that stunning, untainted acreage—into a playground for the powerful and the privileged?" Mike's voice raised a notch. "Tell me you're joking."

"No. I am most assuredly not joking. Look, I know this town holds your heartstrings, but Clinton Farley's land is just that—a patch of land. A good-sized patch, granted, but goodness, there's enough of these hills and hollows to go around. Frankly, your possessiveness seems odd and more than a little..." Sally Sue's eyes narrowed, and her mouth gaped open. "If you hadn't heard I was in town or why, how would you know I'd made an offer on Clinton's property? *Oh. My. Word.* You made the other offer. You're the one I outbid."

This had to be a dream. Any moment he'd awaken from this nightmare and Sally Sue Messmer Ribeck and her grand designs would be a figment of his overactive imagination.

Mike closed his eyes. Counted to ten. Opened them. Nope. Still there.

Sally Sue cleared her throat, and once again, reached across the table to touch his hand. Only this time, she not only touched it, she wove her fingers through his, and clasped it tightly.

"What is it that you're more afraid of—the tourism and dollar signs this project will generate...or me?"

A movement at the entrance of the diner caused Mike to glance that direction. *Erin.* How long had she been standing there?

The call from her service hadn't been an emergency after all. Though, it had prompted an eight minute follow-up with a DVM friend regarding a consult.

Now, Erin's feet refused to move. She swallowed the golf ball in her throat as her heart thwacked the inside of her chest like an out of balance washing machine. Customers' curious glances bounced from her to Mike and the woman who sat across from him. In this very public place—among many who'd become friends—unease silenced any greeting she might have bid them. *Interloper* her mind screamed. Did she turn tail and walk or should she stroll to the counter as if she hadn't noticed the two at the far end of the diner? Which, of course, would be ridiculous.

In what seemed like an eternity, but probably mere moments, Erin had observed enough interplay between the two to realize this was no ordinary reunion. Space and time sparked with an intangible electricity and an intimacy that bespoke knowledge and connection. Never mind the hand holding. It wasn't so much that as it was the history they wore on their sleeves, linking them to a past Erin had not been privy to. Their past *before* her and Mike's present. *Sally Sue Messmer.*

Only when Mike's eyes darted toward her did Erin's feet unstick themselves. Quickly, she turned, scurrying back outside, the clanging cow bell overhead chiming with exhuberance at the sudden one-hundred-and-eighty degree reversal.

Caught with his hand in the cookie jar. Just like Phillip. No! You know that isn't who Mike is. There's a rational explanation. For him to meet his former fiancée in the Come and Get It, the most popular hub in Ruby, there has to be. Mike loved her. He wouldn't jeopardize what they had to revisit Memory Lane with the woman who'd nearly crushed the life out of him.

Still, what had she witnessed? As she drove home, Erin tallied the possibilities. A chance encounter? What were the odds? Sally Sue had left the area over a decade ago. Why suddenly return? Maybe a planned encounter? Doubtful. Mike had no desire to resurrect the past. A vacation? Nuh-uh. Visiting friends? Unlikely. Shopping? There were no malls in Ruby.

Maybe none of those fit the bill. Maybe Mike's former love simply came to reconnect with her roots. *Right.* That made as much sense as a diva returning to her lemonade stand after she'd already tasted the stage.

No longer hungry, Erin navigated the incline that was her driveaway, seeking temporary sanctuary only her cottage afforded. Like always, Miranda met her at the door and immediately rubbed against her legs and began purring. Erin scooped her up and snuggled her face against her soft, warm body.

"Hi, baby. Did you have sweet dreams today?"

Mee-oww.

"Yeah? Well, let's get some sustenance. Even if I'm not hungry, I know you are."

Here she was, carrying on a conversation with her cat again. Oh, well. Only a fellow fur baby lover could understand. She kicked off her shoes and padded over to the cabinet, reaching for a clean kitty bowl.

Try as she might to channel only positive vibes, Erin's mind drifted back to the scene at the diner. Again, she sucked in her breath as images of Sally Sue linking hands with Mike, taunted her. In hindsight, maybe she should have stayed. Maybe she should have marched to the booth and plopped down beside Mike, demanding the other woman keep her hands to herself. That would have told her.

Told her what? That she was every bit the pretentious prima donna Sally Sue was? It wasn't in her nature to be so childish. Or so bold. On the job, she took charge, assessing situations quickly, addressing them without hesitation. In her personal life, however, Erin leaned toward restraint. Without knowing all the facts, who was she to judge? Acting rashly rarely solved the problem.

Was Sally Sue a problem? It certainly seemed that way. If not a problem, a complication.

Mike unlaced his fingers from Sally Sue's. He inched back against the seat, as if putting the additional space between them would insulate him further from her devices. He'd say his piece and leave. No telling what Erin thought. He had to talk to her. He couldn't leave her with the wrong impression.

First things first.

"Clinton won't sell the land to you once he knows your motives. You realize that, right?"

Sally Sue batted her lashes and laughed. "Why do *you* want the property? From what I understand, you have your cabin in the woods, so I doubt you want the land for another home."

So...she'd done some digging. Naturally, in a town the size of Ruby, that didn't require much. "That's my business."

"Ahh." Sally Sue leaned forward and looked him directly in the eye. "Well, if that isn't the pot calling the kettle black. You want it for the same reason. To develop it."

He veered away from the topic for the time being. This

would get them nowhere. No way could he match the amount of cash she could throw at this deal, and likely, she knew it. Maybe, though, he could talk some sense into her.

"You've been gone for twelve years. You don't honestly expect anyone to believe you've acquired a sudden fondness for the area? That would be a bit much to swallow...considering the...uh...circumstances...and your swift departure back then."

"That's ridiculous. Business deals are executed all the time, and no one bats an eye. I doubt Ruby will give two figs about my plans once they realize how Hotel Ribeck will benefit the community."

Benefit? What a crock. Then again, to a degree, she spoke the truth. Except her intentions weren't completely altruistic. Far from it. The girl he'd loved and been engaged to had merely morphed into a woman with similar motivations. After all this time, she still thought of only one person. Herself.

Mike resisted the bait. There'd be no reasoning with Sally Sue. He should have known. He slid from the booth and stood. "Good evening. I pray you rethink this."

"You *pray?* That's a new one." Sally Sue flicked her hand and snorted. "I don't remember you praying when you were sweet-talking me in the back seat of that old Buick you used to drive."

God in heaven. She nailed him. Just like that, she brought it home. Reprisal. For missteps he—they'd—made in their youth. It all boiled down to that. She'd found out where he lived and what he did for a living and deduced correctly what his plans were in going forward.

He'd underestimated her. That, in itself, sent alarm

bells clanging in his head. But why now? Why, after all these years, with a marriage and a husband behind her, would she return to Ruby? To taunt him with money and moral failures?

"I can see this is a waste of time." He turned to go, but she grabbed his elbow.

"It doesn't have to be. There's still a way we can collaborate and clinch this deal."

"And that would be what exactly?"

A smug calm crept into Sally Sue's features. "Marry me."

Chapter Eighteen

At eight o'clock, Erin almost never received visitors. In fact, she couldn't remember when anyone visited her at this hour. Normally, on a late fall evening, the good citizens of Ruby retreated inside their homes to camp out by a warm fire and television. If one enjoyed a vibrant nightlife, they'd best find another town.

Miranda yawned and remained on the upper berth of her cat condo as Erin answered the door. Obviously, it would be the only person who'd drop by unannounced.

"Hi. Can we please talk?"

Erin stepped aside. She bit back a preliminary retort, silencing the inner voices that warred in her head.

"Thanks." Mike shoved a hand through his hair and trudged past, his grim countenance mirroring an internal struggle.

Had he come to let her down gently? Or would he play it cool and offer some inane explanation? Erin closed the door behind him, waiting.

"I went home to check on Blackie, or I would have come sooner."

Good. Despite the evening's upset, she appreciated the fact he hadn't disregarded Blackie's needs. Humans could take care of themselves. Pets were at the mercy of their owners.

"I understand."

"Thanks." His slight smile quickly faded. "Erin, I'm not sure what you think you saw earlier..."

"Maybe you could enlighten me?"

"Sally Sue's back in town."

"Yes. I gathered that."

"For the record, she made advances toward me, not the other way around." Mike grimaced and shook his head. "Well, maybe 'advances' isn't the correct term. In other words, she held my hand. I didn't initiate that."

"Okay."

"She's no longer Sally Sue Messmer. She's recently widowed—or at least within the past year. Last name's Ribeck now."

Erin knew that name. *Not Ribeck as in Ribeck Industries?*

"Sound familiar?"

"Of the electronics sphere?"

"Yeah. One and the same."

"I see."

But she didn't. She didn't see at all. Why on earth, after over a decade away, would a woman of her position return to the very area she despised? For that matter, what would make her assume she could pick up with the man she abandoned right where they left off?

"I know. I can see it in your eyes, Erin. They're the same questions I had when she sashayed through the door." Mike paced to the sofa. "Mind if we sit down?"

"Not at all. Please do." It came out far more formal than she intended. She softened her voice. "Would you like anything to drink?"

Mike lifted an eyebrow. "Scotch on the rocks?"

"Afraid not, buddy. The strongest I can offer is soda, tea, or coffee."

"Kidding. I don't even touch the stuff. Guess it sounds good in the movies—something business magnates order at the club after a long day wheeling and dealing. Anyway, no thanks, I'm good."

"All right then." Erin joined him on the sofa, not next to him, but nearby. "What is it she wants?"

"Interesting you honed in on that. What Sally Sue *wants* is Clinton's land. For the Shangri-la she intends to build there. It'll cater to the rich and famous and draw more money than flies to a picnic.

Erin gasped. "Oh, no. She's the other buyer?"

"Yep. Sally Sue Messmer Ribeck is my competition. Hotel Ribeck is her pet project."

"Clinton won't sell to her. He won't." What kind of cruel twist of fate was this? With her financial means, the woman could build anywhere. Except... she'd done her homework. She'd also lived here. She knew exactly how to market this area as the unique retreat that appealed to guests' inner adventurer.

Erin could just envision the taglines and tactics Sally Sue would use. None of them complimentary, nor necessarily true. "He won't see that property wrecked— trees bulldozed down, flora and fauna destroyed, land basically razed—for the sake of a few measly dollars. Clinton's smarter than that, and certainly, more devoted to his birthright and ancestry than she gives him credit for."

"We're not talking about 'a few measly dollars,' remember? We're talking thousands upon thousands here, Erin." Mike rubbed the back of his neck, then leaned forward, resting his elbows on his knees. "To be clear, I have assets. I have cash. But there are always risks. Besides, that's not the point. Sally Sue pranced in and offered an obscene amount of money for that acreage. Way more than Clinton's asking price. While that should raise questions in his mind, as long as she has the capital, Clinton can accept or reject whatever offer he wants."

Erin bit the inside of her cheek. A sense of foreboding lit on her shoulders. "I still don't understand why she'd be remotely interested in something of this nature. She has her husband's electronics company. Why on earth would she want to launch out in a completely different direction?"

"If it were anyone else, I'd say for the same reason I'd like to. Except it's not anyone else. It's Sally Sue and her plans are a complete contrast to mine."

"There's more, isn't there?"

"Yes."

Somehow, she knew there must be. Erin sat up straighter. "What? She's coming back? She's moving here?"

"She claimed she wasn't. She did, however, suggest a solution to our impasse...or varying viewpoints."

"Which is?"

Mike squeezed his thighs, as if needing to do something with his hands. "She suggested we join forces. That I marry her."

"She *what*?" For once, Erin appreciated the fact that she'd missed a meal. If she'd eaten the Come and Get It's fried chicken special, she might have lost it on the floor.

"Yeah. I know. That was my reaction."

Mike recounted the conversation with his former fiancée, summing up their visit with a few parting thoughts. "The woman's a conniver, but she's sharp. She may have walked out on this town twelve years ago, but apparently, she's kept her ears to the ground. She knew much more than I would have guessed after being away so long."

"Why do you think that is?"

Erin had her own ideas. She wanted to hear his.

"Well, obviously, there's money to be made from a venture here of the magnitude she's entertaining. Also...I suspect she's fonder of her old hometown than she's willing to admit."

"Fonder of Ruby or fonder of you?"

Mike's jaw tightened. "No way. The day she shook the dust from this place she made it clear what she thought of me."

"How do you explain Sally Sue's offer? The marriage one."

"It's a stupid joke. She knows I don't love her, not after all these years."

Is that why his brows pulled in and his voice faltered—because he didn't love her?

When Mike gathered Erin close that evening, he'd intended to reassure her. Instead, it was like embracing a block of wood. Something had shifted between them and his mind reeled with the implications.

Erin couldn't possibly think he still had feelings for Sally Sue? Yet...what if the shoe had been on the other foot? What if she'd been the one sitting in the booth holding hands with a stranger AKA her past love? Even if he hadn't actually been holding Sally Sue's hand willingly, Erin hadn't known that. He agreed. It looked bad.

He grazed Erin's lips a second time. Coaxing without expectation, but hoping she'd respond. Her mouth moved ever so slightly beneath his, except she drew away before the kiss deepened.

"Erin, I—"

"It's been a rather long day and I'm tired. Let's talk tomorrow."

"All right." Mike stepped back, dropping his arms to his sides. "I'd like to say something. I have to admit, seeing my fiancée again was a jolt. I can't deny the history between us or change it. I can tell you, unequivocally, I have no romantic feelings for the woman whatsoever. I love you. *You* are my future."

He paused, watching Erin absorb his words. He needed to add more. "That being said, I sure don't want to see this part of the Ozarks turned into some shiny tourist bauble where only those with affluence and distinction can come and enjoy God's bounty. I don't know how, but I'm going to try and convince Sally Sue to scratch this deal. Will you trust me?"

"Of course, I trust you. It's her that I have reservations about."

On her way to the clinic the next morning, Erin pulled into the Come and Get It's parking lot, intending to grab another cup of coffee and a box of homemade donuts for her and Vangie. She and Vangie took turns bringing snacks and goodies for their little makeshift lounge so when their schedule got slammed, they could sneak in a bite to eat.

A handful of vehicles lined the lot, with two others pulling in alongside hers. One was Edwin Ramsey, the older gentleman who resided at The Meadows. The other, Dander Evans, dressed in a fine new pair of blue jeans and a teal-colored, long sleeved shirt.

"Good morning, Miss Erin. Dander. How're you two on this glorious fall morn?"

"Great, thanks." Erin adored the silver haired senior. He always had a kind word and a pleasant smile. "How are you, Edwin?"

"I'm pretty peachy, my dear. Sun's breaking through, there's a bite to the air, and the holidays are just around the corner. Fall's my favorite season."

What a super attitude. Erin's spirit immediately brightened.

"I have a full load of barberin' ahead of me today," Dander supplied. "Wouldn't have it any other way, though. Love keeping the men lookin' sharp for their gals. Oh, and you might have noticed—I dropped another five pounds. I'm down to one-eighty-five now. Still running a mile or two every day."

Edwin clapped him on the back. "Good for you, youngster. Say, you got a sweet tooth for someone?"

"Ask me no questions and I'll tell you no lies. I'm fifty-six next month. Maybe it's time to think about settlin' down."

Erin quelled a giggle. Good for him. Certainly, love could bloom at any age. Look at Clinton Farley. Word had it he'd been a widower for many years. Now, he and Minerva Walters, a widow who resided at The Meadows, too, were engaged. *Ah, Clinton. Please, God, work in this property deal.*

Dander held the door open for both her and Edwin, and the three entered together. Betsy chimed overhead as delicious scents of toast, bacon, and eggs made Erin's mouth water. Other than a cup of cherry yogurt after Mike left last night, she hadn't eaten anything since noon yesterday. If she'd had time, Erin would have ordered one of the Come and Get It's crazy big and mouth-watering breakfasts, but today it would have to wait.

Edwin and Dander seated themselves at the counter. Erin headed toward the cash register to order a half dozen, fresh made donuts, and a cup of coffee to go.

Ida Mae flashed her a bright grin. "The donuts will take about ten minutes, darlin'. Sorry. They ordered a couple boxes for the ladies group down at the church, and we're making a fresh batch."

"That's okay. I can wait. Hey, what are you doing here anyway? I thought you'd hired extra staff and were taking some me time before the babies arrive."

"I did. I am. Hired a few teenagers from the high school and the new gal, Vale, over there at the pass-through." Ida Mae lowered her voice. "Vale Masters. I'm training her today. Such a sweet young thing—like you. New to town. Early thirties. Recently divorced. Two kids. Never waitressed before, but doing a mighty fine job. We're tickled to have her. Anything else you want to know?"

"I think that about covers it."

Ida Mae snorted, her round belly bouncing. "Glad to be of service. Now you have a seat, honey, anywhere you like, and we'll have those donuts boxed and out to you in a jif. Oh, and I'll send Vale over with your coffee."

"Thank you. I appreciate it."

Erin slid into a booth mid-way back, determined not to replay the interchange she'd witnessed last night between Mike and Sally Sue. The day was new and fresh and filled with promise. Why jinx it by calling to mind a bad memory?

She'd only been seated for a moment when Vale

brought her coffee in a to-go cup. She smiled shyly at Erin. "I'll fill it up again for you before you go."

"Thank you, Vale. By the way, I'm Erin." Erin extended a palm toward the woman with short, wavy brown hair and beautiful cheekbones. "I'm rather new here myself. Welcome to Ruby."

"The veterinarian. Yes, I've heard of you. Thanks."

"I know what it's like moving to a new place, making new friends and all. If you need anything, I'm happy to help."

Vale's shoulders lifted. "Gee, thanks again. That's really kind of you. We...my kids and I...have a cat. Boots. He's overdue for a check-up. I'll try and make an appointment soon."

Erin instantly sensed the woman's financial picture. The reticence beneath her smile spoke volumes. Probably strapped for cash and on a strict budget. Perhaps, shouldering a heavier load than one Vale's age should.

"Yes, please call the clinic, and Vangie, my office manager, will get Boots scheduled. We have a fifty percent off special on all new patient exams."

It was actually twenty-five, but Erin would fill Vangie in.

Vale nodded and slipped away. Erin tugged out her cell from her mini backpack and began scrolling through e-mails and a few messages. Nothing hanging fire today, so she could breathe easy for now. Though her days were fairly well-ordered here, sometimes, life could toss in a few surprises and unexpected craziness. As word spread about the new clinic, business had doubled over the past year. Daddy would be proud.

Erin sipped her coffee—strong, black, and delicious—

and set the cup down as Betsy chimed and another patron entered the diner. *Not again.*

This morning, she wore fashionable black slacks and a pink cashmere sweater that accented every curve and contour of her perfectly gorgeous figure. Large gold hoops danced beneath twin earlobes, flanking blonde tendrils that fell from the poofy blonde mane which crested her very blonde head in a colossal up-do. Without hesitation, cherry red lips widened into a confident smile as she yanked off wide rimmed sunglasses and peered around the room. Her gaze landed on Erin.

Chapter Nineteen

How in blazes had he overslept? Mike yawned, hitching himself up on his elbows as Blackie stirred beside him. How much sleep had he gotten last night? Five hours? Six? He couldn't even hazard a guess. Holy cats, how had life taken such a nosedive in recent days? One moment, he'd been planning a future with Erin, as well as considering new business ventures. In a heartbeat, his past collided with his present like a brick through a window pane. Which end was up? Which was down? For the love, he didn't know.

What am I supposed to do, God? Probably, a stupid question. For all intents and purposes, the offer to Clinton resembled peanuts compared to Sally Sue's circus. Such a fitting analogy and the old guy didn't even realize it. He'd been hornswoggled. Somehow, she'd devised a sweeter'n cotton candy proposal that sounded legit. Had Clinton gobbled it up?

Aside from that, Sally Sue's marital reference made Mike want to holler like a banshee. Did the woman really think him crazy enough to go down that ravine again? For her to suggest they join forces—taunt him with possibilities of what could be—*Lord, have mercy.* He'd rather be walloped by a two by four three ways from Sunday before entertaining that harebrained notion. He loved Erin. Wanted to marry her. It made his gut ball up in knots to think about the nearby hills pulverized into a cleverly marketed mishmash. It sickened him more to recall Sally Sue's crazy as a loon suggestion—insinuating if they marry, that together, they could transform this area into a proverbial goldmine.

Oh, man. The look in Erin's eyes when he'd laid that on her. He'd never forget it. Then again, it wouldn't do any good to keep dredging it up. He'd have to crawl out of this bed and face the day at some point. Maybe breakfast would make everything clearer. It'd been a long time since he'd gone to bed without supper.

His belly rumbled like a train zipping down the tracks. Before he'd even set feet to floor, he could almost taste the Come and Get It's morning special. Ham, eggs, and more, and all the coffee his bladder could hold. *Whowee.* This Little Piggy Went to Market lit his rump afire and made him shake off the covers and tug on a pair of jeans.

"Mind if I join you?" Sally Sue glided into the vinyl seat across from Erin. She snapped her fingers at Vale and called, "I'll have a half-caff dark roast blend. A large. To-go. Hurry, please."

The yellow pad wobbled in Vale's hand as she finished taking another customer's order. Incredible. Had the woman no manners?

She redirected her attention back to Erin and exhaled in dramatic fashion. "Hi. Sally Sue Ribeck."

Since Sally Sue had faced the opposite direction last night when Erin entered the diner, maybe it was her first time seeing her. She had thought Mike's reaction might have caused the other woman to glance her way, but she couldn't remember. Some of those moments remained fuzzy in Erin's brain.

"Erin Shaye."

"Yes, I know. The veterinarian."

That summed up that. The woman knew exactly who Erin was. Did she know about Mike and her, as well?

"That's me." Erin sipped her coffee. She refused to be goaded. "The veterinarian."

Sally Sue remained smiling, yet she pursed her bright, red lips together, shuttering perfect, white teeth. A visible flush stole into her cheeks and her expression grew guarded. Had she expected Erin to wilt beneath her gaze and insolent bearing? As if regrouping, the woman crossed her arms at her midsection and circled the diner with her eyes.

"This place hasn't changed much. New paint, new booths, and new décor, but otherwise, the same, weary diner with the same kitschy ambiance. You'd think with Chuck's success as a big-time cookbook author, he and Ida Mae would invest some of their wherewithal into a major renovation."

Here, she threw in an eyeroll. "Guess it simply goes to show that one can take the boy out of the country, but you can't take the country out of the boy. Makes one wonder, though, after major press—including book tours—why on this massive earth he'd ever want to return to this." Sally Sue gave the room a final going-over. Her gaze landed back on Erin.

"I suppose he returns for the same reason a lot of people do. Revisiting one's roots fulfills a need."

"Do tell."

Erin circled her coffee cup with her hands. So, she wanted to dance around the obvious. "Some derive a deep sense of satisfaction from belonging. Coming home to someplace comfortable and familiar is soothing. Others gravitate toward the love and acceptance they remember there."

"Oh, that's sweet." Condescension dripped from Sally Sue's brisk reply. "That gives me warm fuzzies all over."

Vale arrived and parked Sally Sue's to-go cup in front of her. "Careful. It's hot. Would you like to see a menu?"

"No, thanks. Coffee's all I want."

Vale nodded. Then she turned slightly toward Erin. "The donuts are almost ready. May I top off your coffee, Erin?"

"Yes, please. Thank you, Vale."

"Certainly. Be right back."

Vale was hardly out of earshot before Sally Sue commented, "I see this town continues to draw in strays. Ruby is a wandering soul magnet."

"Indeed." Did she even realize her own comparison? How much longer would this chat fest continue? "Ruby's as welcoming as ever to us."

"How magnanimous."

Vale returned with Erin's coffee cup and the box of variety-flavored donuts she'd ordered. "Mr. Ramsey over there said to tell you they were on him and to enjoy. The same with your coffees, ladies."

How kind. Erin cast Edwin a smile. No wonder everyone in this town treasured the old fellow. No doubt, he remembered Sally Sue. She couldn't have changed that much. *Wonder what he thinks?*

"Please tell him thank you for us."

"Yes," Sally Sue added. "So lovely of him." The inflection in her voice had a bite. Vale hurried away and the other woman snickered. "Like always, Mr. Ramsey is still minding everyone else's business."

What a piece of work. How had Mike almost married this woman? Where he was sensitive and warm, Sally Sue's popsicle vibes could freeze a pan of boiling water. Maybe, in high school, he hadn't known her as well as he thought. Or perhaps, over the years, her personality and what positive traits that once attracted Mike, devolved. After all, they were teenagers back then. Who knew?

Erin had no desire to make additional small talk with this woman. She had her coffee and box of donuts, and she could be on her way. She started to gather her things when Sally Sue cleared her throat quite pointedly.

"You know who I am, and I know who you are. Enough with the niceties. I came to Ruby to transact business. I've also decided something else. What an opportune moment to find you here."

Erin's scalp prickled. She needed to shut down this conversation, yet, she wouldn't run off like a frightened rabbit. "How can I help you?"

"Kind of you to ask. I want the acreage Clinton Farley has for sale. It's all but mine anyway. The other thing I want is..." Sally Sue uncrossed her arms and leaned forward. "Mike."

Certifiably nuts. Had the loss of her husband addled her brain? Had the trauma unhinged her in some way? *Easy, Erin. She wants you to react. Remain calm.*

"Why do you feel the need to tell me this?"

"Do I have to spell it out for you? Mike and I share quite a history. We go back a long way."

"That's just it." Erin remained poised to leave. She kept her tone light and even. "History. It's past. You left Mike and this town. You did that. Not the other way around."

"Ah. I've underestimated you. Fine." A slow smirk formed on the woman's face. "It seems you have some experience in that department, too. Good. Canceled nuptials can be such a beast, can't they? First, there's all the expense. Not to mention effort. A packed church. The decision to return wedding gifts...or not. Oh, and of course—in your case—the philandering fiancé. What's a girl to do, right?"

Erin's heart began to race. Sally Sue had her investigated? Why? Suddenly, it hit Erin. The land deal and her visit here weren't as much about an entrepreneurial venture as it was a fishing expedition and subsequent catch. Surely, she realized Mike no longer loved her? She'd been a widow, what, less than a year? Etiquette wasn't the only thing this woman lacked.

"I'm not biting. I won't play games with you, Sally Sue. Now, if you'll excuse me, I have patients to see." Erin stood, maneuvering her backpack, box of donuts, and coffee cup.

"Patients? Doggies and kitties and the like? Use whatever vernacular makes you feel important, I guess." Sally Sue flicked her hand dismissively and laughed. "Regarding games, I don't mind them. I play to win."

A reply wouldn't advance this conversation. Erin walked away without looking back.

Whoa. Mike barely had a chance to wave before Erin drove past in a flap. Not speeding, merely hustling more than usual even for a weekday. Perhaps, an emergency had arisen at the clinic? Clearly, she'd been too distracted to wave back, which roused his curiosity. He'd text her in a sec.

However, as he approached the Come and Get It's parking lot, Mike's spine went rigid. Only one vehicle appeared out of place. The red Bimmer had to be Sally Sue's. He'd assumed so last night when he'd hurried out of the diner and saw it on the lot. *Oh, my mercy.* Had there been a replay in reverse? Had she and Erin run into each other?

He angled his rig in a parking spot and cut the engine. Did he even want to go in? His stomach rumbled as delectable scents of frying bacon, ham, and eggs filled the air. A coward he wasn't. Reluctance be hanged. Ignoring the problem wouldn't make it go away. It also wouldn't assuage his hungry belly.

Mike stepped down from the cab of his pickup and made his way toward the diner's entrance. Probably best if he waited to text Erin until he knew more anyway.

Once inside, familiar faces greeted him. Several folks waggled their fingers or tipped their heads in acknowledgement. Some cast curious glances, most likely wondering if there'd be any additional morsels to chew on besides their breakfasts. In a booth mid-way down from the door, the source of his discontent sat facing the opposite direction. He almost gave thanks for small favors, when she turned and immediately spotted him.

Sally Sue's countenance, a combination of glee and smug satisfaction, communicated everything he needed to know. *Great.* Erin's hasty exit could only mean one thing. Obviously, there'd been an exchange of some sort. How much of an exchange? Who knew? Being the loose cannon that she was, Sally Sue could've fired off anything. Affluence hadn't refined her. It'd only sharpened her tongue.

The acid in Mike's gut churned. How in blazes had it come to this? A girl from his past. The woman who was his future. They were worlds apart, yet at the moment, only one world mattered—the one where he'd built a new life by moving forward after his old one caved in. It had taken years, but loving Erin had made him realize good things still lay ahead. Except now, the present had become a convoluted mess. Leave it to Sally Sue to wreak havoc and set off more destruction in her wake.

Rather than join her, which she probably assumed he'd do, Mike took the last bar stool at the counter beside Edwin Ramsey. No way could the woman insert herself there unless she wanted to sit in another customer's lap. *Don't even imagine that, buddy. Knowing her, she just might do it.*

"How ya doin', friend?" Edwin extended a weathered palm. "I reckon there's a lot goin' on these days." His old eyes conveyed an understated message. One that neither necessarily needed to address. They both knew the implication.

"I'm fair, Edwin. You?"

"Good. Good. Knees have bothered me some, but then at my age, that's to be expected."

They pumped hands once, and Edwin took a sip of coffee. He set down his mug on the counter and held Mike's gaze, inviting him to talk without really saying so.

"Holy cats, Edwin." Mike lowered his voice. "It's like seeing a ghost. I can't believe she's back in town."

Edwin matched his pitch. "It is a wonder. I suppose she has her reasons."

"You've heard?"

"Son, this is Ruby. We hear a lot of things. Some,

factual. Some, creatively manufactured. What I've heard is beside the point. You wanna set the record straight?"

Edwin and Clinton had become good friends. Maybe Clinton had confided his intentions to Edwin. Likely had. Being the confidante and gentleman he was, Edwin would never share confidences. That's why folks here respected him. The old guy had seen a lot. Heard a lot. Knew a lot. He'd served as a church deacon as far back as Mike could remember, and his entreaties to the Almighty on others' behalf were legendary. Known as Ruby's local prayer warrior, Edwin must have a direct line to God. *Like everyone does.* Except, sometimes, Mike struggled with his own measly prayers to the Lord.

"Well, for the record..." Mike hesitated. Everyone knew about his and Sally Sue's broken engagement and wedding debacle. He didn't want to go into anything beyond that because, as much as he found Sally Sue's maneuvering appalling, what purpose would it serve to share the intimate details of their history? "I guess you probably know we both made offers on Clinton's parcel of land. Naturally, with her financial means, Sally Sue has the upper hand. Privately, I'm well off, but not as well off as she is." How'd she marry into the Ribeck fortune anyway? That one he sure couldn't figure out.

"I see. Nevertheless, I wouldn't let that discourage you. God's ways are higher than our ways."

"Thanks, Edwin. I appreciate that."

However, in spite of Edwin's sentiment, being outbid on the property was only the beginning of his worries. After Sally Sue's outrageous solution to their impasse, Mike had assumed high alert status. He shuttered his eyes for a moment against the memory. *Marry the woman?* For the sake of a tour de force—the most dazzling diamond in this region to top them all? Her resources in exchange for matrimony. Yeah. Seemed like a fair tradeoff.

"Excuse me, may I pour you some coffee or are you ready to order?"

Mike's eyes popped open. He'd heard Ida Mae and Chuck had hired additional staff. *Vale* her nametag read. Pretty with a warm countenance and a tentative smile. Somewhere near thirty, he'd guess.

"I'll start with coffee, please. Thank you."

"Certainly. You take all the time you need to look at the menu and I'll check back." Vale filled his coffee cup from the glass carafe, then made her rounds at the counter pouring refills.

"Miss Vale Masters," Edwin whispered. "New here. Two sweet young'uns. Say, what's those brothers of yours up to these days?" The old fellow's wink mirrored his thoughts.

Mike chuckled. Let the matchmaking commence.

"Ahh. The sound of mischief afoot. Is there anything more telling than the shiftless glee of two grown men?"

His snicker immediately dissolved. Sally Sue wedged herself between them, leaning back against the counter, her right hip perilously close to Mike's kneecap.

"Must be a luscious snippet. Reminds me of when I was a kid and all the fine church ladies would slice and dice their women friends like they were fat, ripe garden tomatoes on a cutting board." Sally Sue shook her head. "Just harmless chitchat, Mama would say. She's still like that. Likes to believe the best of everyone."

"How are Violet and Arch these days?"

She clapped her eyes on Edwin, narrowed them, as if

vexed that he would try deterring her thoughts. "Retired now. The picture of vitality. They always hoped for grandkids, but Shel and I didn't have any. They keep busy with their retiree friends and volunteer work."

Mike's throat constricted. Was Sally Sue's reference to children intentional? He honestly didn't think so, yet he couldn't help but remember the child—their child—Sally Sue had miscarried so long ago.

"It's good to keep busy," Edwin offered. "Keeps us young. Please tell them hello for me when you return home."

Sally Sue's chin jutted out. "Sure. But I don't know when that'll be. I've decided to stay in Ruby indefinitely."

"You what?" It popped out of Mike's mouth before he knew it. He'd intended to play it cool. Blast it if the woman didn't know all the buttons to push.

"I'm staying here. For a while anyway. I rented that apartment of Edna Powell's, north of town. Certainly not a five-star hotel, but quaint and tidy. It'll do until I make further arrangements."

That Sally Sue Messmer Ribeck would temporarily forgo her fancy digs in the city nearly stopped Mike's heart. What other motives could she possibly have in mind?

Chapter Twenty

"Are you sure you're okay?" Vangie asked after they closed the clinic for the evening.

The day had turned out to be busier than planned and Erin barely had time to share the details of her encounter with Sally Sue. They spoke briefly about it over donuts and coffee mid-morning, and later, over sandwiches in between a neuter and a spay. Mike had texted her, too. Apparently, Ruby was abuzz with all the latest.

Wonderful. A love triangle on full display. So much for maintaining privacy and professionalism in a town where neighbors knew the shape, size, and color of other neighbors' undergarments purely by glancing at their clotheslines.

"Yeah. I'm good. Today's hectic schedule helped take my mind off things."

"Did Mike say what happened when he ran into Miss, or I guess I should say, *Mrs.* High and Mighty after you left the diner?"

"Apparently, she marched over to the counter, insinuating herself into his and Edwin's conversation. Said she'd rented an apartment over at Edna Powell's and would be staying on a while."

"The apartment over Edna's garage? Golly. That's a super cute place, about a thousand square feet, I believe. Except...I don't imagine it's up to Sally Sue's standards. She's lived the Ribeck life for six years. Why in heaven's name would she stay there?"

Erin shrugged. "Because she doesn't simply want Clinton's land."

Vangie's eyes widened. "You don't mean...you aren't saying..."

"Uh-huh. I do mean and I am saying. She wants her former fiancé back."

"That's crazy! She's twelve years too late. Back then they'd just graduated high school. They were a couple of eighteen-year-olds who were too young for marriage to begin with. Besides, I was at that wedding—the one that didn't happen. *She* ran out on *him*. Lickety-split with no looking back."

"I know. I think the woman may be struggling emotionally. She's a fairly recent widow."

"Oh. I guess I didn't realize that."

"Mmm-hmm. Sheldon Ribeck died of a cardiac event last year, and his brother Sid heads up the business now." Erin shut down her laptop and stretched. "The Ribecks are old money. Interestingly, they're known for their philanthropy. Good people. Ribeck Industries builds electronic components for medical devices and equipment, that type of thing."

"I didn't realize that. Wonder how on earth Sheldon met the barracuda?" Vangie mused. "I guess the family's amity didn't rub off on their more recent addition. You'd think after being away for twelve years, and being married for six of those, the woman would have matured and developed a heart for others. Instead, she's become a greedy, manipulative shrew. A complete contrast from how Arch and Violet raised her."

Certainly, a mystery. Erin stood and paced to her office window. Sunshine's golden embers set the horizon afire, slowly melting into the tree-lined dips and hummocks. Almost dusk. Never in a million years would she have thought to find herself in this position—caught in a three-sided relationship, forged by past, present, and future—with Mike's first love at the crux of it all.

"It's like I'm trapped in a movie-of-the-week."

"It's a weird situation. I'll grant you that. Say, why don't you come over for supper? My crew would love to see you. Plus, it'll take your mind off this nuttiness for a while."

Erin pivoted back around. "Thanks, I appreciate the offer, but Mike's dropping by the house in an hour. We're heading to Sapphire—away from here so we don't risk a rewind of last night."

"Good plan." They stepped into the hall and began switching off lights as they made their way through the building. Before heading out, Vangie reached for her jacket and tote that she'd stashed in a nearby closet and then flipped on two of the security lights they left burning at night. "Lots of yummy choices in Sapphire. Where are you guys going?"

"I'm not sure. Mike says it's a surprise."

"Alrighty then. Guess we both better skedaddle so I can go tame the hungry beastlets at my house and you can change into something more fitting for your date. See you on the flip side."

Erin nodded. "You bet. Have a great evening with your family."

Family. Would she ever have one of her own? If Ida Mae Farrow could conceive twins at forty, then anything was possible. Thirty was the new twenty. Or something like that. Anyway, in two weeks Aunt Bea would be here and Erin couldn't wait to see her. It may only be the two of them for now, though, a girl could still hope. Besides, this latest cloud on the landscape wouldn't last forever. She and Mike were still on track, and at some point, Sally Sue had to go home. Except...what if she decided Ruby was *home?* Again.

It had been a while since Mike had eaten at The Fryin' Pan and Into the Fire, but Mel and his brother-in-law Matt often ate here when up this way. When he was a kid, this restaurant had been a family fave. With its vintage vibe and magnetic appeal, the family-owned eatery hearkened back to days gone by, yet catered to all palates by blending the old with the new.

Thank the Lord, they'd ventured beyond Ruby's borders and far enough away from a potential repeat of last night. Partial as he was of his hometown, eating establishments were limited. That upped the chances of bumping into Sally Sue again, and no way in blazes, did he want that.

"You're looking especially beautiful tonight." He clasped Erin's hand across the table. "I meant to tell you earlier."

The red in her hair shimmered beneath the lighting's soft glow. Save for blonde undertones, almost a complete redhead, with lashes the length of a pencil eraser, the same beautiful shade. He bet their babies would be redheads.

Easy, fella. Getting a tad ahead of yourself, aren't you? Fantasizing about Erin being his wife wouldn't make it so. He'd best formulate a plan if that was to happen.

"Thank you. I put a lot of effort into this garage sale

sweater and three-year-old blue jeans."

The lilt of her voice lifted his spirit. Sally Sue's arrival had been difficult for Erin. No doubt, upending her as much as him, yet her relaxed demeanor quelled the darts of unease.

"I couldn't wait to see you tonight." Mike raised her hand to his lips, brushing it with a kiss. "I'm sorry you've been placed in the middle of this awkward mess with Sally Sue. I never, in my wildest dreams, imagined she'd return. Other than a possible business deal, there's nothing here for her."

"Well, apparently, there's one thing. One person, that is. You."

Oh, man. Now, Erin had that in her head.

"I honestly don't know where the woman's mind is at. I don't believe she knows what she wants. This bizarre idea to buy property in an area she couldn't wait to leave, and then return only to build some sort of swanky escape for the well-to-do, leads me to think she's lost her mind. I'm merely a pawn of some sort. She cares for me about as much as a match in an inferno."

"You know, I've been thinking. I'm not sure if she's unhinged or...grieving. Grief makes people say and do crazy things."

Did she speak from experience? Still, Sally Sue hardly presented the picture of a grieving widow. Impeccable dress. Flawless makeup. Condescending attitude. Other than a brief flicker of something he wouldn't quite define as sadness when speaking of her husband Sheldon, Mike didn't detect the sorrow one might expect when mourning a spouse's death.

"I suppose her demeanor and decisions might be a

reaction to loss, but I don't know. What I've seen are glimmers of her old personality. She's more fancified. Talks differently and what not. Except, beneath the shiny façade, lies the same self-centered woman I knew as a teenager."

"I suspected that. Why don't we change the subject, at least for now?"

"Great idea. Tell me about your day."

Two steak dinners later, their conversation had drifted into new territory. They were winding down their meal with chocolate pie when Mike's cell phone chimed with a familiar ringtone. *Jerry.* Unless it was something important, his real estate agent usually texted.

"If you need to take that, it's not a problem," Erin reassured him.

"I'm sorry. It's Jerry."

"Go ahead. Really."

He nodded and slipped his cell from his pocket, tapping the screen. Thankfully, when he'd made restaurant reservations, Mike had requested seating in one of their more secluded dining areas. At the time, he hadn't been thinking about phone calls, rather, how nice it would be to slip in a kiss over dinner.

To be as unobtrusive as possible, he didn't hit the speaker function. "Hi, Jerry. What's up?"

"Are you sitting down?"

"I am. As a matter of fact, I'm having dinner with Erin."

"Oh. My apologies for disturbing you. I can call you later."

"No need. We're seated at the back of the restaurant and I don't have you on speaker."

"Okay. Great. There's been a new development. I'll give you the brief version."

A line appeared between Mike's brows. A puzzled expression crossed his face. "Thanks for the update, Jer. I don't know whether to be disappointed...or relieved." His head bobbed up and down in agreement over something Jerry said and they wound down the conversation.

Good news? Bad? Erin couldn't tell. She swallowed the bite of pie. "Clinton accepted your offer?"

"No. I wish."

"I'm sorry. It would be hard to turn down the other one."

Saying her name would only add insult to injury.

"Not only did Clinton reject my offer, he rejected both. Mine...and the other party's. He's decided to sit on the property a while longer."

He's decided what? That's a lot of money to turn down.

Apparently, Mike didn't want to say her name either. Musing about being disappointed or relieved must mean Clinton's about-face saddened him, but in a strange way, brought closure. His former fiancée could return to her tower in the city. She would, wouldn't she? A knot of dread formed in Erin's chest.

"What now?"

Mike tapped his fork against his dessert plate. If she had to guess, Erin would say he wondered the same thing.

"I'll continue doing what I'm doing. Building homes and contracting remodels, while keeping my ear to the ground for anyone else wanting to sell some land. Placing my dream on hold for now doesn't mean it's forever."

She had to hand it to him. A step forward. A step back. Yet, not giving up. Merely, regrouping. "That's a great attitude. I wonder, though, what made Clinton change his mind about selling? The other...offer...especially. It doesn't make sense."

"I have to admit, I'm pleased that there won't be a tourist mecca sitting on that mountain any time soon, but I agree. There must be something more at play here. Something else Clinton has in mind."

"Did Jerry have an idea what that could be?"

"I don't think he knows either. He said we'd talk more later."

They finished dessert and the waitress brought the check. For a weeknight, the restaurant hummed at a busy pace and Erin understood why. The service, food, and dining experience were all superb, and many patrons liked to linger and chat long after their plates were removed. Getting away from Ruby for the evening had been a wonderful idea. There'd been no unwanted intrusions upon their meal, and it'd been nice to focus on the two of them without adding a third wheel.

Even if Jerry had phoned Mike with the latest twist, Clinton rejecting *both* offers hadn't dampened their date. It added a measure of poignancy maybe. Yet, Mike seemed to take it in stride, concentrating on the silver lining. She must, as well.

The hour started to meld into the next, and as much as Erin hated to mention it, tomorrow was a work day.

"Is that a yawn you're trying to hide?" Mike teased.

"Not a yawn. More of a contented stretch."

"Good to know. Glad it's that and not because I'm boring you."

Erin clasped his hand, smiling. "You could never bore me. What you're seeing is a happily appeased appetite from a woman who's worked a ten-hour day with some surprises tossed in."

"That's a polite way to put it." His eyes softened. "About those surprises...hopefully, we won't have any more of those."

But Erin wondered.

They drove the twenty miles back home beneath a star-filled sky and moonlit night. Traffic thinned, and the gentle rise and fall of surrounding knolls and nooks grew more prevalent. As they approached the sleepy town of Ruby, secrets lingered in the shadows—secrets known only to God and the select few who chose to keep them.

As they passed Edna Powell's century-old home—a French provinicial beauty, partially obscurred by the birch, pine, and cedar trees—neither Erin nor Mike mentioned the familiar red BMW parked in the additional space of the breezeway, which connected the two-story garage to the main home. In the converted apartment above, soft shafts of light emanated from closed curtains, a silent reminder of the one who temporarily dwelled there. No need to ponder whether secrets remained within those walls. There were plenty, to be sure.

Once home to Edna's niece Megan, the space now welcomed a new boarder. One whose Ozark roots ran deep, but now a city transplant with a hidden agenda that was anyone's guess.

"Thank you for the scrumptious steak dinner." Erin tried to divert their thoughts. "Just what the doctor ordered."

Mike glanced at her as he drove. "I figured we both needed some alone time. Together, that is."

The insinuation vibrated between them, bouncing around the truck interior like a bad word. Each recognized the other's apprehensions, though, they didn't want to jinx a perfectly good evening by voicing them.

"Aunt Bea will be here soon. She wants to meet you, of course." An obvious shift, but a pleasant diversion.

"I've been meaning to talk to you about that. Mom and Dad would love it if you joined our family for Thanksgiving dinner. It'd be a great way to break the ice. You know, to introduce her to the entire clan at once."

"Oh, I'm sure my aunt would love that. That's very kind of your parents."

"Super. It's a date. I'll let my parents know."

Erin ticked off all the signature dishes she could bring. "I could also bake the pies if your mother would like."

"Mom will say 'No need to bring anything. Just yourselves.' But I know you, and I know you won't rest unless you whip up some fabulous culinary creation. So, I'd cook, bake, or create whatever your little heart desires. Our crew will eat it and enjoy it all."

Erin rested her head against the seat, her mouth inching upward. It would be her first family holiday meal with the Brewers in what she hoped would become tradition. That is, if she and Mike continued down this path. Except for some vague concerns, there was no reason to think they wouldn't.

She thrust those concerns aside as slopes and dips gave way to roads and lanes dotted with various signs and golden-hued street lights. Small and mid-sized homes stood sentry over dormant, dew-covered lawns—many strewn with wayward leaves awaiting their fate of leaf blowers, or worse—the burn bin.

They navigated deeper into town and crested the incline where Erin's cottage awaited. She'd left lamps on inside and soft light dribbled into the yard.

"There's Miranda. Waiting for me, like always." Behind the curtain was the shadow of her cat's outline. The fabric rustled slightly, revealing Miranda's kitty condo with her perched on the highest level. "She's a terrific watch-cat."

"Yeah. Blackie does that, only he does it from the windows in the loft. It's higher there, of course, so that's where the best view is. Then, when I get home, he bounds down the stairs and meets me at the door. Kind of like a kid. It's the darndest thing." A note of wistfulness lined Mike's voice. "I suppose they get lonesome for us during the day. They probably wish they had someone to keep them company."

He pulled alongside the curb and cut the engine. His lips parted, as if to say something else, then changed his mind. Was he thinking what she was? That having a pet was grand, but adding human companionship, incredible.

Erin traced the outline of his jaw with her fingertips. "What's on your mind?"

"Honestly?"

"I wouldn't have asked if I didn't want to know."

Mike reached for her hand, kissing each fingertip, one by one. "I wish we didn't have to say goodnight. I hope one day, we won't." He heaved out a sigh. "I want to hold you in my arms until the sun comes up and all the hours in between. That. That's what's on my mind."

She didn't know when the kiss began, but his touch underscored the need for restraint. It wouldn't do for the two of them to unwittingly initiate new buzz—the blush-worthy kind that induced clutched bosoms and frantic chatter. And yet, the tender way his lips caressed hers made Erin want to lose herself in the moment. *This could be dangerous...*

"Mike, I..."

"I know. Say no more." Slowly, he backed away and took a deep breath. "I want to be clear about something. Our commitment is new...but on the heels of something that's actually developed over the past year. Sometimes, love is weird like that. It tiptoes slowly, then smacks us upside the head with the force of a two-by-four. Because of that—because I've fallen in love with you, Erin, I understand the need for caution. And rest assured—I'm not the same guy that I was at eighteen, destined to make the same choices. To coin a terrible cliché, I'm a changed man. I hope you believe that."

Oh, dear. She didn't want him to think she judged him for past mistakes he'd made in his youth...or whom he made them with. Everyone chose differently. That was a fact. She was glad no one judged her for her stupid choices. She hadn't slept with Phillip, but she'd come close to it a few times. Thank God, she hadn't, but she could have so easily. She'd been young, naïve, and in love. All the ingredients that made people act rashly. Then she ditched him at the altar after she learned he'd cheated on her with her best friend...and hadn't spoken with Patty since.

"You don't need to revisit it." She clasped Mike's hands within hers and said softly, "Good and bad choices don't necessarily define the person. Especially when we change and grow from lessons learned. By the way, I love you, too."

"I probably shouldn't say this, but I have a feeling our love is about to be tested."

He didn't have to mention why, but Erin agreed. He probably shouldn't have said it.

Chapter Twenty-One

By the second week of November, the weather turned sharply colder. Unusual, but not unheard of. After all, weather in the Ozarks had a mixed bag reputation no matter the season, and during late fall, anything could happen.

As Mike signed off on a new build, and completed the remodel over at Mitch's place, folks bustled about town chockful of good cheer and holiday happiness.

Only one thing burst his own festive bubble. Sally Sue remained in Ruby. Going on two and a half weeks and counting. Why? *Dimwit, you know why.* Still, Clinton hadn't relisted his property, and to his knowledge, there were no other new listings. The woman continued to breeze around their little community like nobody's business, coming and going at all hours, promenading in and out of various establishments and stores as if she were royalty on a silver platter. Her presence kept him on edge and gave him a permanent headache.

Fortunately, he'd managed to avoid any further personal encounters with her—a feat, given Ruby's modest population and the fact that most of the buildings on Main Street and in town stood in close proximity to each other. He didn't know what the woman was up to or why she stayed, but the town buzzed with various theories. Some folks speculated she'd returned to open a new fashion venue, which Mike found laughable. *In Ruby?*

Others hypothesized she lingered until Clinton caved and eventually sold her his land. *Maybe.* Some suggested she was following in Chuck Farrow's footsteps and writing a book. Not a cookbook, but a tell-all of where the Ribeck Industries' wealthy widow grew up. *Nutty.* She probably didn't want her fancy friends to know her humble beginnings. Then, several assumed another reason. The one that pestered him the most. *Me.* The girl from his past believed she could revisit history. Relive it, change it, or begin a new chapter. Whatever Sally Sue's motivation in staying on at Edna Powell's spare apartment, Mike could not care less, save for the vague unease it gave him. Like the next shoe waiting to fall.

"Hi. Sorry I'm late." Erin slid across the vinyl seat as she offered a breathless apology. "I met a patient's owner at the clinic this morning and the visit took longer than I expected."

Normally, Erin didn't go in on Saturdays. "Everything okay?"

"Yes. It's all good. Simply a well exam for a kitty cat, and weekends are the owner's only days off."

"So, you made an allowance."

Erin nodded. "I did. It actually worked out well. Sweet family who's had a rough go of it. I'm glad we were able to visit beyond normal clinic hours without other patients there."

Vale Masters. She didn't have to tell him. A few weeks ago, Vale had enrolled her kids at Ruby Elementary. A preschooler and a kindergartener. Gabe casually dropped the Masters' name over supper one evening. "Our most recent transplants. Great bunch. Dad's no longer in the picture, and I get the feeling he hasn't been for a while. They have a cat named Boots, which they're crazy about."

Gabe suggested the Masters could maybe use a wood

delivery as a "Welcome to Ruby" gesture, and everyone agreed. Mike and Garrett had shot each other a knowing look. Vale would probably appreciate the kindness, though, the gleam in their brother's eyes birthed another thought. One of the romantic variety. When they'd teased him about it, Gabe gave a flustered snort. "I'm the school principal, remember? It wouldn't be appropriate for me to initiate anything beyond friendship with students' parents."

"Since when?" Garrett snickered. "You're not their teacher, so there's no direct correlation there. Anything outside of school and off the premises is nobody's business."

Mike set down his coffee cup, remembering. He wanted his brothers—both of them—to have what he and Erin had. What Mom and Dad had. Nothing better than this falling-in-love business. When waiting for the right person, life took on new meaning. Suddenly, everything came into focus. Doubts and misgivings fell away as the bigger picture sharpened.

Erin removed her navy-colored beret, leaving her strawberry-blonde bob slightly tousled. Pink cheeks, slow smile, eyes that brightened as she spoke of her newest patient, made him grin. "Anyone ever tell you that you have a heart as huge as Heaven?"

"Thanks. I really love what I do, and if that means occasionally adjusting my schedule to help someone, I'm happy to. In this case, it was a blessing all around. I made new friends."

"See? The way you put a positive spin on things is an art." After life dealt her a cruel blow as a youngster, no one would've faulted Erin if she'd developed a jaded outlook.

Instead, loss had refined her nurturing side and empathetic nature. "The way you love on people through your profession, or simply by way of who God made you, is an inspiration. It's a ministry."

"I appreciate the compliment. That's one of the nicest things anyone's ever said to me..." Her voice fell away as Zook brought Erin a cup of coffee and poured Mike a refill.

The boy was getting to know the regulars and their particular tastes. He did a dandy job at reading customers' cues and body language and displayed a genuine desire to please. Since this was Vale's day off, Zook had to work quickly as the diner bustled with more activity, but he seemed to enjoy the brisk pace.

"G'morning, Miss Erin. Good to see you."

"Good to see you, too, Zook. How's school?"

"Great. I'm finished with my senior credits, and I've picked up another course at the community college in Sapphire. By the time I graduate in May, I'll have a head start on furthering my education."

"Way to go!" Erin congratulated him. "You've worked hard, and it'll pay off."

Everyone knew Zook wanted to study medicine. Had since he was about fourteen, at which time his grandpa suffered a heart attack. If it hadn't been for Zook's quick thinking and administering CPR until the first responders arrived, the fellow would've died.

"Thanks, Miss Erin. I'm really pumped about everything. What can I get for you two this morning?"

They ordered the Sweethearts Desire—the pancake special for two, which included a stack of four monster pancakes, sides of thick, crisp bacon, two eggs over medium, hashbrowns, and orange juice. Oh, and all the coffee "your bladder can hold," as the menu boasted. "I'll have that out to you in a jiff." Zook picked up their menus and bounced away.

"Great kid, that young fella." Mike watched him turn in their order and begin making coffee refill rounds. "A hard worker and a fine soul. He'll go far, that one."

If anyone deserved all the good life had to offer, Zook Mercer certainly fit that bill. The eldest of seven siblings, money had always been tight for the Mercer family. His parents, dairy farmers and hard workers themselves, loved their children immensely, but they'd fallen on difficult times in recent years.

In a day and age where small farms were being gobbled up right and left by commercialization, the Mercers were determined to hold onto their century-old farm, at all costs. Trouble was, it was costing them plenty. Even with friends and neighbors doing their best to buy local, it seemed the good, ol' days of small family farms were fading into the sunset. *What a shame. Lord, please cut that kid a break. Let him reach for the stars and lasso the brightest ones.*

"Something the matter?" Erin followed his gaze. "Is Zook okay?"

"Yeah. I'm just mulling over some things."

"Must be a deep well."

"Kind of. The family's had some struggles. I'm hoping God will open up some big doors so Zook won't have to sweat bullets over college finances."

"Maybe he'll apply for scholarships?"

"Hope so. He's a brilliant kid."

Mike took another swig of coffee, weighing life's quandaries. Specifically, circumstances and struggles.

How the two correlated closely with choices people made and the roads they traveled. Had he inadvertently set Sally Sue on a course for heartache? Even though she'd been the one to call off the wedding and ultimately leave town, could he have handled that season differently?

Yeah. He could've done a lot of things differently, starting with adult decisions he'd made in his youth. Still, after the pregnancy, he'd wanted to do the right thing. Tried to do the right thing. Her leaving the way she did upended him at the time. Though, looking back now, if they'd married, it would've been disastrous. Young love wasn't mature love.

If he were honest, neither of them were equipped for marriage then. Truthfully, he didn't think Sally Sue ever loved him. In her note, she'd said as much. Admittedly, what he had with Erin was far different than what he'd had with his high school crush. His feelings for Erin were unlike anything he'd ever known. His love for her tapped into his deepest reserves, drawing on every emotion, filling the empty cavern that had been his heart.

"...so, it's something I think I'll consider."

Huh? Lost in his reverie, Mike had obviously missed something.

"I'm sorry?"

Erin tipped her head and cast him a quizzical look. "You ventured away for a minute, didn't you?"

"Yes'm. Sorry. Not because of the company, I assure you."

"I understand. You have a lot on your mind."

Did she always have to be so gracious? So empathetic? Yeah. Yeah, she did. Because that's who Erin was and he loved her for it.

"You were saying?" he prompted.

"I said I think my veterinary practice might offer a scholarship this year to the graduating senior with the highest GPA. That, or maybe to the one who demonstrates an exemplary work ethic. Maybe, we'll even offer two scholarships."

"That'd be great. Other businesses in town already offer some scholarships, mine included, and one more would certainly be appreciated. Knowing Zook, he'll probably apply for any and all."

"Good. I'll speak to Vangie about it on Monday. I'll enlist her help with wording, requirements, and other legalese."

"That's super. I'll speak to the Chamber of Commerce and give a heads-up about adding that to our next community e-newsletter."

Zook delivered tall glasses of orange juice, then a while later, followed up with their breakfast special. With a grand flourish, he removed the pancake platters from the circular tray he carried at his side. Then, he reached for additional plates of bacon, eggs, and hashbrowns, and with faultless precision, positioned those next to the pancakes he'd set down.

The boy's agility and eagerness reminded Mike of himself at that age. Except this kid could've out maneuvered him by a mile. Coming from a large family, Zook probably had a lot of experience helping his parents with his younger siblings. A family of nine meant lots of action on the home front, but the kid worked as hard here at the diner as he surely must at home.

"Can I get you anything else, folks?"

"I can't think of a thing," Erin answered. "Thank you,

Zook."

"You bet, Miss Erin. How 'bout for you, Mr. Brewer?"

"You can call me 'Mike', and I'm good. Looks amazing. Thanks."

Zook nodded and bounced away to grab another order.

"Oh, wow. We'll barely make a dent in all this," Erin gasped.

"Hey. Speak for yourself, young lady. I bet I can clean up most of my share."

"That's because you're one of those fortunate souls who has a fast metabolism. Now, if I ate my entire portion? You'd have to cart me out of here on a stretcher."

Mike chuckled as she slathered her pancakes in a river of blueberry syrup. He deliberated over her prediction when, thirty minutes later, they'd both finished every last, lip-smacking bite of breakfast. Instead, he simply stacked their platters and plates and scooted them to the end of the table, at which time he exhaled a slow, satisfied sigh, and gave her a wink.

"What do you think? Should I call 9-1-1?"

Erin's eyes danced with laughter. "I think I might be able to hoist myself up. Though, I probably won't eat the rest of the day."

"Well, isn't this just the coziest?"

Blast it. Where in blazes had *she* come from?

The smirk on Sally Sue's face raised goosebumps on Erin's flesh. For almost two weeks, she'd managed to avoid the woman, and now here she was—in her bling-studded jacket, blue jeans, and boots—long, blonde mane pouring over her shoulders like new spun silk and arrogant attitude completely intact.

Without so much as batting an eyelash, Sally Sue plopped down beside Mike, forcing him to quickly scoot over lest she land in his lap.

"If you'll excuse us, we were about to leave." Mike motioned to Zook for the check, but Sally Sue didn't budge. "Pardon me, please."

Most people would've taken the cue, but then again, most people wouldn't have insinuated themselves in the middle of a couple's meal, disrupting it with an obvious play for attention. Bless his heart. Mike tried to maintain his composure, when clearly, this woman was doing her best to rattle him.

Erin didn't have to glance around the diner to know that countless eyes and ears observed the drama unfolding. *Good grief.* Didn't Sally Sue have one shred of pride? Why was she doing this?

"No, I don't think I will. Pardon you, that is." She locked eyes with Erin, sending a chill down Erin's spine. "You best run along, sweetie. Mike and I have some things to discuss."

Erin didn't know a ton about mental illness, but what she did know, began to click. This woman's lack of regard. Her histrionics and perception of reality. Her tone. Her posture. Her odd mannerisms. All possible signs of instability. Then again, perhaps by-products of loss and overwhelming grief. Certainly, Erin did know something about that.

For years, after the loss of her parents, she struggled with intense feelings of helplessness, and at times, anger. Counseling helped her make sense of her reordered world. Slowly, she moved past survivor's guilt and learned appropriate coping skills in dealing with her palette of emotions.

With sudden loss, grief was even more severe. The grieving process, twice as devastating. If Erin and her aunt hadn't had therapy, who knew what would have become of them? Instantly, understanding coursed through Erin.

Empathy softened her reply. "Sally Sue, what is it? How can we help you?"

For a moment Sally Sue's eyes flashed with surprise. Then, her spine stiffened, her gaze narrowed, and her red lips lifted in a weird smile.

"How can *you* help *me*?" The other woman choked out a laugh. "Oh, darling. Do you know who I am?"

Mike shifted in the seat, as if the subtle movement would encourage her to move, but if anything, her body became one with the booth. Like a block of cement, she remained next to him, bonded to the spot. He cast Erin an apologetic grimace, and tried a different tack.

"Erin's right. If there's something we can do for you, we'd like to try. Is there someone we could call?"

Sally Sue planted her palms on the tabletop and slowly turned her head sideways, facing him. "Don't condescend to me. I'm not inept or crazy. Look, I didn't want to do this in front of her, but whatever."

Poor Zook chose that moment to spring to their table and hand off the ticket to Mike. Upon clapping eyes on Sally Sue, the teenager's face turned three shades pinker than a newborn piglet. He could hardly get the words out fast enough.

"Oh, hi! Are you joining Miss Erin and Mike? Should I bring water? Juice? Coffee? A menu?"

Sally Sue turned and tossed the boy an eyeroll.

"Wouldn't you say if I'm sitting here that, obviously, I'm joining them? No, I don't want water, juice, coffee, a menu, or an elephant in a pinstripe suit. What I want is not to be bothered. Okay?"

Zook's grin slipped. The pink in his cheeks turned crimson. "Uh...sure. Sorry."

Mike gripped the table with his hands and attempted to stand, which was virtually impossible still positioned in the booth as he was. "Stop it, Sally Sue. There's no need to—"

"It's okay." The boy backed away, his shoulders visibly sagging. "Have a great day, folks." He bounded toward the drink station, disappearing behind the soda fountain, leaving onlookers open-mouthed and incensed.

Erin's empathy morphed into irritation. More than irritation. Sally Sue's treatment of the teenager made her see stars. Not in a good way. There'd been no cause to chew Zook out for being friendly and doing his job. Grief-stricken or not, her behavior needed addressed. But before Erin could get the words out, Mike took matters in hand.

"Sally Sue, I don't know what your motivation is in remaining here, or who you think you are to run roughshod over an eighteen-year-old kid who works his butt off, but you should know attitudes like yours wear thin on a body. Money and stature mean nothing when you're tactless, friendless, and cruel. And I gotta tell ya— I'd hoped you'd grown beyond this. I'd hoped that light and love would've found you, and I'd hoped that you'd latched onto some beauty in this life. I'm real sorry for the loss of your husband. I'm sorrier still that you've lost yourself." Mike gave a final scoot—not rough, but decisive—leaving Sally Sue no choice but to rise.

He plunked down several bills for their meal, including a generous tip for Zook, and tipped his head toward Erin. "Ready?"

"You bet." She couldn't have been more ready unless she'd been sprung from Aunt Bea's old Jack-in-the-box childhood toy.

As they stepped out into the bright November sunshine, Sally Sue stormed past them, casting a final glance their way. Half-way to her car, she stopped and pivoted.

"You may think you have him now." She nailed Erin with a hard stare. "But give it some time. Has Mike told you about all the fun we used to have? Think about it. Do you really want my leftovers?"

Chapter Twenty-Two

Lord. Lord. Lord. Sally Sue had been a lot of things. Spoiled. Bossy. Self-absorbed. But Mike had never known her to be so cruel or crude. Time and twelve years had transformed her into someone he barely recognized.

"I'm sorry," Mike told Erin as they walked along the leaf-strewn path near Jaden Pond—a quiet, picturesque escape north of town and also a secluded respite, ideal for reflective moments and deep thinking. "I honestly don't know what to do. I don't know what Sally Sue's intentions are or why, in heaven's name, she's still here. You'd think she'd have to return home at some point to weigh in on business matters at Ribeck."

Erin's footsteps slowed. "In today's world, a lot of business can be handled online. With many professions, it isn't even necessary to show up at the office every day. People work from everywhere—they do it all the time."

"I guess. But with someone of her prominence, I can't believe she'd hole herself up in Edna Powell's garage apartment, far removed from her life of ease and convenience. Clinton gave his answer. Why doesn't she move on?"

"You said why."

"Because of me? That's so absurd. Sally Sue has to know that. There must be something else. Something more."

"Seems there's only one way to find out." Erin ceased walking. The afternoon grew cool, as the sun slipped behind iron-gray clouds. "Why don't you ask her?"

"Are you serious? Town's already having a heyday with her return. How do you think it would look if I were to visit her at Edna's? Besides, I don't want to give the woman the wrong impression. I think she's troubled."

"Do you think by avoiding her and hoping she disappears, that will make this go away?"

As much as Mike hated to admit it, Erin was right. Still, the idea didn't set well with him. Meeting Sally Sue in private could very well be a recipe for disaster. Who knew what the woman might say or do? Yet, unless he heard her out, she could hang around Ruby indefinitely.

"No, I don't think she'll go away. but I do think I should use prudence in seeing her."

"I agree." Erin drew in a deep breath and released it. "Obviously, she doesn't like me and wouldn't want me along. What about meeting her in a public place—Cusick Park or someplace there's bound to be other people?"

"Good idea."

He mulled it over. How would he contact her? She probably had a private cell number. He could leave word with Edna, though, in that case, he might as well shout it in a megaphone, because the dear soul had a definite penchant for gab. That meant only one recourse. Mike would have to drop by Sally Sue's apartment anyway, which her landlord's sharp, old eyes would surely not miss.

He guessed he'd have to rely on his sturdy reputation and hope that folks gave him the benefit of the doubt. Maybe, he needn't worry at all. Sally Sue may have overstepped today, but at least she'd refrained from causing an all-out scene. What mayhem could she cause in private?

Plenty. That's what worried him. But the sooner he got this out of the way, the better.

When Mike kissed Erin inside her doorway later that afternoon, his lips sought hers without preamble. Tender, yet with barely restrained urgency, his mouth moved over hers with a sweet familiarity. She gave herself fully to the kiss, reveling in this sweet love of theirs, recognizing the storm that brewed on the horizon, yet wishing it wasn't so.

"When will you try to see her?" She practically whispered it, because if she said it too loud, it would breathe reality into existence. She trusted Mike, but she couldn't help wonder...

"Tomorrow after church. I think it best if I let the dust settle a bit. Don't want to wait too long because I need to confront this." He stepped back and trailed Erin's cheek with his fingertips. "I'm committed to you. Only you."

That he felt the need to say it reinforced a thought she hadn't wanted to consider. Who was he trying to convince? Himself or her?

"Son, I know I don't need to tell you this...but be careful." Dad walked with him out to his truck.

Over Sunday dinner, his family had voiced their concerns over Sally Sue's erratic behavior, but eventually, that talk died down as they moved on to sunnier topics— like his mother's Mississippi pot roast and taters and Gabe's interest in Vale Masters. They'd also congratulated Garrett on Sticks and Stones' new milestone—landing a big furniture contract for a new office building in Sapphire. Mel and Matt commented on the rousing success of The Meadows' fall carnival and noted that the proceeds far outnumbered last year's, affording a generous boost to the retirement community's art fund.

Eventually, chatter gravitated toward Erin and her aunt coming for Thanksgiving, and that topic fueled further speculation. Specifically, whether there might be a wedding on the radar sometime next year.

"You'll know when I know." Mike sidestepped the subject with the skill of a handyman in a roomful of chainsaws.

At the time, Mom pinned her gaze on the apple pie she'd been cutting, though she didn't miss a beat as she remarked, "Erin looked lovely at church this morning. We wish she would've joined us for Sunday dinner today."

"I think she planned a little R & R for this afternoon, Mom." At least that's what she'd told him. Except Erin's polite decline to dinner at his parents' house seemed out of character since they'd established somewhat of a routine and had been spending so much time together.

Mike faced his Dad now, noting his father's drawn brows and heavy gaze. "Don't worry, Dad. I'm not about to place myself in a compromising situation with Sally Sue. I'm simply going to speak to the woman calmly and rationally. Find out what she's up to. What it is she's really after. I don't buy for one bloomin' minute that it's me."

"The thing is we don't really know her anymore. She's changed. Grown harder, and she may be disturbed. Be on guard, son. Okay?"

"I will, Dad. If I get the slightest inkling our meeting is about to go south, I'll hit the road. I'm not one to willingly put my head on the chopping block."

"Don't let your mother hear you use that analogy.

Might make her a tad squeamish."

He gave his dad's shoulder a squeeze. "I won't."

However, as Mike drove the few miles out to the Powell residence, he began to wonder if this had been a wise move, after all. Why hadn't he simply phoned Edna and left a message with her? So what if she'd dropped the tasty crumb at her ladies sewing circle, who in turn shared the bounty with all their kith and kin? Folks might salivate for a while, but in the end, the nattering would die down, and they'd come to realize the embellished morsel was just that. A mere snack of no real substance.

It'd been a while since he'd driven out to the retired school marm's abode—an architectural masterpiece, complete with twin turrets, tall chimneys, and lots of windows. He and his crew completed a renovation project there a few springs ago.

An historic gem, the brick and stone architecture evoked stirrings of a different era. Reminiscent of a French estate, the Powell home dated back several generations, and in recent years, had undergone subtle metamorphoses to update interior aspects, as well as replace archaic systems such as wiring, plumbing, and heating and air, while preserving the home's original character. The transformation also included the added apartment over the detached garage, separated from the main house by a generous breezeway. After her niece Megan moved out, Edna occasionally rented out the space to boarders, as she liked the extra company.

As Mike steered his pickup into the space behind Sally Sue's Bimmer, his breath stalled. What in thunder was he doing here? A fine time now to think about that. Not that he hadn't before. Just that now, his decision in coming to talk sense into his former fiancée seemed more asinine than it had earlier. What if she claimed he tried something disreputable and spread tales about town? That'd be bad enough. But what if the woman did something totally outlandish like call the cops or whip out a weapon?

He forced the *what ifs* away and parked, switching off the engine. No sooner than he set his boots on the paved drive did Edna come bustling out the kitchen door, her silver-tipped, pitch-black coif and minimally wizened features belying her seventy-three years.

"Well, now. What an utter delight to see you, Michael. To what do I owe the pleasure?" Edna wore a navy-blue sweat set, accented by vertical, white stripes down the length of both pant legs. A widow of ten years, it seemed in recent weeks, she'd suddenly developed a new lease on life. She strolled down the length of the breezeway and held out her palm, welcoming him. "Have you come to share the recent Chamber minutes?"

"No, ma'am." Perhaps, as a generous benefactor to various causes about town, Edna considered it the Chamber of Commerce's duty to apprise her of community affairs. "Not much to report in way of news. Minutes are always accessible online though."

Edna gave a clipped nod. "I see. How's the family then?"

"Good. Good. Mom and Dad and the gang send their best." Not exactly a mistruth. They knew he'd offer their greetings. "I...uh...actually..."

"You're not here to see me at all, are you, Michael?"

Well, he couldn't fib when asked so pointedly. "No, ma'am, I'm not. I'm wondering if Sally Sue's available?"

"Hmm. Not real sure about that. As you see, her vehicle's here, but I'm not certain she's receiving visitors. You're welcome to go on up and check."

Edna flicked her gaze to the wide, wooden staircase that led to the apartment addition over the garage—the addition he and his crew had completed back in April 2020.

The older woman retracted her palm, crossed her arms, and smiled. Whether in sympathy or with genuine kindness, or maybe some of both, Mike didn't know. Edna and her late husband Bob had been wedding guests on that fateful day so long ago—the day Sally Sue ran off and decided he and this "one horse town" no longer fit the bill on her long list of wants. Embarrassingly, Mike had been the one to return the Powells's unopened wedding gift—a set of gorgeous crystal goblets—according to hearsay.

"Never you worry, dear boy," Edna had soothed. "I can take the gift back. No need to feel badly. That child will come to her senses one day and realize what a keeper of a man she gave up."

Bless Edna's heart. That never happened, but even if Sally Sue had realized it, Mike would never again saddle up for that rodeo. Which brought to mind poor Sheldon Ribeck. He must've been a saint of a man to contend with his wife's chaotic moods.

"Thank you, Miss Edna. I believe I will pay Sally Sue a visit. Excuse me, please."

"Certainly."

Thinking she'd swivel back around and go about her day, Mike headed up the staircase, attempting to quell a thousand reservations. Yet, half-way up, Edna called, "How's the Shaye girl these days?"

"Fine," Mike answered. Now, what was the purpose of that? Had she felt the need to remind him of proprieties?

"Wonderful. I'm happy to hear that." Edna clamped her mouth closed, and that time, she did retrace her steps.

However, she didn't fool him for one Missouri minute. Inside the kitchen, beyond the pale-yellow curtains, she watched. Waiting, possibly, for something she could really sink her teeth into. He couldn't blame her. Who wouldn't want to spy on what might happen? For years, his and Sally Sue's history naturally generated a lot of story fodder. Since she'd returned, the past reignited itself like a bonfire ablaze.

Mike climbed the final steps, inhaled sharply, and lifted the heavy brass door knocker—the repurposed antique treasure he'd secured at an estate sale when they were finishing Edna's renovations. Shaped as a hand holding a doorknob, he gave three firm thwacks to the door.

Within seconds, the door opened slowly, and there stood Sally Sue, with no make-up, wearing blue jeans and a simple tee shirt, long hair slightly mussed, and eyes swollen and red. She'd been crying?

She sniffed and wiped her nose with a tissue. "Oh. Mike?"

"I'm sorry. I would've called first, but obviously, I no longer have your correct cell number."

"Wha... What do you want?"

He knew their voices carried down below, well within Edna's hearing range. "I thought we might talk."

"About what?"

This wouldn't be easy. Why should he be surprised? After their last encounter, Mike expected as much. He regrouped and ran the words through his mind before saying them aloud.

"I'd hoped we could sort through a few things. Resolve issues. Could we try to do that, Sally Sue? Please?"

"You're kidding, right?"

"Not at all."

"What things? What issues?" She pressed.

"Our history. What bearing it has regarding present decisions." Mike attempted to project a calmness he didn't feel. Keeping his tone even, he restated the obvious. "Surely, you'd agree there are matters we need to discuss."

"Like why am I still here? What it'll take to make me go away?"

"No. I wanted to—"

"Uh-uh. Bye, Mike." She started to close the door and retreat inside.

He couldn't leave it like this. It would always be a storm brewing on the horizon unless he attempted a stab at understanding and closure. "Wait. Ten or fifteen minutes. Can't you spare that?"

Sally Sue halted in her tracks, her eyes narrowing. "All right. Ten minutes. I just made a pot of tea. Want some?"

Though wary and unsmiling, her countenance somewhat softened. Without cosmetics and her fancy duds, she looked more like a beaten down waif versus the strong, confident hotshot who had the world by its coattail. Mike weighed the invitation as Sally Sue fidgeted with the tissue and stepped aside from the door frame.

This wasn't a social call. Nevertheless, in the deep recesses of his brain, a note of empathy registered. How to play it smart without being a total jerk?

"Tea sounds good." He rarely drank hot tea, but no sense in telling her that. "How 'bout we have it on your deck here?" A nice spot with the right amount of sun and within full view of Edna's kitchen window. At no time would Mike enter the apartment alone. *Perfect.*

"Okay." Sally Sue nodded, as if understanding his intent. "I'll be right back."

She left the door ajar, and when she returned, she carried a wooden tray with a rose petaled teapot, matching teacups, saucers, spoons, and a sugar bowl. In the midst of those were tea biscuits arranged on pink, heart-shaped doilies, butter and jam, and linen napkins. *Oh, Lord.* Even this seemed too...too intimate for the pointed conversation he'd planned.

He had no choice but to rise from the bistro set and help her maneuver through the door, close it, and situate the tray on the small table. This surprise visit grew stickier as Sally Sue quietly poured their tea and asked, "Sugar?"

"One teaspoon, please."

"Biscuits? I made them this morning."

Since when did Sally Sue bake? Then again, he remembered the Sally Sue he'd known in high school.

"Maybe one, thanks. I'm pretty full from Sunday dinner."

"Oh. Your mother still does that?"

"She does. The entire crew comes, like always, plus one extra now—Matt, Mel's husband."

"What about Erin Shaye? Does she join you?"

"Sally Sue," Mike cleared his throat. Stirred the sugar around in his tea. "I dropped by today to clear the air between us, not to slice open old wounds or create new ones."

"Right." Sally Sue seated herself on the tiny chair across from Mike. "Contrary to what you may think, I'm not some wounded soul who needs patronizing. I came to Ruby to conduct business. I also considered some other possibilities, true. Stupid, I know. See...I had to make sure."

"Make sure of what?"

"That there was absolutely nothing here left for me. I've been completely unmoored since Shel died. Gravitated toward all sorts of ideas and flights of fancy. I realize I've acted insane. Spoken harshly, even for me."

Holy cow. Sally Sue unmasked? All right. Now they were getting somewhere. Mike took a sip of tea, buying time, sensing she wanted to say more.

Her voice broke as she spoke again. "I...loved...him. I loved Shel with all my heart and soul. And he loved me. It didn't matter to him that I was a simple country bumpkin from Nowheresville. He saw attributes in me that I didn't see in myself for a very long time. He saw goodness and kindness and a heart to serve others before I recognized those myself." She stared off into the distance somewhere, as if lost in thought.

"I told him about you, of course. About us. The baby. None of it mattered. He loved me, despite my faults and insecurities. He wanted to give me the sun and the moon and the stars. All of it. He just ran out of time."

Goodness and kindness? A heart to serve others? *Insane.* Mike almost spit out his tea. Obviously, Sally Sue's husband knew a side of his wife that no one else did. As perplexing as he found that, all the knowns and unknowns didn't negate what he needed to do.

"I'm sorry for your loss. I really am." Mike rested his

palms on his knees, contemplating his next words. An apology long overdue. It was something he'd always wanted to say. He never thought he'd have the chance, but funny how God orchestrated time and events beyond the ordinary. "I'm also sorry for taking our relationship to the next level when we were dating. I was wrong. I shouldn't have crossed that boundary. Please forgive me."

Sally Sue's gaze whipped around, unshed tears glistening. "I share in that responsibility, but thank you. Knowing you, I believe you really mean that."

"I do."

Her spine slumped against the back of her chair. "Since we're knee-deep in sorries here, I'm sorry, too. I'm sorry for running out on you on our wedding day, for hurting you the way I did. For the horrible way I broke it to you—in that childish, insensitive letter—which, by the way, that last paragraph? It was awful of me to say what I did. That you lacked ambition, that you'd never amount to anything. I cringe when I think of it. I'm especially sorry for popping back into your life and being horrid all over again to you and others. I'm not the Sally Sue Messmer you used to know. Hard to believe by the way I've acted since I've been here, but I thought I had something to prove. I only ended up humiliating myself and causing people to hate me."

"Sorrow makes people act and react in unintentional ways."

"Understanding and sensitive, as always. Thank you for that."

Somewhere in the distance, a crow cawed, the sound echoing through the nearby woods, reflecting the somber mood. Mike wanted to ask so many things, except he sensed Sally Sue had yet to finish.

"Shel loved me, his family, and his business. Most of all, he loved God. He lived to serve. Ironic that he died so young. He was thirty-six, a few years older than me, but who dies at that age? No one expected it. At the time, he was at a medical convention. He'd just given a rousing discourse about Ribeck Industries' latest and greatest new thing—revolutionary components that would enhance new devices on the horizon." Sally Sue took a deep breath, and exhaled, followed by a sip of tea.

"Afterward, he and his brother Sid returned to their hotel room, where Shel collapsed. I never knew Shel had a faulty aortic valve. No one did, I guess. We'd spoken earlier in the day and he seemed fine. Excited about the convention. He told me he loved me."

Mike's throat tightened. How utterly awful for any wife to lose her husband in that way. In the prime of life, too. *Why, God?* He wished he knew the innerworkings of his Heavenly Father's mind. One day, though—one amazing, breathtaking day—like Paul the Apostle assured in the book of First Corinthians—we'd understand many things.

"For now we see through a glass darkly; but then face to face; now I know in part; but then shall I know even as also I am known." That passage in the twelfth chapter had comforted him during the bleak days of his and Sally Sue's break-up and many days after.

"It sounds like Sheldon was a tremendous man."

"The best. We met at a children's benefit, at the hospital where I worked at the time. We talked of starting a family soon." No longer able to stop them, tears leaked from Sally Sue's eyes.

What could he say to reassure her? False platitudes wouldn't help. Something Dad once told him came to mind. How odd that he should be impressed to say it now. "God knows the desires of our hearts. One day, I think you'll love again. And one day, when the timing's right, I think He'll fulfill your desire for a family."

Sally Sue pressed a palm to her heart, her eyes widening. "That's exactly what someone else said."

"Maybe you should listen."

The creases between her brows relaxed. She straightened in her chair and leaned forward, resting her chin on steepled fingers. "Yes. Maybe I should."

Chapter Twenty-Three

That evening, as Erin curled on the sofa and watched the sun turn the sky orange, purple, and pink, Miranda snuggled close, her warm, furry body vibrating with pure joy. If only she could be so content. So certain of what tomorrow would bring. But ever since Sally Sue Messmer Ribeck came to town, contentedness remained elusive. The woman had poked a pin in Erin's shiny balloon—the life in Ruby she'd come to love.

After losing her parents, it'd taken a long while to emotionally invest in a seemingly sure thing. Then Phillip came along. Perfect in every way, except when he wasn't. Afterward, she'd thrown herself into her education and work until that led her here, to Ruby, another seemingly sure thing. The town dotted all her i's and crossed all her t's...and then she'd met Mike. Fallen in love. Given herself completely to the notion of it. *Again.* And again, a blip on the radar appeared. A pretty big blip, no less.

He could deny it all he wanted, but Mike's first love shook him in ways that, perhaps, he didn't realize or want to admit. Erin had seen it in his eyes. That dazed look that crept into his face at the mere mention of her name. *He isn't over her. Even after all these years.* The thought crossed her mind more frequently now because it seemed she was all they ever talked about. Sally Sue returning to Ruby had resurrected a host of feelings and unresolved issues. It was no longer Erin and Mike. There were three of them in this relationship. The knowledge of it almost choked her.

He'd gone to see her. She'd known he'd planned to meet with her because they'd discussed it. Though, when she'd decided on a whim to take a Sunday drive, what Erin hadn't counted on was seeing Mike's vehicle parked in the breezeway at Edna Powell's home...and he and Sally Sue nestled pretty as one pleased, immersed in deep conversation, at the little table on her apartment deck. What happened to the idea of meeting in a public place?

The picture of the two of them together, a mere thirty-second snapshot, imbedded itself in Erin's brain the rest of the afternoon. Not normally given to jealously, initially, she assumed there must be a rational explanation. However, as the day wore on, she continued to replay the image in her head. Like a movie reel, over and over, the picture scrolled past until she assessed every detail of what she remembered. Together, the two of them, Sally Sue's blonde mane waving in the fall breeze, leaning in toward Mike, their body language open and receptive.

So in tune to each other, Erin doubted they saw her drive past. She'd driven the speed limit, which only afforded her an abbreviated view, but unless they'd been watching the passing vehicles, hers was just another distant whoosh on the winding stretch of highway.

Granted, Erin still didn't know the full story. She chided herself for jumping to pre-drawn conclusions. Until she heard from Mike, it wasn't fair of her to sit in judgment or imagine worst case scenarios. The problem? He had yet to call or text.

Six a.m. Man, when did morning come so early? Mike flung an arm over his eyes, despite the room's darkness. As if on cue, Blackie bound back onto the bed and licked his jaw in greeting.

"Hi ya, boy. Listen, you probably still have kibble in your bowl and I already unlatched the security panel on your doggy door. How 'bout giving Dad another fifteen minutes of shut-eye?"

Woof! Woof! The canine wasn't having it. The slobbery kisses grew more intense as he forced his master to lift his arm and fully recognize him.

"All right, buddy. I get the hint." Mike patted Blackie's head and tossed off the covers, the morning coolness nipping his bare legs. "Gotta get started anyway, I guess." He wished Mondays were a mite more forgiving. He also wished he'd called Erin last night. It'd been stupid of him not to. He didn't have anything to hide.

The visit with Sally Sue lasted only an hour. Maybe an hour-and-a-half, tops. Long enough for revelations and apologies, short enough to be appropriate. Truthfully, the last few minutes, right before he bid her good-bye and well-wishes, had been weird. Telling in a way, yet not completely clear.

He'd seen familiar aspects of Sally Sue—the girl he'd fallen in love with way back when. He thought they reached an understanding. Gained clarity and perspective. Broken new ground. He'd thanked God for it. But when he'd commented on the possibility of a new beginning, a future with someone else, she'd as much as admitted the thought had already crossed her mind. In fact, apparently, someone else had suggested it, too. *Good gravy.* Surely, they weren't going to ride that merry-go-round again.

He'd dropped the subject and that's when he'd stood to leave. Sally Sue rose to her feet as well. Then she leaned in to hug him. *Holy cats.* He hadn't anticipated that.

"Thank you for coming even though I doubted your intentions at first. Your perspective's been helpful."

Mike had disengaged himself from her embrace and stepped back. Caught off guard, he'd bumped the table, where cups and saucers clattered. Blessedly, he hadn't broken anything. "What are your plans? Will you return home?"

He'd meant to couch it with a bit more diplomacy but the hug, quick and light as it was, unraveled years and years of memories. The physical contact with Sally Sue dredged up stuff he'd long since filed away. Stuff he'd worked through...or thought he had.

"It would make your life easier if I went home, wouldn't it?" She plucked at the stack of heart-shaped doilies that remained on the tray as hints of pink bloomed in her cheeks. "I'm sure it would for Erin."

"I'm asking because I care what happens to you, not because I want to make life easier for myself."

"Though it would make things less complicated if I were to head home, wouldn't it? It's okay to admit it. I shouldn't have come here. I'm sure you're not the only one who thinks so. Plus, making an offer on the Farley property was a mistake to begin with."

Mike hadn't known what to say. Yeah, it would uncomplicate matters if Sally Sue would pack her bags and hightail it out of Ruby. Yeah, her offer on Clinton's land had muddied the water on what could have been a great thing. And yeah, she should well understand how her behavior would affect everyone in this town—the town that had been nothing but loving and kind to her since the day she was born.

His silence must've revealed volumes. Sally Sue swallowed hard. "In answer to your questions, I plan to leave within a week or so. Edna's been a complete dear to me and she said I could stay however long I wanted, but I know I have responsibilities elsewhere."

He hadn't tried to probe. He reminded himself that grief had driven her to extraordinary lengths. Made her do and say stupid and cruel things, which he could certainly identify with.

Mike gave a quick nod, and turned to go. Even so, as he plodded down the stairs, he prayed. *Lord, please heal the vacant spaces in Sally Sue's heart. Please place someone special in this woman's midst as she seeks new footing. She needs your touch, Father. Amen.*

That he could pray for the very one who'd once upended his world taught him something. He'd reached a new spiritual milestone. Who would've thought it? Not him, that's for sure. Another page flipped in this very long chapter that was his life.

He'd been about to haul himself into his truck when Sally Sue called to him. "Maybe we'll see each other again? Before I leave town, I mean."

"Maybe. But in case we don't, I'm rooting for you, Sally Sue. I hope nothing but the best for you."

"Thanks. Backatcha."

Now, as Mike went about his usual morning routine, he tried not to let his mind wander. He washed his face, tugged on jeans, shirt, and socks, and padded downstairs with his trusty companion by his side. As he dished up Blackie's breakfast, his resolve to not revisit the past crumbled. Pangs of regret nicked his determination and intermingled with bittersweet moments of first love—those

246 | HIS HEART RENEWED

innocent days of youth, ripe with dreams and passion.

He'd come to realize, of late, when one loved deeply—particularly in the case of first love—some memories would always linger. That was normal. Human beings' minds were miraculous, created by a miraculous God. It was what one did with those memories that either caused one to wither or bloom. What we nurtured, prospered.

His marriage to Sally Sue hadn't been God's plan. He'd told himself that over and over again. He'd accepted it. Yet, he'd questioned the Lord at every turn. Dressed it up in theological meanderings to assuage his conscience. Over the years, he'd physically moved forward, but hadn't mentally moved on. *Until Erin.* Then, just as they'd hit their groove, just when he'd believed himself to be free of the past's stronghold, his first love burst back into his life full throttle, accompanied by her own vices. Why in the world would God orchestrate such a thing? *I'm over her, Lord. Truly. Why would you do that?*

Because you needed to forgive one another. Mike stopped in his tracks. Glanced around. Where had that come from? It hadn't been an actual voice, but more of a thought that floated on his subconscience. Could it be true? Could Sally Sue's stint in Ruby have been the remedy to renew his heart and mend his mindset? By the same token, could he have somehow ministered to her? *Not likely, bud. You gave back what she dished out. Not one kind word, initially.* Yesterday, something changed. His heart softened—again—toward the girl he'd once loved. Not in a romantic way, but instead, with compassion.

See? My ways are higher than your ways.

Mike's skin became gooseflesh as a rush of adrenaline seized him. How on earth would he explain all this to Erin? He needed to chew on it.

Erin stood at the sink rinsing her coffee mug. Other than at church yesterday morning, she hadn't seen or heard from Mike. Now, well after seven, dusk had settled over this Ozark town, and Monday would soon be a fleeting memory.

The kitchen window didn't afford the same breathtaking panorama as Erin's living room, but it did offer a snowglobe version of the community many called *heaven*. Remniscent of another era, softly lit homes and storefronts glowed against the backdrop of moon-dappled night, coaxing a sigh from those fotunate enough to observe from higher elevations. Of course, a bird's-eye view from the mountains—say, from Mike's cabin—offered its own spectacular view.

Why doesn't he phone? For the umpteenth time, she weighed the implications of his silence, drawing the only conclusion that made sense. There were unresolved issues between him and Sally Sue. She'd known it for a while now, nevertheless, knowing didn't ease the waves of sadness that washed over her.

Last night, when she heard nothing but crickets, Erin wondered if she was being overly melodramatic and suspicious. Now, more than twenty-four hours later, and still no word from Mike, his lack of communication confirmed what else she suspected. In his mind, saying nothing would buy time. It would allow him space until he could think things through. Good for him.

Thankfully, she'd held the tiniest piece of her heart in reserve after they'd started getting serious. Making a clean break after any failed relationship was easier when one retained a little part of themselves.

Erin set the mug in the sink, her eyelids growing hot against the onslaught of tears. *Liar. You didn't hold back one sliver of your heart and you know it.* From the moment of Mike's all but bungled apology after he'd delievered wood to right now in the present, all her pent-up feelings for the man sloshed to the floodgates with ridiculous vigor.

She'd fallen in love with him over the course of a year, and when he'd finally admitted he shared her sentiments, all bets were off. She'd let down her guard. Albeit, slowly—but still, she had—and really, how ridiculous. Who falls for someone when there's no measureable interest on their part? Except that was the thing. Nails to magnets. That's how it had been for them. They'd been drawn together at the outset. If Mike hadn't spent so long running from it, his judgment might not be so clouded now.

Erin switched on the fairy lights over her kitchen cabinets, bathing the room in soft, shimmering warmth. There was something about twinkling lights that boosted one's spirit. She'd added them throughout her cottage, scattering them here and there, wherever she wanted to create extra ambiance and sparkle. That meant the kitchen, living room, and even her bedroom, woven strategically around the posts of her four poster bed. A little light went a long way in adding dollops of joy in one's life.

Padding to the living room, Miranda tagged along after her, eager to have a comfy lap to curl up in. "Come on, princess. Guess it's you and me tonight."

The feline gave a happy *meow*, as if she totally understood her, and barely let Erin situate herself on the sofa befofe jumping in her lap.

What to watch on television? Let's see. Christmas movies had started airing. Common this time of year, since Thanksgiving was only a week and a half away. Erin loved Christmas and usually loved the seasonal programming, including the many classics that went with the holiday, but tonight she didn't care one festive whit about the hoopla. She could choose a romance, another favorite genre. Nope. Wasn't feeling that either. How about a series? She searched the cable and then scrolled through the choices on her premium service. That, too, was a bust. Maybe she didn't want to watch anything at all. Though, silence didn't particularly appeal.

In a few days, Aunt Bea would arrive and they'd have fun catching up, baking, and visiting. Her aunt would be the perfect balm to her wilted disposition. Aunt Bea could brighten a mausoleum with her infectious laughter and positive outlook. Okay, maybe a bad analogy. The comparison fell flat even to Erin.

In the end, she grabbed a cozy throw and stretched her legs on the sofa, which Miranda maneuvered herself on, as well, immediately assuming her familiar position, completely euphoric with the state of matters.

"Looks like we'll visit Bedford Falls tonight, Miranda. Sound good?"

Miranda yawned.

"What? This is a full blown, four alarm, American classic. Show some appreciation, please."

Good grief. Erin really needed to get a life. She loved her cat. Miranda loved her. The problem? Cats weren't necessarily the best communicators. Granted, Miranda was an exception in that department, but still, Erin could really use some relationship feedback. Never having a boyfriend, she doubted Miranda would be particularly helpful in that area. Never mind the fact, the cat hadn't learned to talk yet. At least in human form.

"Being single does have its merits though. You live by your own rules and your own clock. No waiting for the phone to ring, huh?"

Girl, you're in sad shape. Talking outloud to her cat as if her fur baby totally understood. She gave a sad laugh and lolled her head back against one of the plump throw pillows, watching the opening credits roll. She loved good ol' Jimmy Stewart, but Clarence, the lovable eccentric, was her favorite. Everyone needed an angel like him in their lives.

As if on cue, suddenly, a very distinct ringtone began playing and Erin almost jumped. Not an angel. *Mike.* He'd finally decided to call? She gazed at her cell phone screen for a few seconds before letting it go to voicemail.

Chapter Twenty-Four

Eleven p.m. Since 7:27, the time he'd left the voice mail at Erin's number, Mike had stared at his cell, as if doing so would make her return his call any faster. Even a text would have been welcomed. Something to let him know she'd received his message and that, yes, she was available to talk tomorrow evening. So far, nothing.

Why was he surprised? He'd started this. He'd been the one to press mute after his meeting with Sally Sue yesterday. He should have called Erin afterward. He'd known it then, but he'd been too emotionally fatigued following the conversation with his former flame to utter another word. He'd needed to rest his brain for a while before dissecting the encounter with another soul.

Mike snapped off the bedside lamp, placing his cell on the nightstand, and slumped back against the pillows. He hadn't spoken to Erin two nights in a row. Forever, it seemed. They'd gone from seeing each other practically every day for weeks to this. Then again, maybe he'd magnified the issue in his mind. Maybe Erin simply got busy and forgot to text back?

Nope. He'd promised to let her know how the meeting went with Sally Sue and he'd blown it. Besides that, he'd agreed that he should meet Sally Sue in a public place, and he'd blown that, too. Even though nothing inappropriate had occurred, guilt squeezed his brain. It lay there between slumber and wakefulness, daring him to debate it.

All right. Nothing to do about all of it now. Unless he

heard something from Erin, he'd pay her a visit where he knew she couldn't ignore him. After all, she couldn't very well run out on a clinic full of critters.

"Something different today, my friend. Here." Vangie held out the humongous cardboard box and flipped open the lid. "Pumpkin bread drizzled in a cinnamon cream cheese glaze and all the calories removed, I'm sure."

"*Ooh.* Don't mind if I do." Erin helped herself to a slice, immediately taking a bite and savoring the treat. She noted the Pennies from Heaven stickers on the box and wondered how Charla Packard was these days. Not quite as far along in her pregnancy as Ida Mae Farrow, the Ruby transplant's bakery continued to thrive. "Absolutely delicious."

"I know, right?" Vangie also reached for a slice of the bread. "As you can see, I purchased several slices. Oh, and for lunch? We have some cute, little hors d'oeuvres that look mighty tasty. I set those in the fridge already."

Erin raised an eyebrow. "Tell me."

Her friend giggled. "Okay. Smoked turkey and cream cheese pinwheels...and a darling charcuterie board shaped like a puppy dog!"

"You're joking."

"Nuh-uh. The Pennies from Heaven staff made it especially for us in celebration of the clinic's one year anniversary. It has all kinds of goodies—Vermont white cheddar, Italian salami, prosciutto, Kalamata olives, crackers, dates, nuts. You name it. I'll pull it out of the refrigerator afterwhile and we can sample the goodies between appointments. Blessedly, we have a light schedule today."

"Sounds great. Now, please, go hide this box before I do something crazy like eat the rest of the pumpkin bread to sweeten my mood."

Vangie promptly snapped the box lid shut and shot her a curious stare. "Do you want to talk about it?"

"Not particularly." Erin dusted at the crumbs on her navy blue scrub top. "I'm still trying to decide how I feel about all of it."

"Way to pique my interest. But if that's what you want, you got it."

"Thanks. Sorry I'm being evasive."

"Hey, don't mention it. All of us have a right to a secret or two." Her friend winked and pivoted toward the makeshift lounge. She tossed Erin a backward glance, inclining her head toward the front door. "Oh. Here yours comes now."

Sure enough, as Erin whirled around, Mike stepped through the front door, the corners of his mouth slightly turned upward. "Morning, ladies."

Erin's heart thumped against her chest at the sight of him. Boy, did the guy wear work gear like a boss. Since when did blue jeans and a denim shirt look so striking on a man?

"Good morning, Mike." Vangie twisted around to acknowledge him. "How's the world treating you?"

"Dandy, I s'pose. You?"

"Stupendous. Mitch and I are loving the new addition and all the improvements you and your crew made to our humble abode. We're not even waiting until after Thanksgiving to put the Christmas tree up. Gonna do that this weekend before the ol' turkey bird is set to cook and we have extra family in next week."

"Sounds like a plan. Glad you like the reno and the extra space. Let me know if you guys need anything else."

"Will do. I better slip into work mode now before the boss chides me. She's such a taskmaster." Vangie's eyes twinkled as she waggled her fingers, casting Erin a mischievous stare.

She disappeared into the front office, but left the sliding partition closed, Erin assumed to afford her and Mike privacy. Obviously, Vangie read the cool vibes between them and would probably wait for a few more minutes to open the glass barrier.

"Hi," Erin said finally. "Our first appointment's in thirty minutes."

"Understood. Could we slip into your hive for a bit?"

Erin gave a brief nod, recalling his recent voice mail. *Hey, honey. Since you aren't answering, I can only deduce you're upset with me. I'm sorry I didn't reach out earlier, as promised. It had nothing to do with you. I needed time to work through some things. Could we get together tomorrow evening and talk? Please? Give me a call. I...* His voice had trailed off without completing the rest.

In her office, Mike shut the door behind them. He wasted no time in reaching for Erin's hand. "Did you get my message?"

"Yes." Of course she did.

"I see." A few seconds ticked by. His mouth set in a firm line. "I'm sorry. I should have called. It was out of character for me to go MIA without an explanation."

When Erin didn't offer anything, he asked, "Did you *listen* to my message?"

"I did."

"I see. You're angry with me."

The sensation lodged itself deep in her gut. That he hadn't contacted her immediately after meeting with the ghost from his past might seem like a minor infraction to some, but there were so many angles to this situation, it only added further confusion to this already peculiar dynamic.

"Not angry. Hurt. You not following through on your word disappointed me. A lot."

Mike's shoulders slumped. "I'm so sorry. I messed up. I needed to... I had to..." He inhaled a gulp of air, and exhaled it just as sharply. "I visited Sally Sue."

"Yes. I know." What was she supposed to say?

"You know?"

"I saw your truck at Edna's Sunday."

His forhead furrowed. "You did?"

"Yeah. I did." She loosened her hand from his and paced the short distance to her desk where she began shuffling through file folders. "Sunday was so gorgeous. I decided to take a drive."

She offered no further explanation.

"I didn't intend to meet with Sally Sue at the apartment. I didn't have her cell number anymore. It's a private listing, I guess. Anyway, that left me no choice but to visit her out at Edna's. I didn't even go inside. We spoke on the deck."

"I know that, too."

Mike raked a hand through his hair and laughed without mirth. "Then you know everything was above board."

"What I know is what I saw—the two of you engaged in conversation. That's it. That's all a thirty-second drive-by allowed."

"And you're drawing conclusions based on that?"

"No. Of course not. I'm considering *implications* based on your silence afterward."

"I understand." Regret underscored his words. "I wish I would've responded differently. Again, I'm sorry."

She wasn't intentionally trying to be unfeeling. She realized there were other issues at play. Small ones. Big ones. Whether or not they could navigate the main one remained to be seen. "What happened? Would you mind enlightening me?"

She'd asked a fair question. It was only right that he'd give a fair answer in return.

"It isn't me that Sally Sue wants. Not really. It's as we suspected. The woman is grief-stricken. I think, quite possibly, she's had an emotional breakdown." In the weeks she'd been here, Mike had seen various sides of Sally Sue. Reflections of who she used to be when he'd first fallen in love with her—or thought he had—and a hard, steely side, the person she'd grown into. Then, there was the gentler side—the one he saw Sunday. The wounded spirit of one ravaged by sorrow and loss by way of a traumatic event. Something Erin should identify with.

"I'd be lying if I said my heart didn't go out to her. We share a history. A history that resulted in an unplanned pregnancy, a miscarriage, and an ill-fated trip to the altar. I can't pretend that doesn't exist."

Erin's hands stilled over the files. "I know you can't. I never asked you to pretend anything. All I've ever wanted—expected—is mutual honesty."

"That's what I'm trying to do here."

"I believe you are. Except there are three of us in this

relationship now, and it feels awkward and strained."

How could he explain this without sounding like a babbling idiot?

"Look, Sally Sue and I did something that we needed to do a long time ago. We cleared the air. After all this time and tons of water under the bridge, we apologized to one another." Mike shared some of the details of their exchange, as Erin listened. He couldn't quite read her closed expression, only that she cocked her head and remained attentive. "The thing is—"

Erin's phone buzzed. "My appointment's here. Can we resume this later?"

"Uh...sure. My place? I'll make supper for you."

"Okay."

"Six'o'clock? Is that too early?"

"No. My last patient's at four. See you then."

The kiss he wanted to give her remained a mere wish as Erin strode from her office leaving him standing there. He had no right to be hurt or disappointed. He'd set this ball in motion and he'd fouled out.

Erin's last patient of the day—Wally's owners anyway—rescheduled, allowing her and Vangie to wrap up early.

"One of the perks of running one's own business." Erin commented, slipping on her jacket. "We can set the pace and adjust accordingly."

She didn't lack for business. Since she also kept her overhead low, Erin had started to occasionally vary her hours. Again, a plus of a small practice in an equally small town. She might make more money in the city, but she did quite well for herself in Ruby and there was more to life than money anyway. Not that she attributed that thought to anyone in particular. Though, her mind did wander. Had Sally Sue left town yet? Mike hadn't mentioned that.

"FYI I added Wally to an open slot on Friday. Since we're closing the clinic for Thanksgiving break next week, that day's shaping up to be pretty full, but we'll make it fine. Wally shouldn't take long. Shoot, I could do that sweet collie's pedicure in my sleep. He's such a gentle baby." Vangie powered down her computer and began tidying up her office.

"Are you and Mitch having a crowd for the holiday?"

"His parents, my parents, our siblings and families, and maybe a few friends from church. What about you? Is your aunt still coming?"

"She is and I can't wait. Aunt Bea arrives this weekend."

"I remember meeting her the last time she visited." Vangie poked her arms in her coat sleeves. "She's a hoot. What are your Thanksgiving plans? Will it be only the two of you?"

"We're invited over to Mike's family's." Erin tried to keep her voice light. "Should be fun."

"Should be?"

"*Will* be."

Vangie didn't press. Instead, she gave Erin a quick hug, her face cheery and hopeful. "That's the spirit. The Brewers do the holidays up right, that's for sure. Well, I'm off. See you tomorrow, my friend."

"See you, too. Thanks for the goodies today. Say hello to Mitch and the kiddos."

"You're welcome, and will do. My best to Mike again."

How had she known they'd be seeing each other later? Either the walls here must be a little thinner than she realized, or Vangie simply guessed. After all, most everyone already assumed they were a couple. That they had a future together. It didn't bother Erin in the least. Or it hadn't. Why did she suddenly second guess that

Later, as she changed from scrubs to blue jeans and a sweater, Erin paused over a text from her aunt.

Hey, sweet girl. Looking forward to seeing you soon! I plan to arrive Sunday afternoon. Have some news. Xo

Can't wait! What news? Erin texted back.

I'll share when I see you.

Ooh! That's FIVE days from now.

Correct.

Erin laughed. So Aunt Bea had a secret? How unlike her aunt to be so cagey. Had she started seeing someone? Taken up a new hobby? Had a makeover? She'd already changed her hairstyle and updated her wardrobe. It wouldn't be something as mundane as that. For Aunt Bea to drop that curious tidbit, it had to be something big. They didn't keep secrets from each other.

On her drive up the mountainside to Mike's, Erin contemplated secrets. They could be fun or they could be sticky. She didn't think Mike kept secrets, but since his old girlfriend had returned, things between them felt...off. In the last two weeks, he'd grown quieter. More solemn. Where they'd once been able to talk easily without pretense, lately, their moments together seemed stiff and cumbersome. Not strained exactly. Unexpected.

If the last two days were any indication, she guessed he'd unpacked old baggage. He'd admitted he wanted to sort through the past. *Wonderful.* She thought he'd worked through most of that. She'd never have let things get this far if she didn't think Mike loved her. After Phillip and Patty's romantic liaison and ultimate betrayal, she'd sworn to never let her guard down again. A love triangle wasn't her idea of adventure. Stepping on a rosebush would be more welcome. Yet, here she was—a chapter heading in a very long book. Maybe Mike didn't see it that way, but that's how it felt.

Her side trip to the gas station earlier reinforced those feelings. If only she hadn't overheard Edna Powell at the register...

Erin tapped her fingers against the steering wheel as she began the ascent up the hillside to his cabin. *Am I being childish?* He said he no longer had feelings for Sally Sue. Everything else he'd offered made sense. Why, then, did unsettling thoughts continue to gnaw at the raw spots of her heart?

Chapter Twenty-Five

Mike had planned the meal carefully. Bacon-wrapped pork loin, sour cream and cheddar mashed potatoes, grilled asparagus, French bread, and lemon-lavender cheesecake for dessert. He'd made everything himself, except the cheesecake. Pennies from Heaven helped him out there.

He'd used one of the only two tablecloths he owned—a plain, vintage white number—but it looked nice with the red Fiestaware, and he enhanced the mood with a soft jazz selection, which he streamed in the background. Somehow, he didn't think Blake or Garth would fit, though who knew? If the somberness between he and Erin continued, he might need a little help from those good, ol' boys to liven up the evening.

"Whatcha think? Everything a-ok here?" He gave the Lab's head an affectionate pat.

Woof. Woof. Immediately, Blackie voiced his approval, plopping back on his haunches, his tail sweeping back and forth against the glossy stone. Even his dog cheered him on. Didn't get much better than that.

Yeah, it did. *I'd sure appreciate your help, Lord.*

Until the last few weeks, he and Erin had been on such sure footing. Still were, in his estimation. Sally Sue's arrival hadn't changed how he felt about Erin. Her coming here shocked him, certainly, as it might anyone who'd been dumped by a fiancée...and then revisited again over a decade later. Throughout the entire absurdity of Sally Sue's designs—the land offer, the marriage offer, the apartment rental—he'd never questioned his love for Erin. What he had questioned was the wisdom in moving forward until he effectively dusted away the cobwebs from his past. Nonetheless, he wished he would've handled the last forty-eight hours differently. He didn't want to hurt Erin, and that's exactly what he'd done.

The crunch of gravel outdoors snapped him from his musing, and Mike willed the jitters away with a deep, cleansing breath. Fresh jeans, fresh shirt, and two matching shoes. At least, he'd look like he had his act together even if he was as nervous as a cat in a roomful of rocking chairs.

Before Mike had a chance to fully open the back door, Blackie bound through his doggie door, leaving the metal flap fluttering behind him. Mike hurried out, too.

"Hey, boy! Come." The pooch adored Erin as much as he, and only meant to bestow some beloved kisses on his favorite vet, but Blackie dutifully halted, albeit with a mournful yowl, and returned to his master's side. "Good boy."

"Hi, ya, Blackie. It's great to see you." Smiling, Erin walked the short distance to where they stood. In her hands she carried a generous sized glass bowl. "Seven-layer salad. Is that okay?"

Salad. The one thing he'd forgotten. "Absolutely perfect. I love seven-layer salad." *And you.*

Have mercy. The woman plundered his heart and left him breathless. How could Erin question his feelings for her? *No-brainer, bud. How would you feel if her former fiancé ambled into town, full of arrogance and attitude, flaunting preposterous notions like land deals and marriage? Rotten.* Real rotten, all right.

"How was your day?"

Did she ask to be polite or was she asking if he saw Sally Sue?

"Great. Business slows down a mite this time of year, but I checked on a new build and wrapped up earlier than expected so I took advantage of the extra time."

"I hope you didn't go to a lot of trouble. Cooking can be draining when you've put in a full day...or most of a day."

Enough of the niceties.

"Erin, I'm pleased as punch you're here, okay? I wanted to cook for you. Spend time with you. Thank you for coming."

Her blue-green eyes sparked with awareness. She handed off the salad bowl, as if needing to fill the awkwardness of the moment.

"Smells fantastic...like bacon and apples and...cinnamon?" She sniffed the air and her mouth curved upward. "Pork chops?"

"Close. Baked pork loin. Wrapped in bacon with apple slices and orange rind, and cinnamon for that extra zing."

"*Wow.* I knew you cooked, but it's really coming home to me what a culinary whiz you are."

"Ahh... Thank you. I've been boning up on my skills since you came into my life. I enjoy cooking now more than I did."

They entered the kitchen, with Blackie prancing ahead of them like he owned the place, which in his mind, he did. He nudged Erin's hand then for a pat.

"I love you, too, buddy." Erin stoked his fur, making soft, cooing noises, talking to him, praising him, warming Mike to the core. "Miranda sends her regards."

Mike let out a chuckle. "Well, how very nice of her." He set the glass bowl on the kitchen island. "Oh, I'm sorry. May I take your jacket?"

"Sure." Erin shimmied out of the lightweight coat. She sniffed the room, her gaze resting on him. "Oh, golly. It smells even better inside."

"Hungry?"

"Ravenous."

"In that case..." Mike fanned out his arm toward the table, motioning her to have a seat. No eating at the kitchen island tonight. He wanted to make a grand production of serving her. He planned to pamper her in every way. "The view here is stunning when the sun sets."

Erin regarded the mountainside beyond the windows, where sunlight and shadow played across the surrounding hills and the valley below, framing their world in crimson, purple, and pink. "I can't believe you get to see this every day."

"Sunrise from one vantage point of the cabin and sunset at this end. I designed it that way."

"Great planning." She stood for a moment, mesmerized by the dwindling shafts of light. "The view from my cottage is gorgeous—I love how it overlooks town and the colorful crests and peaks beyond—but this...this is spectacular."

"One of the reasons I'm partial to this sliver of paradise. God sure knows how to use a paintbrush, doesn't He?"

"He certainly does."

Erin stepped backward, seating herself in the chair Mike had drawn from the table. As he scooted her forward, a soft, powdery fragrance played upon his nostrils, making him want to lean down and trail kisses along her collar bone where surely the pleasant aroma teased. Of course, he refrained, though he did give it some serious thought.

In the flickering glow of candlelight, he served dinner, as Blackie observed from his dog bed in the great room. The hound's dark eyes followed his master's movements, until at last, Mike sat down and he and Erin began eating. Then, the pooch relaxed against the soft, chenille fabric of his bed, his sturdy frame sinking into the squishy oblivion.

"Heaven on earth, in a dog's mind." Mike flicked his head toward the Lab. "I sometimes wonder what the fellow dreams."

"It's probably similar to what we humans dream, only in a canine context. When animals are loved, they equate that love with their favorite people and pastimes—their owners, eating, activities, companionship—preoccupations that stir their greatest joys."

"Makes sense. Sometimes, I declare Blackie laughs in his sleep. You'd have to hear it. It's a cross between a bark and a whimper and a satisfied sigh. His legs get to moving like he's chasing a ball or maybe digging up a bone, and a few seconds later, he's either off on another mission or drifting further into dreamland."

Erin inclined her head toward him, smiling.

"What?"

"I was just thinking. I'm not sure what I would've done had I fallen for someone who didn't love animals."

He considered that for a moment, a grin finding its way to his mouth. "Me, either."

As Erin's fork moved about her dinner plate, Mike's chest ballooned. Every now and then, she'd hold the food in her mouth, presumably, thoroughly enjoying it before swallowing.

"Everything's *divine*. The pork loin is magnificent."

"Thank you. I tried to put all my impressive skills to good use."

"It worked."

For the next hour, they lingered over the meal and dessert, nuances and conversation. They spoke about various topics—family, work, upcoming holidays, even the weather—before the dialogue shifted and the elephant in the room took a seat.

He should have expected it. After all, this evening had been his way of trying to make amends. A way of showing Erin that she represented his future. She alone centered his world, despite the upheaval of the last few weeks. Still, if it hadn't been for his past resurrecting itself, there would be no need for reticence and reassurances.

"I'm glad you agreed to come tonight," Mike began slowly. "I know I hurt you, and I'm sorry."

Erin set down her water goblet, resting her hands beside her empty plate. "Yes, your silence did hurt me, and yes, I know you're sorry. There's no need to rehash it, except to say I wish life's complexities could be resolved so simply. Words like *silence* and *hurt* and *sorry* insinuate understanding, so thank you for that. However—" One hand fluttered to the crumpled napkin beside her plate. The other, she placed in her lap. "The fact *is* Sally Sue's still here. In Ruby. She hasn't left."

"Pardon?"

"Gas station scuttlebutt. The card reader at the pump was broken so I had to pay inside."

Okay. But that in itself didn't surprise him. After all,

it'd only been two days since he'd last seen his former fiancée. She'd mentioned she expected to leave within the week. The week wasn't over yet.

"What did you hear?" In Ruby, one could hear a lot of things. Some fact. Some fiction. Assumptions and vague chitchat. All harmless meanderings. "You have to remember to take things with a grain of salt around here. The old-timers, especially, may embellish. A sprinkle becomes a monsoon. A snowflake, a blizzard. So on and so forth."

"Well, not a monsoon and not a blizzard, and I hardly think Edna Powell and Tilly Andrews count as 'old-timers,' but apparently 'the Ribeck widow' will be celebrating the holidays in Ruby. Holidays, as in more than one. Christmas, too. Maybe. Oh, and that's not all. 'It's as if the child has developed a new lease on life.' Mrs. Powell further indicated her boarder's countenance is much improved. She thinks a certain young man might be the reason."

Mike flinched. Ripples of alarm rolled through him. *Oh, no.*

"Erin, I promise you, I have in no way, shape, or form given that woman any encouragement."

"I believe you. I simply share this to prepare you. The ladies didn't even realize I overheard their banter, and I don't believe they intended to gossip. They're both tender-hearted women. Upright pillars in the community. I think they honestly care about Sally Sue and her well-being."

Mike scraped a hand through his hair, his dark eyes, narrowing. "Erin...the other day...Sunday...Sally Sue hugged me. It was toward the end of our visit. I thought she meant it as a friendly gesture. A good-bye, if you will. I didn't return the hug. In fact, I stepped back and left shortly after."

Now, this was something she hadn't expected.

"It doesn't surprise me that Sally Sue would attempt physical contact, especially as a last ditch effort to resuscitate old feelings. What I do find curious is why you failed to mention it."

His gaze flicked heavenward before settling on her again. Whether uttering a prayer or searching for words, Erin had no idea.

"At the time, I honestly believed it was her way of letting go of the past—a way of dismantling the fantasy she'd created in her mind. I didn't think any more of it."

But Erin did. She thought a lot more of it now that she knew. "Can I ask you something?"

"Sure. Anything."

"How did the hug make *you* feel?"

"What?" Mike's forehead puckered.

"I'd like to know if hugging Sally Sue dug up old feelings. Did it make you remember how it once was between the two of you?"

"For the record, *she* hugged me. Not the other way around. I'd be lying if I said I didn't remember our past. But like we—you and I—talked, she's my past, Erin. You're my present and my future. How many times do I have to say that?"

"I don't know. What I do know is that your first love is still in town, and it seems she has no foreseeable plans to leave."

"That's my fault?" A hint of irritation punctuated his words.

"No. It's not your fault." Erin scooted away from the table, yet remained seated. Once again, she attempted to rationalize this very odd dynamic, and a dynamic that was getting odder by the day. "But why would the woman continue to stay if you've told her unequivocally there's nothing between you? Is she, perhaps, reading vibes that you, yourself, don't even recognize?"

Mike shook his head. "I can't presume to know what Sally Sue's thinking. All I can tell you is when I left Edna's place on Sunday, it was under good terms, yes. But I certainly didn't give Sally Sue false hope. She seemed encouraged, but in a different context."

"All right." Erin rose from her chair, checking the time. "Thank you for the delicious dinner and dessert. I really appreciate all your hard work."

She needed to go. It wasn't that late, but suddenly, the weight of their exchange exhausted her. She couldn't think clearly anymore.

Mike stood, reaching for her. "Wait. That's it? Please, don't leave. Not like this."

"Everything's okay. It's just that I have early patients tomorrow and I think I better hit the hay earlier." *Plus, I really don't want to expend any more time or energy discussing Sally Sue Messmer Ribeck and what her intentions may or may not be.*

"How about a cup of coffee or hot chocolate before you leave?"

"No, thanks. A raincheck, please?"

Mike released her hands, his arms going slack. "Okay. Just a sec and I'll grab your jacket and mine."

"Only mine, please. There's no need for you to follow me down the mountain tonight. It's a full moon so there's plenty of light."

"I'd feel better if you—"

"Really, I'm a grown woman. I'll be okay," Erin interjected. "I'll drive slow and text when I get home."

He waggled his head, though his mouth angled downward. "Promise?"

"Promise." She wasn't intentionally trying to hurt him. She simply didn't want a chaperone tonight.

Erin trod across the room and gave Blackie a pat. "See ya soon, fella. You be a good boy."

Blackie roused briefly from dreamland to give Erin several affectionate kisses. When she turned, Mike had her jacket and he held it up for her to slip on.

"I really wish you'd stay. Please believe me when I say there's nothing between Sally Sue and me. That chapter ended years ago."

Erin nodded. She knew he believed that. "I can't stay any longer tonight, but we'll catch up in a few days."

"A few days?"

"Yeah. My schedule's jammed the rest of this week because the clinic's closed next week for Thanksgiving."

"Your aunt's still coming this weekend?"

"Yes."

"And you're still planning on coming to Mom and Dad's next Thursday?"

"Yes. None of that has changed."

"I'm glad." He leaned down to brush the lightest of kisses upon her cheek, the faint scent of his spicy aftershave teasing her nostrils, hovering there, even as she carried his kiss with her down the mountain that night.

Chapter Twenty-Six

Mike hadn't intended to follow Erin down the hillside. She hadn't wanted him to. The more he thought about it though, the more uncomfortable he grew. There'd been some road work midway down, and he'd feel better if he at least followed her to the main road, past the trickier winds and bends. Not surprisingly, she realized he shadowed her. His headlights weren't far behind. Well, she could be aggravated all she wanted. What was one more thing added to the mix?

As they came within a quarter of a mile from the main highway, Mike paused. Okay, she should be good from here. He'd honor her wishes from this point and turn around. He flashed his lights and Erin's hand went up in a quick wave as she continued on.

She should have known Mike wouldn't be able to help himself. Yes, the twists and turns of this mountain could be dangerous, but she always negotiated them carefully, slowing down at appropriate junctures. Besides, the full moon tonight offered enough light to easily resemble pre-dawn. If it'd been pitch black, that might be a different story.

Erin made it to the main highway and turned back toward town, marveling at the fact that her vehicle seemed to be the only one on the road. Only eight-thirty, but for Ruby, the highways and byways already slumbered, awaiting a new day. Such was the way of rural life in this

Ozarks region. Considering that she'd once been a city girl with somewhat different aspirations, the fact made her smile. She drove on, cognizant of her surroundings and thankful for the simplest of blessings, even though, sometimes, life doled out unexpected events and surprises. *Boy, did it.*

About a mile outside Ruby, the speed limit decreased, and Erin slowed accordingly. Thick groves of cedars, pines, birches, and oaks began to give way to less populated patches of earth, while other sections remained dense with thickets and underbrush. Up ahead, alongside the road, something stirred. Coyotes? Rumored to be plentiful in these parts, Erin didn't doubt it.

Suddenly, the stirring became movement. Movement transformed to color. Flashes of brown soared up and over the pavement in one, seemingly, fluid exodus. She barely had time to think, much less react, before the herd of deer leaped like a zenith rising through the slight clearing and across the road within mere feet of her SUV.

In the barest of seconds, Erin overcorrected. *No. No. No. Not again. Help me, Lord!* Trying to prevent a rollover, she took her foot off the gas, rather than braking, which slowed her speed and allowed her vehicle to stabilize. Except it wasn't enough to stop her from careening off the road in stellar fashion, bumping and thumping over jagged rocks and bristly terrain and into the ditch where the herd once gathered. *Thwack!*

Ohhh. Had she hit one?

Airbags deployed like exploding marshmallows and her head jerked to the side and struck something hard—maybe the door—as her seat belt sliced into her, holding her securely, doing what it was designed to do. Pops—

possibly clicks—reverberated through the vehicle. Door locks? They were supposed to release in the event of a crash.

In a heartbeat, the world grew still.

How bad was it?

Don't be afraid. I am with you.

"Who's there?"

But the words were only in her mind.

Quickly, other sounds and voices swelled around her. Her location services and security system? Thank God, she'd renewed her service. And yet, everything seemed fuzzy and out of focus...

Fatigue, swift and cumbersome, claimed her as waves of deep, dark blackness drew her into silent oblivion. All she wanted to do was close her eyes and sleep. If it wasn't for someone shining a light in her face and calling her name, she could have.

"Doctor Shaye? Erin?" The voice—familiar and melodic—washed over her. She knew that voice, and yet, she couldn't place it. "Erin, can you hear me? Don't be afraid. Help's on the way."

There were some grunts and groans from someone nearby, but they were muffled by the window. One. Two. Three good tugs and the door made a popping noise. Abruptly, the driver's side door jerked open, and with a touch as soft as butter, the person gently skimmed her face with their hands. Fingers feathered her head—her scalp—as if searching for something. Perhaps, checking for lacerations?

"Don't try to move. I don't see anything that needs sutures, but you've likely suffered a concussion and maybe a whiplash. The deputies and an ambulance should be here any minute."

Erin tried to open her eyes, but grogginess weighted her lids.

"I want you to remain very still. Try to stay awake, okay?" The voice was calm, reassurring, but firm.

"I...c...can't stay awake. So sleepy."

"I know, Erin, but you must. Listen to me. Does anything else hurt besides your head?"

"N...no."

Fingers trailed the inside of her wrist where they rested a moment. Someone was assessing her pulse rate?

"Did I injure them—the deer?"

"No. They're fine. You will be, too."

"I'm frightened." Memories of another time, another place, called to her in the fog. "Please don't leave me. Stay."

"Here, Erin. Hold my hand." The person reached for Erin's palm and held it, their thumb lightly caressing the topside of her hand. "Can you tell me about your family?"

"Aunt Bea? Aunt Bea's my family. She's coming for Thanksgiving. S...supposed to be here in a few days."

"I bet you'll have a grand visit. I'm having family in, too."

"My mama and daddy passed away. We were in an accident a l...long time ago. A rollover. Deer. Ironic, huh?" Erin half-sobbed, half-laughed. What was wrong with her?

"I'm so sorry. It's hard to lose someone we love."

She attempted to nod, but found it too exhausting. Instead, she squeezed the person's hand. They squeezed back.

Somewhere in the distance, sirens screamed. Instaneously, others appeared out of nowhere, all talking at once, as Erin's head throbbed beneath something cold. "Wha...why is a bag of corn on my head?"

"I'd just run out to the convenience store for a few items. It's the only thing I had to use as a cold compress." The voice paused. "My first aid kit's in my other vehicle at home."

"Thanks for staying with her, Mrs. Ribeck," a masculine voice boomed. "We appreciated your assessment of the situation. We'll take it from here."

Mike had been loading the last of the dishes into the dishwasher when his cell phone chirped. Not Erin. She'd promised she'd text when she got home, but maybe since he'd followed her down the mountain, she thought it unnecessary. Or maybe, she was too aggravated with him. He rarely answered calls from unknown numbers, though he sometimes made an exception because of his business. 'Course, this late, his subcontractors or others wouldn't be calling.

All right. This better be good. He tapped the talk icon. "Mike Brewer."

"Mike?"

What in thunder? The way she rushed his name sent shivers down his spine.

"Sally Sue?"

"Yes. It's me. I have something to tell you."

What now? Hadn't they reached an understanding? They'd closed the book on their final chapter. Exchanged apologies, pleasantries, and good-byes. Surely, she wasn't going to prolong this any further. Whatever *this* was.

"Everything all right?"

"Are you sitting down?"

Mike's blood pounded in his ears. When someone uttered those words, whatever followed was never good.

"No. I'm not sitting down." He slapped the dishwasher door closed. "Why?"

On the opposite end of the line, Sally Sue exhaled. An extended pause trailed the gush of air. "I came upon an accident a few moments ago. Mike...it's Erin."

He gripped the counter for support. Normally, not a man of anemic fiber, he'd never passed out in his life. He wasn't about to now. "What happened?"

"Take some deep, cleansing breaths. I'll make this quick."

He tugged on his boots and grabbed his jacket as Sally Sue started to explain. Calmly and concisely, she laid out the facts and shared everything she knew. Even as his world crumbled, something in her voice seemed to anchor him to the present. Her inflection and word choices communicated the gravity of the situation without giving way to hysteria.

Merciful Father. Erin could've been killed.

"So, they've taken her to County General in Sapphire?"

"Yes. I imagine they'll do a full work-up on her. Labs. Various diagnostics. A CT. X-rays. Whatever else they feel is appropriate."

"Thanks, Sally Sue. I can't tell you how much I—" Mike struggled for composure. "I appreciate you being there...for staying with Erin until help arrived."

"You bet. Stay safe as you head out."

He'd barely made it down his drive before his cell started to blow up with further incoming calls. Mom and Dad. Gabe. Garrett. Mel. Friends. He let them go to voice mail, as he focused on getting to the hospital.

As he drove, he prayed. *Heavenly Father, I know sometimes I've not talked to you as much as I should. Please forgive me for that. I'll try to do better. Thank you for protecting Erin tonight. For the divine appointment of Sally Sue. For sending others to help, too. I ask now, please, that you touch Erin from the soles of her feet to the tip-top of her head, healing her body in every way, from the inside-out. Please ease any fear, pain, and discomfort. Oh—and Father—remind her that I love her. Please? It's in your Son's name, I pray. Amen.*

How long had it been since he prayed—really prayed? Too long. How bored and disappointed God must be with his feeble attempt now. But wasn't that what the enemy wanted us to believe—that our appeals and petitions to the Lord fell on deaf ears?

A favorite scripture from the fifth chapter of the book of James assuaged Mike's doubts as he called it to mind. *Confess your faults one to another, and pray one for another, that ye may be healed. The effectual fervent prayer of a righteous man availeth much.*

He knew he wasn't worthy, and he sure didn't feel very righteous, but God could work with that. God knew his heart and heard his cry.

Erin's wreck, and the events following it, unfolded in brief bursts and snippets. A normal physical reaction, according to the doctors. While she didn't remember quite everything about her accident, what she did recall were the soothing hands and the comforting voice of her rescuer—or at least the person who'd found her first.

Now, over thirty-six hours later, the fog began to lift

more fully. Various scenes from that evening played in her memory, similar to the process she'd experienced as a child. The deer leaping across the road. Fighting the steering wheel for control. Her rescuer—whose face she still could not recall. First responders rapidly assessing her injuries, which blessedly—other than bumps and bruises and a mild concussion—weren't many. Though, they didn't know that at the time.

Other things Erin remembered—like Mike's face, pasty white, framed in worry, and Aunt Bea arriving in the wee morning hours afterward looking much the same— and they remained on the fringe of her subconscious. Initially, they'd sat by Erin's bedside, rarely taking a break. She'd finally convinced Aunt Bea to go rest and unpack and give Miranda some attention. She'd had more difficulty in getting Mike to return home for a while, but ultimately, he'd agreed.

Aunt Bea, however, couldn't stay away long. At some point, she popped back into Erin's room, quietly slipping into the bedside chair. Gently, she clasped Erin's hand.

"No need to rouse, darling. I returned because I wanted to share something. News that, I hope, will put a bounce in your step as you recover." Her aunt leaned close. "You rest and I'll talk, okay?"

Erin nodded, groggily. Was this what Aunt Bea had referenced in her recent text? *It must be important.*

"Granted, maybe this isn't the best scenario. I'd hoped we might chat over pizza and breadsticks when I arrived this weekend. Given the circumstances, though, I believe there's no time like the present." Aunt Bea cleared her throat. A smile played at the corners of her mouth and her emerald eyes sparkled. "I'm moving here, darling. To

Ruby. No more shuttling back and forth every few months or communicating via FaceTime. I've sold the house back home and I'm pulling up stakes. Come January, your dear, ol' auntie is here to stay. I've rented a cute bungalow in town."

"Moving? Here?" Erin's heart ballooned with joy. Yet, she could hardly believe it. "I don't understand."

The soft tinkle of Aunt Bea's laughter echoed in the room as she practically bounced on the edge of her chair. "You will. I have so much to tell you..."

Vangie stopped by briefly, telling Erin not to worry about the clinic. She'd taken the liberty of closing it for a few weeks until Erin recovered, diverting patients needing immediate attention to a veterinary clinic here in nearby Sapphire.

"In the meantime," Vangie remarked, "I'll use this opportunity to reorganize the front office, update files, field calls, and rearrange appointments. Oh, and since I'm also your vet tech, in addition to office manager extraordinaire, I can handle the simple procedures like flea and tick treatments, pedicures, and that sort of thing when we reopen. I've got ya covered, my friend."

"Have I ever told you that you're worth your weight in donuts?" Erin had still been woozy at the time, and she'd meant to say *gold*.

"Nope. But hey, I'll take it. You owe me a box of raspberry creams when you feel better."

"You got it, girl."

Flowers, floral arrangements, and balloons soon began arriving. Pastor Bill from church stopped in to see her for a few minutes, as did Mike's parents, with Billie

Gail informing her that Thanksgiving was in the bag. Erin was not to lift a finger and could simply rest and eat. She and Aunt Bea weren't to bring a thing next week—only themselves and "mighty big appetites."

Ida Mae, only a few weeks away from her delivery date now, and her husband Chuck Farrow delivered cards to the information desk. The Sewing Bees sent over a jar of tonic to boost her morale, but hospital staff intercepted it before Erin had the opportunity to sample the contents from the pretty vessel.

"I'm sorry, Dr. Shaye," one of her attending nurses lamented. "We're not allowed to deliver food or drinks from outside sources to patients' rooms. It's against policy, as I'm sure you can understand. Instead, I sent it home with your aunt where she assured me she'd put it away for safe keeping."

"Oh, thank you very much. I'm certain my aunt will do just that." Naturally, she might take a sip or two for medicinal purposes.

Wearing the standard issue, teal-blue hospital gown, Erin leaned back against the pillows, vaguely aware of muscle stiffness and a slight headache. The doctor wanted to keep her at least another day, and although Erin understood from a medical standpoint, she really wished she could go home to her own bed. Nothing like a car accident to reframe priorities and shift one's focus. *Car.* Her SUV. Her *Honda CR-V*, to be precise. *Oh, my.* She'd just paid it off. Had it been totaled in the accident? She'd have to ask.

A soft knock at her door jarred Erin from her thoughts. "Nurse Stickler for Rules said I could visit for a while unless you were resting. Are you resting?"

The sight of him brought a smile. Clean shaven, fresh clothes, and holding a stuffed Teddy Bear with a huge pink ribbon, Mike waited in the doorway.

"Are you kidding? Everyone knows you don't rest in a hospital. Come on in."

He crossed the short distance to her bed and bent to kiss her forehead. The kiss, sweet in its own right, only reinforced her want of a proper one.

"How are you feeling?"

"I think we can do better than that." Erin wove her hands through his hair, drawing him closer. When she pressed her lips to his, Mike responded in kind, his enthusiasm obvious.

"Are you sure this is okay?" His breaths came in short, ragged spurts. "I don't want to get us in trouble."

"What are they going to do? Kick us out?"

At that, he snickered. "You have a point there."

"So, did you sleep?"

"Some."

"Fibber." She knew he hadn't. His eyes were bloodshot and lines of weariness creased his handsome features. "Have a chair. I've been meaning to ask about my vehicle. How bad is it?"

"A vehicle can be replaced. You, on the other hand..." his voice cracked. "Cannot."

"It's totaled?"

"Yeah. Yeah, it is. But as I said..."

"I know. You're right. I have so much to be thankful for." Erin breathed deeply, slowly releasing the gulp of air. "The irony of the wreck though. Deer, again. What's the likelihood of that?"

"Darlin', it's deer season. Deer are moving. We have

lots of 'em in these mountains. I should have reminded you. I blame myself for that."

"What? Don't!" She didn't blame anyone for her accident. It wasn't something they could've predicted. She only wished their dinner together hadn't dissolved into meanderings about the past.

Erin had thought about it a lot. She loved Mike. He loved her. Maybe he had things to work through, but perhaps, her own baggage also prevented her from fully trusting God's plan for their lives. If it hadn't been for her recent accident, maybe she'd still be second guessing His will.

"I want to apologize to you."

"What on earth for?" He cocked his head to the side. His face took on a note of seriousness, obviously not understanding. How could he?

"Besides pressure you've felt from other sources, I'm afraid I added to that. Things have happened in the past few weeks that were beyond your control. Naturally, it placed you in an awkward position. You had a right to examine those things. I had a right to sift through things, too."

"Erin, I love you. Only *you*."

"I know. I love you, too." She melted inside at his words. "When I had the wreck, and I overcorrected and I felt myself losing control of the vehicle, dozens of thoughts ran through my mind. The main one? That I might not get to say those words ever again."

Mike rose from the chair and carefully sat down beside her on the bed, clasping her hand. "On my way here after your wreck, I asked God to remind you how much I loved you. Looks like we were of the same mindset."

"Equally yoked. In Him and with each other." Happiness ricocheted through Erin, warming her from head to toe.

"Yes."

A thought struck her, something she'd wondered, but in her fuzzy state, she'd forgotten to circle back to. "How did you find out about the accident? You arrived at the hospital so quickly after the paramedics brought me here..."

"Someone phoned me immediately after it happened. They—she—came upon the accident. A divine appointment, you might say."

Suddenly, Erin knew. She knew that voice. That touch. Those hands. *Sally Sue.* She'd been convinced it was an angel.

"Oh, Mike. She helped me. Sally Sue comforted me. She attempted to keep me awake when I—"

"She didn't know how you might feel if you realized it had been her that night."

"How I'd feel? I'm grateful!" Erin sat up straighter, remembering again further snatches of their conversation. "I want to thank her."

"Maybe you'll have the opportunity. She's renting Edna's apartment through Thanksgiving next week. Apparently, she and a family member are celebrating the holiday with Edna."

"A family member?"

"Someone who has loved—and loves—Sally Sue very much."

"Who?"

"Sid. Sid Ribeck. Sheldon's brother."

"Her brother-in-law?"

"*Former* brother-in-law, yes." Mike cleared his throat. "Just so there are no secrets between us, Sally Sue and I spoke again yesterday. When she first met Sheldon, she worked as a nurse at a hospital in their area. Apparently, they met at a children's benefit there. Anyway, eventually, she left the nursing professsion to take more of a lead in the family business—Ribeck Industries—assisting with galas and fundraisers and so forth. She fell hard for Sheldon, reciprocating his feelings. But the other Ribeck sibling also fell in love with Sally Sue. He stepped aside out of love for his brother."

"All these years, Sid Ribeck's been in love with his brother's wife?"

"Yes. There was never anything inappropriate between them, however. I gather, now that the situation has changed, Sally Sue is opening her heart to new possibilities. Her coming to Ruby—her whims and erratic behavior—were her way of coping with survivor's guilt."

Survivor's guilt. Yes, Erin well understood that.

"Also—and I have Sally Sue's permission to share this—she's struggled with clinical depression since her husband died. Unfortunately, we're only beginning to demystify the stigma surrounding this widespread illness. It doesn't excuse behavior, but it does help us better understand the disorder and what influences decisions and thought-processes. Honestly, looking back, I believe Sally Sue grappled with issues in high school. I think that's why her parents moved—they thought a change of scenery would benefit their daughter. Sadly, she only recently sought treatment and therapy."

"Goodness. How does knowing all this make you feel?"

"It explains a lot. While I still hold myself accountable for actions of my youth, I realize now that I'm not responsible for Sally Sue's mindset or conduct. I know in my heart I tried to right a wrong with a marriage that was never meant to be. I only want the best for her, as I would for anyone who's loved and lost, or for someone in a similar position." Mike sighed, expelling air from his lungs, as if doing so would also free him from the past

Erin leaned forward, carefully negotiating the I.V. tubing, and wrapped her arms around him. Doubts she'd once had concerning Mike's deepest desires, fled. "It feels like we've negotiated and mastered our first big hurdle."

"Yeah, it does." Mike swept wisps of hair away from her cheek and kissed her there. "I know there'll be others, but that's how life is. The main thing I want to concentrate on now is your recovery. The doctor said it's important you take it easy for the next few weeks. Prepare to be pampered and fussed over."

"What did you have in mind?"

The twinkle in his eye gave Erin an idea of what he meant. The brush of his lips upon hers communicated a better understanding of his intent.

"Oh, some of this and some of that." His lips then traveled down her neck to the cleft of her collarbone. "These hospital gowns are top-notch, are they not?"

"Driving you crazy, huh?"

For the first time in what seemed like forever, Mike threw his head back and laughed, full throttle. "You know it. Well, maybe not the gown. More like the girl."

"*A-hem.*" A shadow fell across the doorway and Nurse Stickler for Rules entered the room. "While I do appreciate the art of romance, it's time for my patient to actually rest.

You may visit again later during visiting hours, Mr. Brewer."

"Aww, shucks. We were just about to make out."

"We were not. He's teasing!" Erin couldn't keep from giggling, though the woman didn't blink.

Nurse Stickler—her actual name—Freda Stickler, RN MSN—to be exact—shoved her sensible, black frames higher on the bridge of her nose. "I'm a mother to six, grandmother to seven, and I've been a nurse for thirty years. Fortunately, I don't shock easily. Making out doesn't bother me in the least."

Obviously.

"What I mean to say," the dour-faced nurse clarified, "*is* what you do on your own time doesn't concern me. What happens on my floor, however, with my concussed patient *is* my concern. Now, please say your temporary good-byes so I can chart vital signs."

"Yes, ma'am." Mike winked as he rose from Erin's bed, then cast Nurse Crabby a solemn glance. "May I ask one last question?"

Ooh. Brave guy.

Nurse Stickler crossed her arms, her face tightening. "One. That's it."

"Do you think women prefer a short engagement or a long one?"

Chapter Twenty-Seven

"Is that your idea of a proposal?

"Ma'am?"

"Because if it is, you're fired." Nurse Stickler then directed her attention to Erin. "I didn't hear a proposal, despite all that smooching. Make him work for it, dear."

"I...um..." Erin rolled her shoulders and raised her hands.

"Just as I thought. Time for you to go, young man. If I were you, I'd make your next attempt a firecracker."

Nurse Stickler's reply made Mike titter all the way home. High time something did. Felt good, too. After the past day and a half—no, make that the last few weeks—Lord knew he needed a good chuckle. And no, it wasn't a proposal. Certainly not. Nope. When he asked Erin to marry him, he'd do it up right. Obviously, Nurse Stickler didn't appreciate his feeble stab at humor.

Blackie greeted him with his usual tail flapping, rump wiggling, yip-yapping self. "Hi ya, boy. Great to see you."

The Lab danced circles around him, immediately sensing the mood shift. Since Erin's accident, no doubt his comrade had honed in on the somber atmosphere around here. Poor fella. He'd known his master had been upended and had tried his darnedest to comfort him.

"No worries, guy. You're tops, okay? Forgive me if I've been distracted." He ruffled Blackie's fur and dished up his supper, then helped himself to a slice of pork loin from the other night. If only he'd followed Erin all the way into town after supper that evening and...what? He couldn't have prevented the deer. Couldn't have prevented the accident. Maybe, though, he would've been first on the scene.

For the dozenth time, Mike thanked God for Sally Sue's timing. If it hadn't been for her, Erin might have panicked...or drifted off to sleep without... *Stop.* Replaying what could have happened would serve no purpose. God had intervened and sent help—albeit from an unlikely, providential source—when Erin needed it.

Whoa. Sally Sue, a registered nurse? He could hardly wrap his mind around that one. She said she'd met her husband at a hospital benefit, but Mike had drawn the wrong conclusion. He thought she'd worked in a non-clinical setting. Perhaps, public relations or in administration. Not in a service related industry, once caring for the sick and injured.

Even years later, she still maintained her state licensure and served on various boards within her hometown hospital. So...a nurse, a widow, a company head, and a woman of influence and means. By her own admission, clinically depressed, and now seeking therapy and treatment. Had he ever really known his former fiancée? Probably not.

When he thought of how long Sally Sue may have struggled, long before pursuing professional help, sadness gripped him. As a teen, her mood swings and behavioral shifts befuddled him. Now, over a decade later, it all made sense. The sudden loss of Sally Sue's husband a year ago may have been the final straw—the chunk of ice that tipped the iceberg and caused her to almost sink.

"You know that old saying 'can't see the forest for the trees?' It's true. For those who work in health care, sometimes, we miss the correct treatment because of the quick fix." Sally Sue had phoned him yesterday in a follow-up call to check on Erin. She'd revealed brief glimpses of herself in the seven-minute conversation.

"We may also attempt to self-diagnose, self-soothe, or distract ourselves with yellow brick roads. There are so many facets to mental illness that we're only beginning to recognize its effects. People from all walks of life navigate it. Even, and maybe especially, those in high profile professions who refuse to believe it can happen to them."

Such a heartbreaking reality. She'd articulated it well. All of it.

"That's a profound assessment. You were brave in seeking help." Mike had been sitting on the deck, chugging coffee, at the time. Wistfulness and regret colored Sally Sue's words, yet it seemed important she say these things and that he listened. "What's your plan in going forward?"

"For starters, stay on my prescribed medication and maintain regular visits with my therapist. Work on my control freak tendencies. Scale back from day-to-day operations at Ribeck since Sid's doing an exemplary job at the helm." There'd been a gap in her thoughts, as if she mulled over additional things. "Maybe someday, I'll create a foundation to raise awareness of mental illness."

"That all sounds real fine. I'm proud of you, Sally Sue."

"I'm proud of you, too. No matter what I said or did in the past."

"Thanks. I know that now."

"Take care. Oh, and I know it isn't until next week, but Happy Thanksgiving."

"To you, as well."

He really prayed it would be a happy one for her.

Mike finished his slice of pork loin and set the plate in the sink. Later, upstairs in his bedroom, he drew out the old container from the closet shelf and found what he searched for. This time, it wasn't to revisit history and muse on a note faded with time and tears. It was to put it to rest. Once and for all.

In the burn bin outside, he purged his trial by fire with a single match.

The tentative knock at Erin's hospital room door came a few minutes after one. "Are you receiving visitors?"

She glanced up from her lunch tray, warmth filling her chest and radiating through her limbs. She'd just finished eating a turkey club on whole wheat, cream of broccoli soup, and something that tasted like chocolate pudding. Not too bad for hospital food, with the exception of the prunes. No way was she going to eat those.

"Sure. Come in."

Recollection and reality meshed, as Sally Sue entered the room, her stride, confident and certain. "You're looking much better. How are you feeling?"

"Better than when you last saw me."

"I would imagine. I'm so glad." The other woman regarded the prunes on Erin's lunch tray and wrinkled her nose. "Not a fan, huh?"

"No. I asked for apricots, but I guess they substituted."

A slight smile played at the corners of Sally Sue's glossy pink lips, her face, a combination of unease and relief, an understandable dichotomy. Dressed in casual jeans and a simple sweater, she wore her long, blonde hair pulled back with a black velvet headband, complementing the black hoops in each earlobe, and she'd toned down her make-up, which added an innocent quality to her countenance.

Erin had wondered if they'd meet again. Now that the moment pressed upon them, the rush of emotion came swiftly. Understanding. Compassion. Gratitude. Grace. She couldn't possibly thank Sally Sue enough for what she'd done, but she wanted to try.

"Would you like to sit down?"

"Yes. Thank you." Sally Sue chose the straight-backed chair, rather than the recliner. "I hope I'm not interfering with your rest."

"Not at all. I'm happy you stopped by." How to convey what she wanted to say? There might not be another opportunity. "Thank you for helping me. I was so frightened and shook up after my wreck, and you kept me calm. You held my hand and talked to me until the paramedics and fire department arrived. I'll always remember your kindness."

Sally Sue cast her gaze downward. When she tipped her head back up, her eyes shimmered with moisture. "I wasn't always kind to you...or others. I'm sorry about that. I won't try to make excuses, except to say, I wasn't myself."

"Loss is so hard," Erin empathized. "I know everyone processes it differently."

"That's true. When I lost Shel, my world fell apart. I'm sorry for the loss of your parents, too, Erin."

"How did you know?"

"You mentioned it the night of your accident."

Oh. She hadn't remembered that. "The loss of parents, a spouse, a child... It hurts so badly. All are tremendously painful and life-changing."

"Yes. For those already grappling with depression, the death of a loved one is sometimes the final blow." Sorrow registered in Sally Sue's face. Then, determination sprang up. "It may take some work, but I'm going to make better choices than I have in the past. That includes not trying to readjust my medication myself. I'm also going to be more in tune to internal cues when I feel off-balance, and I'll continue seeing my therapist."

Were they really having this conversation? The hurricane Erin had come to know as Sally Sue Messmer Ribeck now mirrored a soft, gentle rain. Perhaps, that's why she didn't recognize her the night of the accident. The contrast between the two sides defied logic.

"Sounds like you're on the right track. I know you have a wonderful life ahead of you." Erin hoped that didn't sound phony. She meant it.

They spoke a while longer, then Sally Sue rose to go. "I can see why Mike loves you. You're a special person, Erin."

"Thank you, Sally Sue. So are you."

A month later when snow lay heavy on the ground and the silver-gray morn hugged the Ozarks like a slumbering child, a most unexpected thing happened. Word came by way of a simple phone call, four days before Christmas.

"Are you sitting down, my friend?"

The last time Mike heard a semblance of that, it hadn't been good.

"As a matter of fact, I'm cuddling with my best girl here by the fire, Jerry. What's up, man?"

"What's up? What's up, you say?" Laughter, loud and

boisterous, reverberated in his ear. "I'll give you the long and short of it since you're...uh...occupied." Slurping noises followed, as Jerry chugged, presumably, morning coffee or the like.

"The land deal—the one we thought was a cry-like-a-baby bust? Well, hold onto your bloomers, son. There have been some new developments. Clinton contacted me at the butt-crack of dawn. He wants to sell you the acreage. Clean offer, no strings. You ready for the best part?"

Mike's heart hammered against his ribcage. He looked at Erin, sat up straight, and hit the speaker on his cell. "Yeah. Yeah, Jer, I'm listening."

"All righty then. Not only does the fellow want to sell you the land...he's offering it for fifty thousand less than he orignally asked. So, basically way below what you originally offered."

"Wh...why would Clinton do that?"

"Who knows the inner workings of a Christmas elf's mind? Says he has plenty of money. Doesn't need the excess. He wants you to build your dream, son. A lodge, a bed and breakfast, an airbnb, whatever. He knows your heart. He trusts your vision."

Erin leaned her head against Mike's shoulder and squeezed his mid-section. *Oh, wow!* She mouthed.

"Jer, I don't even know what to say. I'm stunned."

"We'll all gather for a punch and paperwork party after Christmas. Here's another snippet, I think you might be interested in. My, the grapevine in our little community doth proliferate."

"Don't beat around the bush, man. Lay it on me." Whatever else Jerry had to say couldn't be better than this.

"Well, I'm sure it'll be all over the local news by tonight, but I guess I'll go ahead and enlighten you since you seem to be oblivious."

"Guy, would you spit it out before I have to drive down there and give you a head thump?" Now, the laughter rose in Mike's chest. Jerry seemed to take extraordinary delight in being Santa's mouthpiece.

"Ribeck Industries has bestowed a one million dollar gift to The Meadows."

"They *what?*"

"Yes-sir. The wheeler-dealer electronic parts company, known for their business savvy, muscle and philanthropy, is now about to best themselves. They've stipulated the funds are to be used for the retirement community's new arts and activity center, as well as state-of-the-art furnishings, décor, and art supplies. It's gonna be revolutionary—a creative space for our retirees, as well as others who wish to expand their talents."

Mike swallowed. It had once been his brother-in-law's dream to start an art program at The Meadows. Matt wanted to pay it forward through GIFTS—*God's Incredible Free Treasure Supplied*—his brainchild, that would encourage folks in their artistic endeavors, but until financing could be secured, his dream remained on hold.

My heavenly days. Mike could hardly form the words. He merely uttered silent praise. *Thank you, Lord!*

"Oh, and there's more. You ready?"

Ready? He couldn't be more ready than a hound awaiting a bone.

Even Erin's eyes widened. She gripped Mike's hand and bounced on the sofa. "We're ready, Jerry! Spill it!"

"Why, hey there, Miss Erin. You'll like this, too." Long

slurps ensued, followed by a stifled belch. "Whoops. Pardon me. Anywho... Seems that Ribeck Industries is also awarding a Heart and Hands full-ride scholarship this year to the graduating high school senior they deem most deserving. This can be to the university of the student's choice, of course, or wherever the student is accepted for entrance. Mrs. Ribeck—Sally Sue—wishes community input on who that young man or young woman should be. Specifically, your input, Erin."

Mike didn't have to ask Erin's thought. *Zook Mercer.*

He drew out a clean handkerchief and passed it to Erin. He guessed he'd have to use his sleeve.

"That's all I've got today, kids. Happy holidays and merry Christmas."

They fell together in a tearful heap. What in the world had just happened? *And we know that all things work together for good to them that love God, to them who are the called according to his purpose.* The 28th verse from the book of Romans walloped Mike's heart. *Lord. Lord. Lord. Thank you, Father!*

Long after the call ended, Mike held the phone in his hand, as if it were gold. They hadn't heard from Sally Sue since she'd left Erin's hospital room the week before Thanksgiving. Word on the street, AKA Edna Powell, indicated Ruby's most unusual and intriguing soul had returned home from whence she came. Wait until word spread about this latest development. Town would have a heyday. They'd probably make a motion at the next town meeting to enact a Sally Sue Ribeck holiday. *Wow.* How life could change in a flash.

Erin ran her fingertips along Mike's cheek. "A love triangle unmatched. I believe this is the best and purest kind."

"Darlin', triangles serve a purpose, for sure. But I think it's time to retire this three-sided polygon, which leads to my next thought." He savored the warmth of her nearness, her heart beating so close to his. "I'm wondering if you might shut down the clinic for a few weeks...say, in June, for instance?"

"I think maybe I could arrange that. What did you have in mind?"

"I can't tell you quite yet. I'd like to speak to your aunt first."

Erin studied him with a languid stare. Would she understand or would she consider him an old-fashioned oddity?

"Okay, hotshot. You do that. Let me know what Aunt Bea says. But fair warning—my aunt is all roses and truffles and stars-in-her-eyes at the moment. She's likely to say yes to anything."

Yeah. Mike was banking on that. Ever since Beatrice Shaye shared her news of pulling up stakes in St. Louis with plans to move to Ruby, she'd been—to coin a fitting phrase—a busy bee in motion. But it wasn't only the move that had Erin's aunt in a flutter. Nuh-uh. One Dander Evans, four years Aunt Bea's junior, had come courting this past Thanksgiving. Wasn't that a wonder? Apparently, the two had been communicating following Aunt Bea's prior visits to Ruby and sparks ignited. A long distance love match had burst into a full-blown flame.No better time to strike than while the fire burned bright.

It would seem that love bloomed again in these old Ozark foothills.

Epilogue

Six months later...

It's rumored that a June bride is the most fetching. Though, really, *any* bride in love is a most fetching bride. Now, that being said, when Doctor Erin Shaye strolled that petal strewn aisle on the arm of her Aunt Bea, not a soul in attendance could argue that "fetching" was truly in the eye of the beholder.

To Mike, his Erin mirrored an angel—her strawberry-blonde locks adorned in a wreath of baby's breath and roses—her gown, an elegant study in yards of tulle and silk, befitting a princess. Some might argue that Aunt Bea stole the show, whose upcoming winter nuptials would certainly give pause to who outshone who, for today, the sixty-year-old beauty dazzled in lavender organza, rivaling royalty.

"Ahh...look at them."

"You hit it out of the park, brother," Gabe whispered as the two women strode closer. The fact his eye wandered to the pew where Vale Masters and her children sat imparted what many already suspected. Cupid waited in the wings with arrow in hand.

Garrett elbowed his eldest brother, speaking softly, "Watch and learn, man. Could be you soon."

"Or you," Gabe replied. "I hear she has a twin."

Twins.

The Farrows's six-month-old lad and lass snoozed in their mom's and dad's arms, oblivious to the ramblings of three bachelor brothers who'd soon become two. Twins could be fun.

"Hey, fellas. Some respect, please. Someone's getting married here." Mike grinned and nudged them both. Nothing else mattered in this moment except the woman with an affinity for cats and dogs and all of God's creation—the woman who'd rewired his heart and garnered it forever.

Author Note

Is there anything more sigh-worthy than the first tweaks of our heartstrings—those initial days when love is so fresh that tears prick our eyes with the sheer giddiness of it?

As Erin and Mike discovered, sometimes, love happens unconventionally and without fanfare. We teeter around the rough edges and raw spots, navigating the prickles and pauses as we venture toward that which our heart yearns, not knowing the outcome, but believing the thorny patches are worth the journey.

I hope this latest installment in The Welcome to Ruby series has uplifted and inspired you as new seasons come and go. From winter's dark and dreary days to the first blush of spring, may you always sense God's guiding hand as your divine appointment awaits.

A final word... We know some life points are comfortable and even welcomed. Others drop us to our knees. This author knows something of each. Within two years, I lost five family members. My dear mother-in-law passed away in September 2020, my precious Aunt Charlene in November 2020, and my beloved daddy in December 2020. As if my heart could survive more, on the heels of those losses came the most difficult blow yet—my darling sister, my best friend forever—passed away in June 2022. My cousin Todd, whom I adored, followed eight weeks later in August 2022. *Oh, my.*

As I've shared elsewhere, it's a difficult thing to

process and publicly grieve, yet, I know there are others who've trudged this terribly hard road. I believe our unique experience unites us, and in our grief, our journey is part of our collective story.

As I wrote again to deadline during a season of enormous loss and pain, I channeled that emotion into *His Heart Renewed*, weaving elements of faith, hope, and tremendous love into the pages of this novel. At times, I could only utter one word as I plodded along, but that one word sustained me and it was and always will be enough. *Jesus*.

I pray, as you meet your own trials and successes, you'll take His name with you.

Until we meet again, my friend ~ You are loved.

About the Author

As an avid encourager and lover of the underdog, Cynthia writes Heartfelt, Homespun Fiction from the beautiful Ozark Mountains.

"Cindy" has a degree in psychology and a background in social work. She is a member of ACFW, ACFW MozArks, and RWA. She is a 2020 Selah Award Winner, a 2020 Selah Award Double-Finalist, a 2017 ACFW Genesis Finalist, a 2016 ACFW Genesis Double-Finalist, and a 2015 ACFW First Impressions Winner. Her work is represented by Sarah Freese @ WordServe Literary.

Besides writing, Cindy has a fondness for gingerbread men, miniature teapots, and all things apple. She also adores a great cup of coffee and she never met a sticky note she didn't like.

Cindy loves to connect with friends at the following places:

Her online home: authorcynthiaherron.com
Twitter: twitter.com/C_Herronauthor
Facebook: www.facebook.com/AuthorCynthiaHerron
Facebook Readers' Group:
www.facebook.com/groups/195462117765130
Instagram: www.instagram.com/authorcynthiaherron
Pinterest: www.pinterest.com/cynthia_herron
Sign up for her monthly **e-NEWSLETTER** at
authorcynthiaherron.com

Welcome to the family!

If you enjoyed *His Heart Renewed*, please take a minute or two and post a review to Amazon, Barnes & Noble, Books-A-Million, Goodreads, BookBub, and additional book sites. A book review needn't be a long, drawn-out missive. Without revealing spoilers, simply sharing a few thoughts why you enjoyed the book and why you'd recommend it to others is a huge blessing to authors and readers. Thank you so much for your support!